BLOOD OFFERINGS

Robert San Souci

*No power can stay the mojo
when the obi is purple
and the vodu is green
and Shango is whispering,
Bathe me in blood.
I am not clean.*
　　　　　—*Henry Dumas,
　　　　　　from the poem Rite*

LEISURE BOOKS ∞ NEW YORK CITY

To my sister and brother-in-law
Ellen and Fred Cebalo
Who first gave me the newspaper clipping
That started the train of thought
That arrived at the following book.

And to my good friend
Mary Ann Shaffer
Who, as a favor, took her ax
And gave the needed forty whacks.

A LEISURE BOOK

Published by

Dorchester Publishing Co., Inc.
6 East 39th Street
New York, NY 10016

Copyright©1985 by Robert San Souci

All rights reserved. No part of this book may be reproduced or transmitted in any form or by any electronic or mechanical means, including photocopying, recording or by an information storage and retrieval system, without the written permission of the Publisher, except where permitted by law.

Printed in the United States of America

Excerpts from PLAY EBONY PLAY IVORY by Henry Dumas, edited by Eugene B. Redmond. Copyright 1975 by Loretta Dumas. Reprinted by permission of Random House, Inc.

BLOOD OFFERINGS

ONE

THE DREAM was always the same. Her grandmother, dead some twenty years, always stood at her left. The old woman, tiny, her skin filmed with sweat, gleaming like polished ebony, rocked gently back and forth. She looked just like Suzanne had remembered her, when Suzanne had been a teenager growing up in Oakland, living with her grandmother, mother, and sister in the little house on East 14th Street.

The old woman's name was Charlotte, but one of her common-law husbands had nicknamed her "Chicory," and that was the name Suzanne had always known her by. In the dream, the old woman was chanting something in a near-whisper; Suzanne could never quite understand the words, but she recognized the cadences of one of the ritual obi chants her grandmother would use when she summoned an *orisha* to help her in healing a friend or punishing an enemy.

Always, in the dream, the two women—the aged crone and her lighter-skinned granddaughter—were joined by a third presence. Suzanne could feel a power, like the change in the air before a storm, gathering somewhere on her right side. It never took on the physical presence of a man, though she could sense a *maleness* in the energy there.

She never bothered to turn her head, because she knew that what she was feeling must always remain unseen. Instead, she kept her eyes focused on the old woman and on the mounded earth in front of them.

They stood at the base of a gently curving knoll. Suzanne could feel the blades of grass pricking the bare soles of her feet, for the two women were barefoot. Suzanne wore the shift her grandmother had made her as a child; the old woman wore the white blouse and nearly ankle-length black silk skirt that was the only outfit Suzanne could recall her wearing.

Suzanne could feel the invisible presence around her, at her back, seeping into her and heightening her senses. She felt she could see with greater clarity, could hear the wind stirring the dead leaves on the ground and green leaves in the surrounding trees so acutely that she could distinguish the individual sound of each leaf, living or dead. There was a smell of ozone in the air, as though lightning had struck nearby.

"In time," her grandmother said, her voice rasping from the cigarettes she had smoked unceasingly in life. "For now, this."

The old woman handed her granddaughter a knobbed stick, the wood as blackly shining as the skin of the hands holding it out to the younger woman.

"Let it pass to another," Suzanne pleaded, in the same words she used in every dream.

Silent, obdurate, the old woman held the staff at shoulder height extended toward Suzanne. For an instant, the pale blue power of the *orisha* was upon the old woman. *Shango* was the one summoned; god of thunder; grandmother Chicory's special intercessor. The staff in the withered hands seemed to writhe for a moment like something alive. A serpent.

"Let it pass..." she begged again.

The wood was rigid again, but a line of faintly visible power rippled along its surface as though it were charged with St. Elmo's fire.

"It is yours now; the choice has gone out of your hands. Shango is your master; his power will fill your body. Open yourself to him."

Reluctantly, helplessly, she reached for the staff, felt it burn in her left hand, freeze her right hand.

"Now!" the old woman commanded.

She grasped the staff in her right hand and struck the ground in front of them one-two-three times. After a moment, she repeated the action. Then she took a step back, letting the wooden staff slip to the ground, holding the tip of it in her still-frozen fingertips.

The little hillside now floating on a sea of indeterminate fog began to suspire, swelling, receding, swelling again as though massive lungs filled the ground underneath. The old woman nodded, taking up her mumbled chant.

Fissures appeared in the grassy soil, cracks that

exposed the wet earth underneath the way ulcerated skin might burst. The clay seemed alive with seething, soft white and black shapes.

Then, from deep within the earth, chill white light, so thick it seemed to spill *moistly* out onto the ground, seeped out through the cracks.

"No . . ." Suzanne whispered. She was unheard or ignored by the old woman, who continued the *obi* litany. Suzanne shook her head, willing an end to the dream, which was now following the familiar pattern into nightmare. But she could not move, could not turn her head away or close her eyes to the horror that had come.

Clots of wet, steaming black mud were pushed up from below. A hand, then another clawed into the twilight. More earth fell away; a figure began to extract itself from the resisting earth. There were only the wet sounds of the settling earth; the excited breathing of the otherwise silent old woman. Suzanne felt her own heart and lungs smothered in the grip of this familiar, yet always terrifying, drama.

The corpse, free of the grave to its waist, began to crawl forward toward the two women. It was the body of a slender young black man whose skin had the lividness of a fish-belly or grub. His once-white shirt and stained jeans were caked with mud, soaked with moisture that seemed to ooze from the body more than the earth in which it had lain.

"Now, now, *now!*" the old woman urged.

The corpse knelt on the ground in front of them, raised its head up. The lids opened, revealing curdled white light, like soured milk, filling the sockets; it opened the mouth as though to speak, but no sounds emerged from the mouth that was also filled with the viscous light. A narrow tongue, blacked, fissured like the earth, slid forward, lay moistly on the lower lip. The milky luminescence began to drip from the eyes, from the mouth.

"Time is short," the ancient woman warned. Again she raised her hands and held out to Suzanne a long splinter of wood and a bone needle.

Caught in the inevitability of the dream, Suzanne took the splinter and, reaching down for the smooth rock that was always near her feet, she placed the point of the wooden splinter just above the bridge of the man's nose, then swung the rock, driving it suddenly into the dead brain.

Instantly the light spilled out of the eyes entirely, leaving only a faintly blue-veined darkness, the cold light vanishing on the dead face, leaving not a trace.

"Now he is mindless; he is almost yours."

Her stomach heaving, Suzanne took the bone needle and jammed it through the tongue. Whiteness gushed from the mouth, splattered her hands, then vanished. Doing what had to be done, with shaking hands she pushed the tongue, still transfixed by the needle, back into the mouth and clamped the lips shut.

"He can only speak when you command it. He is your servant now."

Kneeling before Suzanne was a skinny, living, and breathing (or so it seemed) man, wide eyes regarding her impassively, a hint of smile shaping his sealed lips. The half-inch of splinter was gone; the smooth, black forehead was unblemished. Her knowledge that this was a mindless, helpless creature somewhere between ghost and corpse was the most horrible part of the dream. That look of obedience, empty complacency, was too much for her.

"It begins soon," the old woman said. "Shango's will be done."

Suzanne took a step backward; the corpse raised its hand to her as a child might.

"You have your servant," she heard her grandmother say. "Now you must begin the work."

"No . . ."

But the old woman was gone. She felt the touch of a breeze almost like fingertips brushing her right arm; turning suddenly, she saw no one.

She was alone with the dead thing that was waiting for her command; its arms stretched out to her, but held back, as though even its mindlessness sensed the forces stirring in her.

She turned suddenly, running away from the horror, running blindly into the gathering fog, shouting her denial of everything she had been forced to do or was expected to do . . .

"What did you say, dear?" asked the woman in the bus seat beside Suzanne. A plump black woman, with her hair in a close-cropped afro and her arms folded comfortably across the green-and-purple pattern of her dress, just below her generous bosom.

Suzanne fumbled awake; the dream fled, largely unremembered. She shifted uncomfortably in her own seat, rubbing the back of her neck with her hand.

Through the grimy windows of the Greyhound she saw that the rising sun was tinging the flat landscape blue-green, cobalt, silver-blue, silver-gray. The distant hills on both sides were shaded deep purple.

"Where are we?" she asked.

The woman smiled and whispered, to avoid disturbing the other still-sleeping passengers, "Getting near San Francisco, soon." She sighed pleasantly and settled back into her seat, appearing little the worse for wear in spite of the long hours cooped up in the transcontinental bus. "Not long now," she added. "Not long at all. Isn't that a good feeling? And isn't California a nice place to be?"

"Real good," said Suzanne, feeling nothing but a need to get away from her neighbor and free herself from the taste and feeling of the dream that still clung to her as a bitter film in her mouth, an uneasiness that lay like static electricity beneath her skin. "Excuse me," she said, rising and retreating to the little washroom at the back of the bus.

When she had secured the door behind her, she felt some of her suffocating nervousness subside.

Taking a comb from her purse, she began drawing it through her hair, trying to undo the effects of dozing in the bus seat. Her vigorous combing helped a little, but her thick, black hair still looked lifeless, the few gray streaks in it seemed more pronounced than ever. How long would it be before her hair was as white as an old woman's? she wondered. Feeling faintly ill and lost, she could almost imagine herself shriveling up as time accelerated and made her look like her grandmother, just before the old woman died at ninety-one. The unhealthy sallowness of her skin was accentuated by the harsh overhead lighting. Even her lips were chapped from the dry air in the bus. She smoothed some lip gloss on, to soothe her irritated lips. Then she stood back to survey the result of her hasty repairs.

She was still an attractive woman. Her cafe au lait skin was even-toned and rich; her eyes wide, clear; her lips full with just a suggestion of a pout, a nicety of features which she had always called her "Egyptian look," but which her grandmother had said was the beauty of the secret priestess-queens of Buckawai from whom the women of Suzanne's family were descended, all the way back to Queen Naii.

Someone banged on the bathroom door, startling her out of her daydream. A man's voice said, "Hurry up, lady—there's only one can for all of us."

Suzanne grabbed up her few personal items and shoved them back in her purse. She had hardly opened the door, when a fat white man pushed his way past her and closed the door behind him, clicking the latch noisily. She could feel her panic —momentarily abated—returning, drawing every nerve in her body taut. A wave of dizziness, coupled with the pitching floor of the bus, threatened to spin her into the laps of sleeping passengers.

She groped for the back of a seat to steady herself, and found herself face-to-face with a wide-eyed, terrified infant.

The child cried suddenly, twisting violently in its mother's arms. Startled, she called out, "No!" The infant continued to whimper; but its mother—hardly more than a teenager herself—looked apprehensively at Suzanne, startled by the intensity of her cry.

One of those moments was closing in on her when the terror of what she was involved in overwhelmed her, when time collapsed in on itself and her world imploded into a blazing awareness of her own powerlessness and her paradoxical new powers. Corridors opened in her mind filled with purple light, choked with blood and stillness, echoing with screams of anguish and triumph. Screams from her own heart, remembered screams from a time she could not escape. She might even scream now—

But she held her arms across her stomach and kept the screams inside her. She took control and the pain subsided enough to allow her to walk towards her bus seat. With a sigh she dropped into the narrow seat, letting her head loll back, supported by the head rest. She closed her eyes, letting her lids hold in the pressure that was threatening to burst out through her eyes from her swollen brain.

"Are you all right, dear?" her neighbor asked,

concern and curiosity both evident in her voice.

"Fine," Suzanne said, not daring to open her eyes. "Just a little—motion sickness, I guess."

"I'm sorry to hear it," the other woman said. "I have the constitution of a horse. Never been carsick or airsick in my life. Not even as a kid."

Suzanne made a sound she hoped would pass as acceptable response. The woman chose to hear it as encouragement.

"Where are you heading, dear?" she pressed.

"Oakland," Suzanne answered, hoping her tone of voice would discourage her interlocuter.

Undaunted, the woman plunged on. "Are you visiting friends in Oakland?"

"I have—" she hesitated, then decided, *What does it matter?* She said, "Family here. My sister. I have some . . . family matters . . . to take care of." After a moment, she added, "My sister and I haven't seen much of each other since our mother died. This will be the first time we've set eyes on each other in almost thirteen years."

"I see. And where are you from?"

"New York, now. But I was born in Oakland." She was warming to the conversation, finding that her panic was retreating—defeated by the mundane business of making small talk.

"Interesting. Where were you born?"

"East 14th Street—near the Diamond District."

"Well, now, isn't that a *coincidence?* I know that district. I lived not far away, for a time. I used to attend the New Bethel Church, when old Reverent Cartland preached there. Do you remember him, by any chance?"

"Yes," Suzanne said, "I remember him quite well."

Old Reverend Cartland must be long dead and buried, she reflected. She remembered the long arguments, earnest but good-natured, between her grandmother Chicory and the elderly pastor, who was constantly urging her to give up her "devil's work and come back into the fold."

Suzanne remembered her grandmother's harsh laugh; then she would shake her finger and say, "Mr. Cartland, you're a smart man, but you're not *that* smart. You know some of the answers, but you think you know them all. No man alive can know them all."

"Jesus was a man; Jesus knew all there was to know."

"Jesus was spirit. I'm not talking *orishas*, I'm talking *men*."

The old man would shake his head and sigh. "You're pavin' the way to hell, and you're doing' the same for them two granddaughters of yours." He would set his hand gently on seven-year-old Suzanne's head and look at her sadly. She let his hand stay there for a moment, but she drew herself closer to old Chicory, feeling the old woman's dry, boney fingers tighten around her own reassuringly.

"That's enough, Reverend," the old woman said gently, "you're scarin' the child."

The man removed his hand and smiled down at the girl. "She'll come around. I keep prayin', and you add a prayer yourself. You'll see. Your grandma, she'll come around."

Then he had moved on, and the elderly woman and child had continued on to do their shopping. After half a block of walking in silence, Chicory warned her, "You go prayin' for me and I'll never speak to you again, child." She laughed suddenly. "Back in Bukawai, where your grandmothers come from, when they were brought away as slaves, we had a special *orisha*, that was Shango, the god of Thunder. In Trinidad, where I grew up, we call him St. John the Baptist, because that was a real Christian place, and we had to give the old ones new names. But now I'm in a new place, I don't have to listen to any more Reverend Cartlands if it suits me. So I'm back to calling Shango by his rightful name; I'm back to discovering the powers of *orishas* that my grandmothers knew."

She stopped, knelt down beside the girl, and hugged her impulsively to her; her breath was a mixture of coffee and cigarettes warm in Suzanne's nostrils. "Honey, you're the one I chose; you're the one *been* chosen for me to pass on what I learned. I got *so much* to tell you. If even a little bit of it be true, you're gonna see how all the thinking of all the Reverend Cartlands there ever was don't add up to nothin' against the powers inside and outside this world."

She remembered Chicory telling her one story: how, as a young woman in Trinidad, she had been walking through a field. Clouds had gathered overhead. Her grandmother's words came back to her.

"I knew somethin' was 'bout to happen. The moon the night before had gone green; now, with them clouds up there, the sun got to lookin' purple. Suddenly, one them big clouds overhead broke loose from the others, swimming like a whale up above. Then, when it was just over me, these gashes opened up on its side. Like it was bein' attacked by invisible swordfishes. And it began to bleed, great heavy drops of red blood come spatterin' down on the field, on me. I started screamin' and run and run, and my dress was covered with blood, my hands and arms, and I'm slippin' in big puddles of it. It's mixin' with the dirt and makin' red mud cakin' to my shoes and makin' it harder and harder for me to run. And it's gettin' in my eyes and in my mouth when I'm trying' to scream. Some of it is so heavy it beats on me like it was hail. I know in my heart this is a sign from Shango—but I'm afraid because it might just kill me.

"And then I tripped over a root and come down hard, my face falling into a pool of blood. I'm gaspin' and swallowin' and chokin' and I feel I swallowed some of it down, that blood. And I try to puke it up, but that blood is in me for good, even though I'm heavin' my guts out.

"Then, while I'm coughin' and chokin', the rain suddenly changes to black water, then clean water. It's clean and warm, bathin' me as gentle as my mama used to bathe me when I was a little girl.

"And when I'm cleaned, the rain stops, all of a sudden. A breeze comes up and dries me while I walk back to town lookin' for Ben to tell him what happened.

"But no one in town had seen that blood rain, 'cept me. It was a sign for just me. They had felt the rain, and they believed what I told them. It frightened Ben . . . I believe that was probably one reason he left me and ran off with that Port-au-Prince whore. He couldn't take the fact that I was marked for somethin' special. That all the women in my family have a special gift that goes right back to our Spirit Mother, who whispered the first secrets to Grandmother Naii in Africa all those years ago."

If even a little bit of it be true, Suzanne remembered. Staring out the Greyhound window at the clouds that had begun massing overhead as the bus rolled steadily south and west, through smaller, then larger towns and suburbs. She added to herself, *It's true. And much more than a little bit is true.*

"Dear," her neighbor said, "I don't think you've heard anything I've been saying. Are you all right? You seem tired."

Suzanne shook her head briefly.

"Well, good . . . if you'll excuse me, I think I'll use the washroom myself."

Suzanne let the heavy-set woman pass, then let her head loll back. For a few minutes she stared at the roof of the bus; then she closed her eyes, letting the hum of the engines soothe her.

A moment later, she was asleep, and didn't wake up again until the woman beside her gave her a nudge and said, "Wake up, dear, we're in Oakland."

Suzanne blinked awake as the bus rolled to a stop beside the terminal waiting room.

She let the other passengers leave first, while she sat looking out the dusty window at the unappealing back facade of the bus station. *Now it begins,* she thought, *the big pieces begin falling into place. Years later. More years later than either of us could dream would come between, Dr. David Palmer, the blood price is going to be paid. And that price is everything you have—and your life.*

Overhead, the clouds gathered as if for a summer thundershower. Suzanne tensed, anticipating a roll of thunder that never came.

With a sigh, she heaved herself to her feet and started toward the front of the bus.

Not now, but soon, she thought, and stepped out into the sulty air.

TWO

DAVID PALMER walked beside his pool, wincing as the morning sun reflected off the water and stung his eyes. As he walked hunched forward, his hands shoved deep into the pockets of his robe, he was enjoying his four-acre estate on some of the choicest land in Marin County. He could feel the sun warming the back of his neck. Today was going to be a scorcher.

He smiled a bitter smile. Someone—correction: *several someones* were going to get some heat applied today. He was going to call in all the favors he could until he found out the leak and put a stop to the newspaper articles in the *Post* and the threat of a CIA check on his involvement in the Bukawai civil war. The arms he was supplying and the monies pouring in from rebels there were all so laundered no one could have traced it. And yet, too many particulars had hit the front pages. The PalmerCo offices in San Francisco's Stritch Building were already targeted for pickets from U.C. Berkeley, and some of the more radical congressmen were demanding a congressional investigation of PalmerCo's involvement with the

Bukawai Provisional Government—a right-wing faction attempting to overthrow the two-year-old, legally constituted Socialist Government of Bukawai Prime Minister Mwala Kwamina.

He stood beside the diving board, leaning the backs of his legs against the molded plastic, staring at the house which lay beyond the opposite end of the pool. The white stucco was painfully bright in the sunlight. As he watched, he had a sudden vivid memory of his wife, Sabrina, standing on the balcony which ran the full length of the upper story.

In his mind, she was dressed in her long, light-blue robe of some silky material; the wide sleeves fell away in loops from her pale arms. She shook her head, letting her long blonde hair fall back behind her shoulders.

She extended her arms, stretching—looking for all the world, David thought, like some high priestess performing some ritual.

He blinked and wished her away. The balcony was empty. Sabrina dead (killed in a drunken car crash while she may—or may not—have been cheating on him) had only a little less reality for him than Sabrina alive. She had married him (he always knew) in a hasty burst of passion; she had repented of it through a leisurely series of affairs with occasional strangers—more often the husbands or lovers of her closest friends.

David had ignored her unfaithfulness, because she was useful to him. Her old Marin family money and her social standing had given him the entry he needed to the San Francisco business world. He provided her the illusion of a respectable homelife that masked her increasingly more flamboyant indiscretions; he gave her more money than her generous inheritance provided; and, of those occasions when neither her current love nor his current mistress satisfied, they coupled with the exhilarating passion of equally matched rivals who brought to bed the vigor of their lovelessness and contempt.

Oddly enough, David reflected, out of those unloving, superheated embraces had come a daughter and a son whom both of them loved as absolutely as they detested each other. David saw in Angelica and Kirk the beginning of a dynasty. With his children to love, and his present mistress, Christine Lee, for sex, David had suddenly found Sabrina so much excess baggage. He considered her fatal crack-up on Wolf Grade Road the year before the only selfless action of their life together.

For a brief moment, things had appeared to come together for him in the best possible way. He had his son and daughter; he had Christine; PalmerCo's revenues—from all sources—were going through the roof. And then, the very moment when everything looked fine, the situation had gone critical with PalmerCo and its multiple overseas involvements—particularly the Bukawai connection. There was talk of the CIA nosing around—armed with more information than they could possibly have gotten without inside help. He had to find the security leak, and *fast*.

With an oath, he dropped onto the end of the

diving board, turning from the terrace to look out over the shore of Belvedere Island, toward the Marine Headlands and the Golden Gate Bridge.

He had come so far, gained so much. Now they were threatening to take everything away from him, trying to bring the whole of PalmerCo's worldwide network under government scrutiny—a move that could destroy his far-flung empire overnight and erase what it had taken him fifteen years to build. PalmerCo was his life—it was almost as important as his children. If he lost control of the legitimate firms and their underground "branch operations," he would lose everything. The crux seemed to be Bukawai. The little West African nation was being ripped apart by civil war. But, *God help him*, he wasn't about to let the Government of Kwamina nationalize the most important copper mines and numerous other highly profitable PalmerCo holdings. The rebel forces of Colonel Obitsebi should, with the sophisticated arms and advisors financed by PalmerCo's African subsidiaries, be able to topple Kwamini's already faltering Government. Then, PalmerCo would be around to help pick up the pieces and act on the guarantees generously provided by Colonel Obitsebi in return for M-14s, ammunition, machine guns, and a variety of the most advanced technological hardware.

David Palmer had come a long way from the child he had been. Life had taught him to be ruthless, whether dealing with a mistress who was unfaithful or the deaths of thousands in a tiny, pivotal nation half a world away.

He was the only child of a father who taught mathematics in St. Godric's Catholic High School (now closed) and a mother who believed that her marriage was a mistaken impulse begun in the arms of her Marine sergeant husband-to-be on V-J Day on Market Street and culminated in rapid succession with her marriage ten days later and the arrival of David just under nine months after that.

She claimed that the labor and delivery of what was to be—emphatically—her only child and heir had so affected her health that, for the rest of her life, she had to live as a semi-invalid. This, she would angrily explain to her increasingly frustrated husband, was the reason she *could not* get a job to supplement his inadequate income. Besides, she would always add, *her* mother and father had raised her to believe that a husband was the provider, a wife the homemaker.

As a child, David had been spared few of their arguments, and none of the bitterness that flourished between them. He hated his father's inability to provide for the family in the manner his mother assured him "true achievers" did. And he hated his mother's whining and pretensions, her endless, blaming reminders that he (and, of course, his father) had robbed her of her youth, her health, her right to a life—any life—that was better than the one she was living.

David grew to despise his father for enduring his mother's abuse; and he despised his mother for not taking him and leaving forever his father, the damp little apartment on Lincon Street, the life that was—according to her—swallowing them alive minute by destructive minute.

More than anything else, he hated the poverty: the endless altercations over his father's inadequate salary, his mother's refusal/inability (depending on which of the two David listened to) to work, the expense of raising a child. As a child, David had vowed to himself that he would never be poor—and he would never let *anyone* control his life in the name of love or duty or any of the fancy names that seemed (on the basis of his experience with his parents) nothing more than putting a respectable face on the pragmatic business of sinking your teeth into someone else's throat and sucking the lifeblood out of them.

His mother grew more reclusive; his father buried himself in coaching the basketball team and the football team for St. Godric's. David recalled those days (he went to St. Godrick's on substantially reduced tuition) with loathing. He hated the Brothers of the Order of St. Godric who taught the classes with little imagination—except when it came to punishments. He could still recall the disgrace of being made to kneel, hands behind his back, gum (the chewing of which, in study hall, had brought the wrath of Brother Nicholas down on him) wadded across the bridge of his nose, while Nicholas smacked him on the ears and lampooned him mercilessly, to the vast amusement of his classmates—who were no friends, finding him standoffish, a "snob," and deserving of everything he got.

His mother took to quiet drinking; his father took to boisterous drinking—whether celebrating a basketball victory or drowning out a football loss.

David considered running away, but had sense enough to know that it was too soon for him—that he would only make more trouble for himself than he already had.

And then, in the senior year of high school, returning home one afternoon and letting himself into the Lincoln Street flat, he found himself delivered.

His mother, the side of her head caved in from a blow by a blood-spattered "Coach of the Year" trophy, lay in the middle of the living room floor, between upended coffee table and an overturned chair. His father, the man's cheeks still wet with tears (drunken tears, David guessed), lay across his twin bed—the right side of his head, his right eye, and most of his cheekbone blown away in the blast from the military-issue revolver that had (so far as David could recall) resided under a pile of stale-smelling linen handkerchiefs and tarnished war medals in blue and purple cases.

For an incredulous moment, the young David had stood in the doorway between living room and bedroom, surveying the ruins that had been his parents. For a moment he was puzzled by the failure of the Wickersons, who lived in the flat below, to respond to the mayhem over their heads. Then, he remembered it was Friday, and on Friday they visited their married daughter who lived in Daly City, forty-five minutes bus ride to the south.

He stood and savored his abrupt, unanticipated freedom for several long, satisfying minutes. Then, in a voice remarkably calm (given the circumstances), he reported the murder-suicide to the San Francisco Police Department.

* * *

In the aftermath, he discovered that his parents had guaranteed him a way to begin working toward everything he had promised himself. While he could not collect on his father's policy, his mother's insurance brought him a substantial amount. And the Brothers of the Order of St. Godric, moved by some obscure sense of duty, paid for all the funeral expenses, and gave him a check for $957 "on behalf of the order."

Two days after the funeral, he had sold the furniture—everything that belonged to his parents he sold, gave away, or threw away. Then he set about making his way towards the goals that had always been clear in his mind.

He moved to the East Coast after graduation with honors. He spent the summer working at a variety of jobs, and—in the fall—using the insurance money and a partial scholarship the Brothers had helped him obtain, David went to Harvard.

Several years later, David had gotten his M.B.A. from Harvard. With such flawless credentials, he easily secured a position with one of the more prestigious investment firms in New York City.

It was while working at Global Development Corporation (GDC) that he had first begun to discover the lucrative potential of third-world countries, where judicious investments and surgical handling of political situations could prove high yield, with multiple factions channeling monies into GDC while they battled to the death—or met a slower (but nonetheless sure) death paying inflated prices for inferior merchandise. While several African or Latin American countries went bankrupt, GDC cried all the way to the international bank.

But it had been GDC's *sub rosa* involvement with American politics in which David had shown his initial flair. Working under the unquestioned (though never acknowledged) blessing of the Herrick brothers, whose brainchild GDC was, David had immersed himself in politics. He worked for the election of whoever was willing to insure that the Herrick Brothers' operations would continue unchallenged by any government —federal, state, or local.

And then, he had made the mistake of his life.

He had met Suzanne Raine, had become infatuated with her, obsessed, finally—*enslaved* by her. There was no other word to describe the hold she had over him sexually, emotionally, *totally*. It was like voodoo, the way she had taken control of him; he had imagined her at the time like one of those black-skinned, many-armed Eastern goddesses who had taken hold of his mind, will, heart, sex and could, at any moment she desired, destroy him in the most painful and devastating way imaginable—eviscerating, emasculating, ripping everything of him away if she desired—

He had never loved her. "Love" was a wholly inadequate description of even the least part of what had happened between David and Suzanne so many years ago in New York. He had wanted her utterly. And then, he had only wanted to be utterly free of her.

Because she would not free him, because the stakes in his own game had suddenly spiraled to unexpected heights, because the baby had arrived to complicate things beyong hope of simple answers, the violence had happened. And, in the end, it had caught him anyway, swept aside everything he had built up, turned his world into a nightmare and sent him scuttling like a frightened child across the country to San Francisco again—like a wounded animal returning to its lair to lick its wounds.

He still hated her, and even now, realized he feared the control she had taken over him. Lately, fragmentary memories of her troubled him. Or dreams. Sometimes she was naked and hungrily stretching out for him from a tangle of silken bedclothes; sometimes, sheathed in the green-white-and-purple African-style dress that made her seem so regal, she sat on a carved ivory throne, dandling her cafe-au-lait-skinned baby on her lap.

Once, a week ago, he had reached out to the naked Suzanne, had embraced her in his sleep, and had wakened to find Christine in his arms. Her automatic response had hidden his momentary confusion at having past and present meld together.

Afterwards, when Christine had fallen asleep again, he lay staring into the pre-dawn darkness, listening to his mistress's soft breathing. He let the sound of her, the traces of her perfume, the feel of her breast under his hand exorcise the dream of Suzanne.

But, he realized with irony, the beautiful black

woman who had shared his bed for less than a year was a constant reminder of that other woman, whose hold he had broken on every part of him but his memory and his dreams. There was something of Suzanne in Christine's eyes, which seemed almost violet in a certain light—and in the shape of her mouth, the color of her skin (like polished rosewood), her stately carriage. Sometimes, when he watched her crossing to his bed, David was reminded of a tall pagan queen out of some ancient African story.

But there was nothing stately or restrained about their lovemaking. She had a passionate nature that also echoed Suzanne's—with this difference: this time, *he*—not the woman—was in control.

He would never—*never*—allow himself to be brought to the edge of lunacy like that again.

He heard a dry cough. Turning, as he stood up from the end of the diving board, David saw his assistant, Dominic Roselli, standing in the doorway to the living room, framed by the shadows inside the Palmer house. The older, heavy-set man had the flat of his right hand tilted across his eyes to shade them from the bright sun. Having located his employer, and having announced his presence, he made no effort to move any further into the daylight. In all the years they had worked together, David had never known his underling to step voluntarily into any bright light—especially sunlight—unless circumstances left him no choice. Occasionally, Dominic spoke vaguely of a sensitivity in his eyes; David privately believed it was long years of acclimatization to activities more profitably (and safely) pursued away from well-lit spaces and prying eyes. Like a successful magician, Roselli produced sometimes amazing results—but David, for whom these things were done, chose not to see the behind-the-scenes machinations Roselli used to deliver the goods. He felt it was better that he knew as little as possible about Dominic's methods.

Dominic Roselli had turned up—long years after the fact—from the largely buried wreckage of David's early New York career. David had only been married a short time to his socialite wife— was just beginning to extend PalmerCo's diversified interests into unexpected but potentially hugely profitable new directions—when Dom showed up. Asking for work. Dismissing David's questions about why the man had left New York with an angry, impatient gesture. Dom wanted work: in return he brought his very real (very specialized) talents and the suggestion (never actually put into so many words) that David's cooperation would guarantee Dom's forgetting certain New York matters that might prove an embarrassment to David's rich new wife and his fledgling company's credibility and respectability in San Francisco's business community.

Ostensibly, Dominic Roselli was head of Palmer-Co's security forces throughout its far-flung corporate mini-empire. In actuality, he was David's right hand: the man whose business it was to secure all of PalmerCo's interests—legal, marginal, or illegal—against interference from outside. Or inside. Now, with the CIA putting pressure on them, with the Bukawai situation poised between paying off and blowing sky-high, Dom had made it a personal crusade to ferret out fifth columnists (if they existed) within the corporate structure—and make sure that anywhere government snoops looked, they saw a clean-as-a-whistle operation that could not, by any stretch of the imagination, be linked to international political misdealings, gun-running, selective assassinations.

The stakes, David knew only too well, were getting higher by the minute. But he had every confidence in Roselli.

Shoving his hands in the pockets of his robe, David walked toward the patio doors. Dominic stepped further back into the cool semidarkness inside the living room.

When David had closed the sliding glass door behind him and glanced around the room to assure himself the room was empty, he said, "Well?"

Roselli shrugged. "Sanders and Channing are clean."

"You're sure?"

The heavy-set man shifted his weight from his left foot to his right, saying nothing. The question, he let David know, was not worth answering.

David crossed to the couch and settled into the cream-colored expanse of it, putting his bare feet carelessly on the ebony coffee table in front of it.

Dom remained standing.

"So, now what?" David prompted.

"I've got some new ideas. And an old one: Christine Lee—"

"No!" David snapped, irritatedly. "It's a waste of time. It's letting your overdeveloped sense of thoroughness run away with you."

"I'm only saying, let me check her out. If she's clean, she's clean. I'm not saying for sure she's an *infiltrator*—" He pronounced this last syllable by careful syllable, clearly pleased to be able to use the word.

"Jesus, Dom! It's a leak—a goddamned leak—there's someone unhappy with his position who's been bought by the C.I.A.—someone who's been around for a couple of years at least. Christine's been—with us—less than a year. And she doesn't have access to the sort of information you're talking about. No—going after Christine—that's a crock. And you've got my guarantee. Drop it—let's look into realistic possibilities."

Roselli shrugged, and shifted from his right foot back to his left.

In a calmer tone, David said, "What other possibilities?"

"Cooper. Halversen. Some others I've got my eye on."

"How soon can you smoke the bastard out?"

Another shrug.

"There's not much time," David said, more to himself than to the man standing across the smooth, waxed-black surface of the coffee table from him.

"I'll deliver," Dom promised.

And David, meeting the man's eyes, knew that

whoever was selling his and PalmerCo's interests out had only a short time before Roselli called him —or her—to a final accounting.

THREE

SUZANNE STARED at the immense orange cat lying in the path directly in front of her. The cat regarded her impassively, blinking its green eyes in the white-hot sunlight.

"His name is Dubonnet," a familiar voice called down from the porch above her. She glanced uncertainly at the sagging steps which climbed sharply to the porch of the Victorian-style house painted a dusty white and trimmed in blue.

She shaded her eyes and located a woman in the shadow of the porch. She called back, "Elenora?"

"Who else was you expectin'?" her sister asked. There was no warmth in the other woman's voice.

Suzanne nodded and picked up the suitcases the cabbie had set carelessly on the sidewalk. She stepped around the animal with distaste and walked up the strip of concrete that led from the sidewalk to the foot of the stairs.

Her sister made no move to help her, made no welcoming gesture; she remained standing in the shade of the porch. Suzanne could feel her eyes even as she let her own gaze take in the flaking paint, the bowed front steps, and the weed-choked remains of a garden burned brown by the sun. Everything she saw suggested a meanness, an unwillingness to make more than a minimal effort to resist the petty vandalism of time. She told herself, as she started up the steep steps, holding securely onto the railing, it didn't really matter that her sister had not changed at all, while so many changes had happened in her own life: all that was important was finishing the things she had been sent to accomplish.

Elenora had hardened into a chunky, aggressively plain-featured black woman in her mid-forties. She was wearing a shapeless tan skirt and a violently patterned green blouse. Some of her graying hair was carelessly restrained by a yellow scarf worn gypsy fashion. Her sandals clopped loosely on the steps as she grudgingly descended three stairs, took the heavier suitcase.

"It ain't much," Elenora said over her shoulder, "but it does fine for me and the boy."

Suzanne followed her through the front door, heavily scarred and hastily covered with thick brown paint. Elenora held the door open for her. "Come on in," she said. Her tone remained guarded, not overtly hostile, but Suzanne heard no trace of warmth. But then, she hadn't expected any. Circumstances—not affection—had caused her to write her sister and come home after all these years.

They passed a small table alongside one wall in the hall on which unopened mail had been tossed.

On the threshold of the tiny living room, Elenora paused and set down the suitcase she was carrying. Suzanne continued to hang onto the overnight case.

There was a momentary silence while they stood uncomfortably staring at the uncarpeted room in front of them.

The room was dark; a mass of drying green-brown shrubbery pressed against the picture window and let in only diffuse light, which seemed to draw out the darkness of the floral wallpaper, the depth of the scarred, thickly varnished hardwood floor, and the browns of the old, cumbersome furniture. Two mismatched arm chairs, unholstered in washed-out stripes of green and brown, faced the couch, which was covered in a dark green material. The rock-and-brick chimney was guarded by two shoulder-high, dusty, narrow windows. Though it was grated, and a new-looking set of fireplace tools stood primly on its brown-tiled hearth, the fireplace had the chilly look of long disuse.

Something about the quality of light and shadow, something in the cool still air of the room, suggested to Suzanne a secret glade buried deep in a forest.

Beside her, Elenora said, "It sure ain't much to look at but it suits us." Again, there was that challenging tone. The older woman had folded her arms across her chest and was looking at Suzanne with a mixture of curiosity and belligerence.

"It's like a clear space in the woods," Suzanne said, and she thought of her grandmother, who often said, "When you most need to be in touch with *ju-ju*, go where there are trees and no one else goes. Shango will talk to you there—you'll hear his voice in the wind shakin' the leaves. He roars in the thunder, but he speaks gentle in the forest."

"—I said, you never did say how long you planned to stay."

"Sorry. My mind wandered. I was remembering Nana Chicory."

Elenora shrugged, then muttered, "Well?"

"How long I'm gonna stay? Just 'till I find a place of my own."

That seemed to satisfy her sister. Elenora relaxed, letting her arms drop to her side. "Well, now—well, I'd better show you the room you'll be stayin' in."

Suzanne nodded, reaching down for the small case at her feet. Then her hand froze in mid-reach. Some trick of sunlight through the dusty window to the left of the fireplace suddenly burnished the wood statue carelessly set amid a cluster of shells and bric-a-brac on the window ledge.

The carved mahogany female stood, leaning slightly on an unadorned staff in her right hand; in her left arm she cradled an infant who suckled at one of the exaggerated breasts. She wore a Bukawai ceremonial kilt and characteristic anklets, bracelets, and necklace of cowrie shells, and a headpiece that displayed the double-headed axe insignia of the Shango cult.

The light faded. Suzanne picked up her overnight case aware that her hand was shaking uncontrollably.

"You all right?" asked Elenora, who missed very little.

Suzanne smiled. "I'm tired and I drank too

much coffee at the bus station, that's all." Trying to keep her voice conversational, she said, "That statue over there—it was Nana Chicory's, wasn't it?"

"Sure. Don't know why I kept the thing after she died. Only, she put such store by it—called it something—"

"The Ancestress," Suzanne supplied in a voice little more than a whisper.

"Yeah, that was it. I guess that's *supposed* to be our great-great-granma or some shit. I tell you, if we had tits like that, Sweet Sue, we'd be richer than Jackie-O right now."

"Yeah, well—that sure as hell wasn't part of what either of us got handed down from the old folks."

"Um-*um,*" Elenora agreed. Lifting the suitcase, she motioned to Suzanne with her head. "Come along, now. Your room is on the second floor—just past Jomo's."

"Jomo?" asked Suzanne, still reacting to the strange effect of seeing the wood carving.

"Your nephew? My boy. *That* Jomo." Anger, poorly concealed, tinged Elenora's voice. "I *know* you've never seen him, but you *can't* have forgotten that you've got a nephew now."

"Of course I haven't forgotten," she said, keeping her own responsive anger just under control. "I'm tired and a little disoriented, that's all."

"You need a rest, *that's* what you need," her sister said. "Come on now and we'll get you settled in. You can have a little sleep before Jomo gets home."

Suzanne followed her sister out of the room, not

daring to look back at the statue nestled on the window sill.

Eleanora led her down the short, narrow hall towards the staircase near its end which climbed steeply upwards. The air was very still; faint smells of cooking, dust, and moth balls lingered. At the top of the stairs, a dilapidated purple armchair nearly blocked their way. Elenora said, "I've *got* to get that thing moved. It's been here almost a month, I'm ashamed to say. Jomo moved it out of my bedroom and got it this far."

Near the end of the upstairs hallway was the bedroom. Elenora pushed the door open, stepped inside, and set down Suzanne's suitcase.

After a moment, Suzanne followed her sister into the room, setting her smaller case beside the larger one.

The smell of fresh paint hung thickly in the warm air. The new white paint had been slathered carelessly over cracks, uneven repairs, small holes, so that every imperfection was evident. The new chocolate-brown carpet was badly bunched in several places.

There was a narrow bed against one wall, an old desk in front of one window, and an old drop-leaf table in the corner opposite the closet. Also a single bookcase and a compact easy chair covered with a grimy-looking, shiny fabric. The windows were wide and covered with thin, over-washed curtains.

"It's homey—nothin' fancy," Elenora remarked.

Suzanne moved around getting the feel of the place. She lifted a copy of an old high school chemistry text with mildewed pages off the bookshelf and leafed through it a moment. She looked into the little bathroom off the hall with a side door from her own room. In it she found an unexpectedly nice marble basin with a wide ledge around it.

"It's real comfortable, Elenora," she murmured, returning to the bedroom, where she went to the window and looked out into the neighboring yard below.

A child about ten was throwing garden clippings into the back of a battered pickup truck. The boy was mulatto, the color of milk chocolate; he had a thick mop of loosely matted, reddish-brown hair.

As if he sensed someone watching, the boy paused and looked up, shading his eyes against the sunshine. Suzanne let the curtain drop back into place before the boy discovered her.

She turned back into the room. Her sister was sitting on the end of the bed. She smiled and said, "Nice, isn't it?"

"Yes," Suzanne said, with no real conviction in her voice, repeating, "real comfortable."

"Jomo and me did the fixin' up." She toed one of the ridges of brown carpet, then laughed sharply. "Well, we ain't the best fixit-people around, but I guess you can live with it."

"I'm sure I can," said Suzanne, returning her sister's smile, feeling a sudden, helpless warmth toward the other woman.

"Say, Suzanne," Elenora began, obviously having just made up her mind to ask an uncomfortable question. "Why did you decide—so sudden-like—to come home? We sure as hell ain't been what you'd call *close* all these years. You

43

didn't come home for mama's funeral. Or Thomas's—"

"I never really knew your husband," Suzanne said softly, "and I hardly had two nickels to rub together back then."

"But you never even came when Nana died. And that old lady *loved* you. I'll tell you, it sure didn't sit well with me at all. I still—well," she made a dismissing gesture, "no point rakin' up old hurts the minute you get back. But, you know, I really don't have any idea about why you come back now." Elenora stared at her sister with frank curiosity.

Suzanne studied the worn felt on the desk top, rubbing her fingers back and forth for a long time. Finally, she said, "I got some . . . business . . . to take care of."

"You didn't mention no business in your letters. What *kind* of business?"

"Old business, new business . . ."

"'Any business but your business'—yeah, I know the old song. And I hear you tellin' me to mind my own business, like you'd do when we was kids. Okay—your business is your business—long as it don't cross over to my side the street and make itself mine."

Suzanne kept rubbing her fingers over the blotter; she was uncertain what reply to give her sister.

"Elenora . . ." There was a worried urgency in the other woman's voice now. "It's *private*, Elenora. *Private* business that doesn't concern you. I appreciate your letting me stay here till I get settled, but it doesn't give you the right to pry."

"Sister of mine, you turn around—*now*—and look me in the eye and tell me this visit ain't gonna make no trouble for me or my boy."

After the faintest hesitation, Suzanne turned and met her sister's stare directly. "I have no mind to involve any of you in anything, Elenora. What I've got to do belongs to me, alone."

"Well, long as we got *that* taken care of, things will run real smooth for all three of us while you're visiting."

"Oh, I expect to be settled in my own place before too long. But," she smiled again, catching her sister unawares, "who can say what the *orishas* have in store for us?"

"Sure, well—" said Elenora, clearly disconcerted by the unanticipated reference to the old religion. Clearly, Suzanne thought with amusement, spirits have never been credited before with any of the events in Elenora Watkins' life. After a momentary pause, the older woman asked cautiously, "Uh, Suzanne, you ain't become a Jesus freak or nothin', have you?"

"No," said the young woman, clearly amused, "I swear Jesus is the further thing from my mind."

"Well good, 'cause I had my fill of God and spirits and devils and I *don't* know *what-all* shit growin' up around Nana Chicory. I don't hold with that stuff no more and I don't like Jomo 'sposed to it."

Sensing the dangerous ground they were crossing, Suzanne changed the subject. "Would you mind if I took a little nap? I never got a decent wink of sleep on that bus."

"Sure, honey, you really do look all worn out,"

said Elenora, sympathetic now that they were back on safe ground. "Everything's ready. Do you need any help unpacking?"

"I can manage very well. Thank you for thinking of it." Suzanne walked over to her sister; the other woman stood up abruptly, uncertainly, her arms dangling uncomfortably at her sides, her fingers twitching nervously. Impulsively, Suzanne embraced Elenora, kissing her lightly on the cheek. "It really *is* good to be here, Elno." After a moment of uncertainty, her sister returned the embrace, smothering Suzanne with a hug that almost, in its ferocity and hunger, cut off the younger woman's breath.

When Elenora let go, there were tears in her eyes. "Have you really come far enough to forget the old shit and be friends again?" she asked hopefully, uncertainly.

"I'd like to think so," Suzanne said guardedly.

"Well then." Elenora beamed, ignoring the cautious tone of the other woman's reply. "Well, then, welcome home, little sister. It's been too long." She fumbled a wad of Kleenex out of her pocket. "You get a rest now. I'm gonna fix something real special for dinner."

She gaze Suzanne a final hug, then walked to the door, stepping around the large orange cat, Dubonnet, who had seated himself on the threshold of the room. The cat was licking a paw and regarding Suzanne with an almost insolent look.

Elenora reached down and scooped the protesting animal into her generous, mahogany-colored arms. "You've already met Dubonnet," she said. "I named him that 'cause he looks like the cat on the wine label. You know."

Suzanne nodded and said, mechanically, "He's a pretty cat."

"Ain't he just? And he knows it. I spoil him something fierce." Elenora stroked the cat's head several times. The creature stretched and yawned, but never took its eyes off Suzanne. "He's a real friendly cat," she said. "I'm sure you'll be good friends."

"I'm afraid I don't much care for pets," she responded.

"Don't worry, old Dubonnet will win you over," laughed Elenora. "Now you get some rest, hear. We'll talk more later." She went out, closing the door softly behind her.

After Elenora was gone, Suzanne glanced around indifferently; then she dropped onto the edge of the queen-sized bed and began unbuttoning her sweater. The room seemed cool enough, but she felt flushed, almost feverish.

She folded her light-green sweater and set it on the nightstand. She crossed to the little bathroom, and splashed some cool water on her face and neck, and patted herself dry with a worn towel; then she forced herself to take several deep breaths. She was relaxed now. For the first time she realized how nervous she had been as she had gotten closer and closer to her journey's end.

She returned to the bedroom. With a care approaching reverence, she lifted the larger suitcase onto the bed and opened it gently, fearful that its contents might have been damaged by careless jostling during her bus ride from New

York.

From its nest inside the softest clothes she owned, Suzanne pulled out a single shoebox. She opened it, examining the contents, packed in thick swaths of crispy tissue paper. She saw at once that everything was safe. She replaced the contents of the box carefully and repacked the tissue paper. Then she returned the box to its burrow within the softness of sweaters and skirts. Finally she relocked the suitcase and slid it under the bed. She told herself, "Everything is going so well, it's a clear sign that the spirit is watching over me and approving."

Afterwards, she took off her clothes, drew the dirty shades, got into bed. She was asleep shortly after her head touched the pillow.

She was lying on her bed in pitch blackness; the air around her had a thick, suffocating quality. Suzanne had the terrifying thought that she was trapped in a lightness space far below the surface of the earth.

Then a pale radiance grew around her; it seemed a quality of the air which was growing less oppressive as the light intensified. With mingled confusion and relief at the familiar, she was back in the old bedroom she had shared with her sister when their parents had still been alive.

She could see the details of her old stuffed animals and toys haphazardly tossed onto cupboard shelves; the zig-zag pattern of the afgan Nana had crocheted for her bed; the kewpie Elenora had won one summer at Playland at the Beach—

Everything was as she remembered it. But it had the flatness and colorlessness of a black-and-white photograph.

She started at the sudden feel of bony fingers clamping onto her shoulder. She was half dragged to her feet and forced to turn around and face her grandmother, Charlotte Chicory Brown.

Bursting into tears like a little girl, she tried to explain to Nana that she had been frightened, but the old woman only said impatiently, "No time for that, child, you've got to watch now. These things are important: the Servant is soon here, you must take him. The sacrifice must be made; you will surrender it. Remember: the splinter and the needle work most strongly on blood kin."

"But, Nana, what does it all mean?"

Nana Chicory had turned and was walking away into a distance beyond the walls of the tiny bedroom.

Suzanne screamed after the old woman to halt, she tried to run after her, felt the walls of the room become no more substantial than cobwebs as she ran through them into the starless night, and was suddenly tumbling down into infinity ...

She awoke suddenly. Her room was very warm; she had forgotten to leave a window open when she had fallen asleep. Now she threw open both windows to the lazy, half-imagined summer breeze.

From her smaller suitcase, she took a large brown envelope. Out of this she pulled a newspaper page and unfolded it carefully. She laid this gently on the floor and studied the yellowing AP

Wirephoto. A good-looking full-faced man in his late forties smiled out of the picture. Her had salt-and-pepper curly hair and a tight, self-conscious smile. Alongside him was a serious-seeming girl and an open-faced boy about sixteen who seemed clearly embarrassed at having his picture taken. The caption below read:

> David Palmer, President of PalmerCo, International, has just announced that his company will open additional overseas branch offices in Manila, Melbourne, and Sydney. Palmer is shown here with his daughter Amy, a student at the University of California, and his son Kirk.

Suzanne sat on the floor beside the newspaper. From the envelope she extracted a blurred sepia-toned photograph of an infant about one year old, Negro, albino, who smiled out at her with an elfin self-assurance from inside his crib. This she set beside the newspaper. She pulled her purse off the bed and took out a tiny hardwood pendant carved like the doubleheaded axe of Shango. The handle was pierced with a leather thong so that the amulet could be worn around her wrist or neck, if she wanted. She set this on the floor below the baby picture.

For a time she simply stared at the collage, letting herself be open and attentive. She heard the breeze stir the curtains, felt it playfully caress the back of her neck, the left side of her face. But the presence she longed for wasn't there . . . all she sensed were wind-imps who mocked her with the pretense that the one they served was standing near her.

She sighed and waited: patience was the one lesson she had learned best over the years between her baby's death and now. The weariness of all that waiting seemed to drain her suddenly.

A soft tapping at her door disturbed her. She heard her sister ask softly, "Honey, you 'wake? It's almost five o'clock. Jomo will be home soon. It would be kinda nice for you to be downstairs to meet him, don't you think?"

Suzanne felt lightheaded. With a tremendous effort she gathered up the newspaper clipping, the photo, the pendant, and pushed them deep into her purse. Rising unsteadily to her feet, she set the purse carefully on the little desk.

"Suzanne, you all right?" Elenora sounded worried; she rapped even more loudly on the door.

"I—" She stopped, licked her lips, swallowed because her mouth and throat were so parched her voice emerged as little more than a whisper. "I'm fine," she said finally. Making her way to the door, she opened it part way and said to Elenora, "I was pretty far gone—guess I must be tireder than I thought."

Her sister studied her a moment, then asked, "You okay to come on down?"

"Sure, sure," Suzanne said, feeling a lethargy so absolute it was almost painful. "Give me a few minutes to pull myself together."

She closed the door before Elenora could ask her anything else.

When Suzanne walked into the living room some ten minutes later, she found her sister sitting in one corner of the couch, a drink in one hand. Elenora saluted her with a raised glass; the ice in the tall, purple-tinted glass clinked with appropriate loudness.

"Feelin' better?" she asked, eyeing her sister speculatively.

"Yes. Lots. Thanks." Suzanne walked over to the fireplace. Until the last of the drowsiness left her, she felt she should keep moving, keep the blood flowing.

"Gin-and-tonic all right?" asked Elenora, heaving herself to her feet as though she already knew Suzanne's answer.

"Fine," Suzanne nodded, "but make it a little on the weak side or I'm not gonna make it through dinner."

Elenora rattled around mixing Suzanne's drink and freshening her own at the impromptu bar she had spread out on a towel over a sideboard, with several bottles of liquor, mix, and a yellow plastic salad bowl half-filled with ice. Suzanne leaned with one hand on the mantelpiece, staring at the Shango-cult carving on the nearby window ledge.

"You sure like to stare at that ugly old thing," Elenora said from behind her.

Suzanne turned to her sister and said, "I almost expect to hear Nana Chicory's voice when I look at it."

The older woman settled back comfortably onto the sagging couch and said, "Poor ole thing: she was completely out of her head the last year she was alive. She used to claim that statue would walk at night into her room and sit on her pillow and give her all kinds of crazy dreams." Elenora shook her head at the memory. "She was all the time seeing spirits and demons and dead folks and I don't know what." She took a long, reflective sip of her drink, before adding, "I don't never want to be that old. If I ever get so old I start seein' spooks, you promise me to put me out of my misery right away."

"She never answered any of my letters," Suzanne said, moving slowly along in front of the fireplace, letting her fingers slide along the lip of the mantel.

"Said she didn't need to, said she spoke to you through the blood. That you two were such close kin, what she felt, you'd feel; what she knew, you'd know. Even across 3,000 miles. You see, she was crazy. 'I talk to Suzanne in her dreams,' she'd tell me, 'so don't you waste time writing her.' Crazy."

Suzanne made a small, non-committal sound and sampled her own drink.

They were interrupted by the sound of the front door opening and slamming shut. A boy—no, Suzanne corrected her first impression—*a young man* stood smiling on the threshold of the room, his eyes darting from Elenora to Suzanne and back again. He had a bulky, blue pullover, with only the tabs of his white shirt visible at the neck. Immediately Suzanne recognized her nephew, though she had never seen him before. He wore faded jeans and sneakers; his hair was clipped into a medium length 'fro. His eyes—open, curious— and his mouth—shaping a hesitant smile—were the clearest marks of Elenora. His coloring, a richer black more akin to Nana Chicory's coloring, and his rugged build were probably his father's gifts to him.

"You must be Jomo," said Suzanne, smiling to put the boy at ease.

"Got that one right," said Elenora pridefully. Climbing to her feet, she threw an arm around her son, pulling him further into the living room. She gave him a flamboyant kiss on the cheek, which clearly embarrassed him, and said, "Suzanne, let me introduce your nephew, Jomo Watkins. Jomo, meet your long-lost aunt, Suzanne Raine."

"Hello, Aunt Suzanne," the boy said, smiling. He held out his hand to her, but she deftly cupped his face in her hands, pulling it down to kiss him lightly on the lips. "Hello, nephew," she said, taking in the faintly sweet smell of his hair, the sharp scent and salt taste of his sweat, and the feel of him—male, uncertain, *real*—as she followed the kiss with a sudden hug.

When she backed off, he grinned at her and said, "Wow, that's quite a greeting—from both of you."

"Oh, get off with you," laughed Elenora, returning to the couch. "I was just tryin' to show my sister we're always so affectionate."

He gave a whoop of laughter, and confided loudly to Suzanne, "Just you watch how *affectionate* she is when there's work to be done or I want to go out to play some pool."

Suzanne laughed, while Elenora made a regal gesture with her hand indicating the discussion was beneath her.

"I'm glad you're here," Jomo said, still smiling at Suzanne.

"Thank you," she said. "It's nice to have kin again." She shot a look at Elenora over the rim of her glass. Elenora pretended not to notice.

Jomo, however, grinned even more broadly and said, "I haven't exactly figured out what it was set you two at each other's throats, but I'm glad it's over. Especially since you're all the family we've got, since Nana and Dad passed away."

"Well," said Elenora, rising suddenly, "I better see about getting us some dinner."

She started toward the hall door, carrying her half-filled drink glass.

"Need some help?" Suzanne offered.

"Not right now. Maybe later. You two take a minute to get acquainted."

They stood motionless in silence, listening to Elenora's footsteps padding down the hall.

Finally Jomo said, "I suppose you're not going to tell me why you two had the fight?"

Suzanne, taking another swallow of her own drink, smiled at him and shook her head slowly side to side.

"I didn't think so," he said, moving toward the little bar. He picked up a bottle of Scotch and asked, with elaborate casualness, "Was it a man? I've always suspected the only thing that would make you fight for all those years was a man. Or money? But there doesn't 'pear to be much extra on your side, either—or did you lose it all foolin' around in New York?" He spun suddenly, clearly hoping he'd caught her off guard enough to read something in her face.

All he read was light disapproval of his drinking. She wiggled a finger at him, asking with exaggerated severity, "Your mama lets you drink like that?"

With only the briefest hesitation, he added a

splash of soda to his glass, his attention entirely on recapping the club soda bottle tightly. "My mother treats me like an adult. Besides, she knows I can get—or do—anything I want anytime I want. It makes more sense all around to deal with things like alcohol in a grownup way." He turned to face her with a smile, raising his glass in brief salute. "Or don't you agree, *Auntie?*" The last word was gently mocking.

Suzanne shrugged. "I got no kids of my own. At the moment, it just seems natural for me to think of you as my sister's little boy."

"Yeah, well, whatever the reason for your fight, you missed my *little-boy* time. I'm a man, now," he said, and took a deep swallow of his drink for emphasis.

"Humm," Suzanne said. "Just give your poor old auntie a little time to catch up with things." Then she raised her glass and tapped the bottom of it against the lip of his glass. "Glad to meet you, nephew."

At that moment, Elenora bustled into the room, saying in a too-loud tone of voice. "Well now, is everybody friends?"

"Sure, ma—we're all a happy family now." Jomo laughed.

"We'll eat soon," his mother said, glancing around to see just how much her son was putting her on. She said, "Run along and get some of those crackers and cheese I bought yesterday."

Jomo made a face at his aunt and said, "That's my real function around here—servant." But he said it good-naturedly, and left the room.

Suzanne stood frozen in place, drink halfway to

her lips. Something in the word "servant" resonated deep in her: another part of the still-not-fully-comprehended sequence of events inside and outside of her that had brought her to this moment, this place, these blood-kin, so long only a part of her memories and fancies. She had the sudden, brief impression of the scent of one of Nana Chicory's healing balms of fragrant wax, honey, and pungent herbs.

The ice in her glass popped noisily. Jomo returned with a wooden tray offering a lopsided cheese wedge and a haphazard arrangement of crackers.

"Well," said Elenora, raising her glass toward the center of the room with one hand, "here we are. All together. God bless every one." She finished with an audible swallow of her own drink.

Jomo grinned and sliced himself some cheese.

Suzanne, not moving from her place near the mantel, looked at her nephew.

It was clear to her from the first moment she saw him that he was going to be a part of her plans. She was certain that the thread of his life and the thread of hers were converging in some pattern that would soon reveal itself.

Jomo was telling his mother a funny story that had happened to him earlier, mother and son were oblivious of Suzanne's stare.

For the moment, she was the outsider. But she also knew that soon—for the time between each event in the pattern grew always briefer—their relationships would alter. She would step surely and irrevocably to the center of their lives, and closer to the moment of offering the ultimate blood price to the power that had set her on her course and had guided her across so many miles and years.

FOUR

CHRISTINE LEE gently removed David's hand from her breast, where the tip of his finger was tracing light circles around her nipple. He stirred in his sleep, nudging closer to her. In a moment he would be awake enough to hook his ankle around hers and draw her to him. She could already feel his sex stiffening, pressing gently against the soft skin of her thigh—not yet insistent, but nearly so.

She leaned over and kissed him lightly on the side of the face and disengaged herself. He made sleepy protest, but she murmured, "Later."

She sat up on the edge of the bed, pressing the heels of her hands to her eyes, yawning. David's hand crept around her waist; his fingers made teasing, tickling, stroking motions on her thigh. She smiled, enjoying the answering stirring inside her. Then Christine stood up; his hand slipped caressingly down her leg, then dropped on the sheets. David pulled a pillow over his head against the light and snuggled back down under the blankets. Christine pulled a filmy robe out of the closet and went out to the living room.

She sat in her Telegraph Hill apartment and

shifted uncomfortably in the expensive designer chair; one of the leather straps slung across the chrome frame was cutting painfully into her back through the thin fabric of her robe. She managed to find a comfortable position; she lit a cigarette and let her thoughts follow the course begun early in the morning, while David slept beside her and the morning sun began filtering through the fog.

This part of the day—like the moments just before she drifted off to sleep or those middle-of-the-night bouts of sudden insomnia—was the only time she had real difficulty with, because it gave her too much time to look at herself, at what she was letting—oh, be honest, girl! she told herself, don't try to lie to yourself the way you lie to everyone else! You've LET yourself become one high-principled, high-paid, high-security-clearance whore!

From the bedroom, David murmured sleepily, then drifted off again. In a few minutes, she'd have to wake him, so they could get ready for the new day at PalmerCo.

She was getting close to the information she wanted: the facts that would link PalmerCo Investments International with the Bukawai crisis—and probably plenty of other *sub rosa* activities. Her sixth sense, which had never let her down, was assuring her her objective—exposure of PalmerCo's far-flung illegal manipulations—was almost within her reach.

But for the first time in her professional career, she felt a growing distaste for what she had become: someone who used a lover as a means to an end, someone who was nothing more than a pawn to her government, someone who was no longer at peace with herself. She had come adrift: she acted out of necessity, out of form, out of any reason but some reason that gave her any feeling of *rightness*. She was feeling estranged from herself—feeling as little love between the inner woman and her day-to-day self as existed between David Palmer and Christine Lee.

At the moment she clung to the idea that this present assignment had an undeniable correctness to it—and that it would, in some obscure way, provide her justification for what she was doing. To be sure, the cost in human terms of what David Palmer was doing was incalculable. But, on a smaller scale, she was being brought face-to-face with the dehumanizing aspects of her own situation.

Moving to one of the windows of her glass-walled apartment, Christine Lee stared out into the foggy morning—the mist just beginning to burn away. She ground her last cigarette out in an ashtray on a nearby table.

As the city came into view, Christine grew aware of memories crowding up from some obscure corner of her mind.

It had been absurdly easy to make contact with David Palmer.

They had arranged the abrupt resignation of Christine's predecessor; had seen to it that no other likely candidates applied for, or followed upon, the job opening; and provided Christine a battery of platinum-grade references and credentials that made her a shoo-in candidate for the position of David's administrative assistant and private secretary.

The morning of her first meeting, she had known everything was going according to scenaria. David talked at length about her qualifications and references; in point of fact, he had candidly let his eyes linger on her calf, her face, the hint of cleavage revealed by her pale-blue silk blouse with only the top two buttons undone. She had flirted with him only in the lightest sense; she had let a sense of professionalism ignore him totally, while reassuring him she was what she seemed—and was not someone out simply to put the make on one of the wealthiest and most influential businessmen in San Francisco.

She had gotten the job two days later—just long enough, she knew, for them to check out her credentials one last time. She particularly remembered being introduced to Dominic Roselli, who had come into David's office that first day. She recalled the way he had scrutinized her from head to toe. There was absolutely nothing sexual in that once-over, but it had chilled her absolutely. David might be a fool for her blandishments, but she knew—and subsequent input from her superiors assured her—that Roselli was nobody's fool. If anyone was going to be a threat to her at PalmerCo, her sixth sense warned, Roselli—not David—was the man to watch.

Now, in the lassitude of morning, she felt herself flooded with bone-deep weariness for the endless games, frauds, lies. She was in too deep to make the getting out a possibility—and yet . . .

Hang onto that sense of rightness, girl, she

warned herself. You've got nothing else going for you.

She went into the bedroom, pausing to look at the bed where David still slept, arm across his eyes, coverless, his limp sex lying against one thigh; then she went into the bathroom and closed the door softly behind her. She stared into the gold-flecked mirror and ran her fingers through her hair, then she pressed her face up close to the glass—yes, definite squint lines were showing around her eyes. She drew up the skin, pulling it back toward her ears, and remembered an article about face-lifting, complete with all-too-vivid diagrams and plastic face models, she had read somewhere recently.

Well, she thought, I'm thirty-six: I've still got a few good years left . . . Her eyes, though, were pretty and . . . She sat on the bench and let the robe slip softly off her shoulders and down her hands to circle around her waist. The flesh was firm and brown and her breasts full; she touched each softly, enjoying the gentle stimulation. She thought again of David's sex against the dark hair on his thigh. She shook her head—too much to do to fool around.

Through the high, rectangular windows she saw that the fog had all burned away now. Christine moved toward the bathroom to shower. She slipped out of her robe and climbed into the tiled cubicle, letting the water pour over her. She realized that her fear had been replaced with the excitement she felt when a big deal was about to be consumated and it looked good. She realized that she was on the beginning of an adrenaline high, but she could go with it.

She remembered her first private meeting with David Palmer. David had set everything up—his own eagerness requiring only the least stage direction from Christine. He had arranged a dinner with her to discuss the reorganization of some key administrative departments of Palmer-Co's San Francisco headquarters.

The meeting was scheduled for sometime around seven at Pengallon's, one of the more exclusive pubs on San Francisco's Union Street.

She had arrived at Pengallon's just before seven.

The bar was nearly deserted. Three men were playing dice at the far end of the counter. On overstuffed chairs in front of the unlit fireplace, a slender, nervous-looking man with a shock of salt-and-pepper hair was talking animatedly to an attractive blonde who looked about twenty—less than half the man's age, Christine guessed. The game the woman was playing seemed the ironic counterpoint of her own particular hustle. With a "what a surprise to find you here," David joined her at the little table she had selected in a quiet, shadowed corner of the bar. The game began in earnest.

When they had ordered drinks David Palmer launched into a discussion of his reorganization plans. She sipped a manhattan, nodding slightly every so often to assure him that she was listening. She always let her eyes linger on his face just a moment longer than politeness dictated.

David watched in fascination as she caught an unexpected dribble on the side of her glass when one of his sudden gestures had struck her hand, almost upsetting her drink. She moved quickly enough so that only a bit spilled. The drops of liquor were caught up on the tip of a slim coffee-colored finger with a cherry-red nail; her eyes still on Palmer, she brought her finger to her lips and licked away the drop in a gesture David found incredibly exciting.

She knew, without even staring at him, that he was watching her every move; she tossed her head in an apparently casual gesture, but managed to turn just enough to catch his eye, hold him a moment, and transmit a conspiratorial sexy smile, before returning her attention to her manhattan. David made an elaborate point of staring at the painting of a cricket player over the fireplace, and then returned his glance to Christine. She put her hand gently on Palmer's arm and drew him slightly towards her so they could exchange a few words in whispers. "It almost seems a shame for us to be talking business, don't you think?" She laughed; after a moment, Palmer laughed too, and then he suddenly took her hand in his own and squeezed it tightly.

Her single ring—an emerald surrounded by tiny purple amethysts—caught his eye for a moment; then he was looking into her eyes. She wondered what he found in them—was the illusion the one she was creating? Or one he was creating for himself? She stared back, and the amusement he had seen a moment before was still there; but now it was muted by an appraising look. She felt herself being scrutinized the way she imagined he might look over a stock portfolio or check a diamond for flaws. Her sixth sense told her: this is the moment when it all happens or falls flat. The man made her feel like a specimen under a microscope.

On the surface, they talked about local restaurants. He appeared greatly interested in what she had to say, but she guessed he was most intrigued by the way she ran the tip of her finger back and forth below her lip and the way she met his own frank stares with a frankness of her own.

Palmer signaled their waitress, ordered another scotch for himself and manhattan for Christine. When their drinks arrived, Christine took a sip of hers and announced, "Perfect. Even better than the first. Well—" she tipped the base of her glass slightly and clinked David's tumbler, "here's to business."

He returned the gesture with a smile. Christine felt the first sip of her second manhattan beginning to go to her head. She let her glass sit untouched for several minutes.

He noticed this and said, "If you're going to nurse that one, we may be here all night. And I've made a reservation for our dinner already and we're due there in, oh—" he consulted his watch, "forty-five minutes. And we've still got to get my car out of hock at that garage."

"In that case, let's go now. I'll have a drink when we get wherever we're going." She looked at him questioningly.

"The Ugetsu in the Japanese Trading Center." He smiled, then added, "I remember you mentioning once how much you like Japanese food."

David signaled the waitress for the check. While

they waited, he finished his scotch quickly in two swallows; she sat smiling at him, nibbling the end of the little plastic sword upon which the cherry from her drink was skewered. He watched the tip of her tongue curl playfully around the bit of green plastic; she knew he was growing acutely aware of how much he wanted her. He reached for her knee with his hand, but she evaded him, smoothly turning the swivel chair away from him, then rising and picking her purse off the table. "Your reservation?" she murmured, smiling down at the still-seated man.

He fished out his American Express card, paying for their drinks and leaving an overly generous tip. Then he followed Christine, who was gracefully threading her way through the crowded tables. He caught up with her at the door, smoothly putting his arm through hers. Together they stepped out into the foggy night, and began walking briskly towards a garage half a block down Union Street.

In the car, she let him rest his hand on her thigh; but when he tried to slide it elsewhere, she put a firm, gentle pressure on it with her own hand. He had the presence of mind to smile and not argue the point, accepting the limits—for the moment— with good grace. They both knew that the evening was only beginning; he seemed willing to play her little games her way. Neither of them, Christine knew, had any doubt of the outcome.

David surrendered his car keys to a white-jacketed Japanese valet under Ugetsu's awning; overhead multi-colored Japanese lanterns swayed uneasily in the rising wind. David seemed uncomfortably cold in his sportcoat; Christine, on the other hand, was quite comfortable in her knit suit —as if the chill and the fog were her natural elements. "Come along," she said. "A rum blossom or two will warm you up. If not—" she paused just a moment. "We'll think of something else." Then she held the door open for him, silencing his protest with a reminder that "in some ways, I'm a very liberated lady." He shrugged and went on past her.

Inside, the kimono-clad hostess escorted them to a private dining cubicle, screened from the hallway and other diners by walls and sliding doors of rice-paper.

They sat on the floor, amid a scattering of brightly colored pillows. The table, barely a foot off the floor, had a little gas brazier in the center. The hostess directed them to leave their shoes in the hall, then she departed. A few moments later a young waitress, also kimono-clad, came in, took their cocktail order, and returned shortly with two drinks on a small black-lacquer tray.

"Tell me again what I'm drinking," David said, looking doubtfully at the glass Christine handed across to him.

"These are rum blossoms," Christine explained. "It's a fabulous mixture of rum and saki—just go easy on it."

He did as he was told, sipping carefully at the drink, telling her he was unable to decide whether he liked or disliked it. They decided to have a second round. This time David decided rum blossoms were his new favorite drink.

When the waitress came to take their food

order, Christine, at David's request, ordered for both of them. The main part of the meal—the tempura, yakatori, and sukiyaki—was all cooked to order over the table brazier by several adept waitresses. David made several jokes about being annoyed at having so many people around. He breathed an exaggerated sigh of relief when the women withdrew, discreetly closing the screen door behind them, to let the couple dine in privacy. For a little while they gave most of their attention to the aromatic, delicious food. David insisted that she give him a "refresher course" in the use of chopsticks, which he claimed he had never gotten the mastery of in all the years he had lived in San Francisco.

She good-naturedly agreed, leaning towards him and folding her slender fingers around his own, which were holding a pair of chopsticks with the exaggerated awkwardness of a little boy.

But when he tried to parlay the "refresher course" into hand-holding or more, she shifted away from him. She laughed and said, "Don't rush dessert until you've finished dinner."

Making a rueful face, he used the chopsticks to pursue a morsel of beef around his plate, pincer it, and raise it halfway to his lips, only to have it drop back onto his plate. "How about you feeding me?" he suggested.

"Maybe," she smiled. "When I've finished my own."

"You're heartless, you know," he said. "Well, necessity and all that—" So saying he abandoned one chopstick and used the single remaining one to skewer the reluctant chicken. Christine just smiled and said, "I see I can take you anywhere but out."

"That's just fine—" he began, but was interrupted by the hostess, who slid open the screen doors. Without comment (though with just the ghost of a smile) she handed David a fork and left, quietly closing the screens behind her.

He looked at the fork, then laughed, saying, "So much for my schemes. I guess, for the time being, dinner is all that's on the menu."

Christine nodded and handed him a porcelain bowl of rice, which he accepted with a shake of his head.

When they were finished, and their dishes cleared away, they lingered over coffee and cognac, talking a little, letting their eyes do most of the real communicating.

Then David shifted closer to Christine; gently he reached over and began to stroke her fingers, which were toying with a single red-lacquer chopstick.

Responding, she suddenly slid her hand over his thigh and pulled him even closer, with a contented little sigh. She began moving her fingertips in gentle circles, moving her hand slowly along his inner leg, exerting just enough pressure to play him like a finely tuned instrument. She felt him becoming aroused; he put his hand gently behind her head and drew her close enough to share a light kiss. When she made no move to pull away, he kissed her with more passion; but when he tried to push his tongue into her mouth, she pulled back slightly. She murmured, "Easy, babe. All in good time." Her hand moved, the fingers caressing his crotch now, one finger stroking his swelling member through his trouser material. He shifted slightly to better accommodate his erection, at the same time pulling her head toward him to kiss her again. Again, she kept the kiss brief and almost demure. She smiled, making it apparant that she was enjoying the exquisite torture she was inflicting as much as he. He fumbled toward her for yet another kiss. While they embraced, he put his own hand over hers, trying to guide her fingers up to his zipper to give him long overdue release.

But she released him suddenly, sliding partway around the table.

"Christ!" he moaned, his pleasure suddenly giving way to real frustration. "That's one hell of a dessert course."

She calmly raised her brandy snifter towards him in a salute. "You're doing fine, just fine," she said. "But this is just a preview: the show's going on for real in more private surroundings."

David lay back at full length on the cushions, breathing deeply, letting the sweet tension in him subside somewhat. "Christine," he said laughingly, rubbing his forehead with the fingertips of his right hand, "you're playing with fire. If you're going to pick up your marbles and split—"

She laughed out loud. "You pick up your marbles and let's both go somewhere where we can show each other a real nice time. Or do you want more coffee and maybe a little more to eat?"

He ignored the joke and remained sprawled across the cushions, breathing deeply, trying to clear his head, trying to let himself relax. He appeared to her only partly successful on both counts. Christine had been calling all the shots since their arrival at the restaurant: he seemed content to let her continue calling them.

Outside, the valet quickly delivered David's sportscar to them, and accepted David's generous tip with an appreciative glance at Christine and a wink at David.

"Let's go to my place," she said matter-of-factly as she slid into the deep, leather-upholstered bucket seat beside David's. "Marin seems just too far away right now."

For emphasis, she squeezed his knee.

"Sounds fine to me, just give me directions."

"Easy enough, we're almost there already."

They talked little on the short ride to Christine's apartment. Once in awhile she would tell him where to turn.

It took them nearly ten minutes to find a parking place on the street. Christine apologized for having an apartment without a garage space. "Working girls," she laughed. "We have to economize somewhere."

Once inside her third-floor apartment, she took him by the hand and led him down a short hallway to a bedroom which, when she snapped on a series of recessed lights, revealed a huge bed piled high with blankets and a thick quilt. He went and sat on the edge; she followed and stood over him. Then she put her hands on his shoulders and pushed him gently down onto the quilt. "Get comfortable, but don't fall asleep just yet," she whispered.

"No danger of that," he answered.

She slipped off his shoes, helped him out of his jacket, began unbuttoning his shirt. Her fingers hesitated teasingly over his belt buckle for a moment, before undoing it and releasing his zipper with the delicate slowness of someone peeling an overripe fruit.

She felt him stiffening, straining to be free.

This time, she helped him, peeling down the restraining trousers, freeing him from his shorts.

She stood up and quickly slipped out of her skirt and blouse. He watched the exquisite slow-motion as she slid her slip and panties down over the curve of her hips and unhooked her bra, letting it drop carelessly to the floor. Then she stood beside him and took his unresisting hand in hers and guided his fingers up into the mat of her pubic hair to the moist folds within, letting his fingers to do their own eager exploring.

This time she withheld nothing.

So they had begun. And now they were locked on a course that could only lead to destruction for one of them. Again she thought of Dominic Roselli's cold, challenging looks. Well, she temporized, the man was the risk that went with the territory. At the same time, in an obscure way, she pitied David for his folly in placing so much trust in her—in the very person who was most certain to bring his international empire crashing down around his head. From their first night together, she had been in control—though she let him think that he, not she, was calling the shots.

Unwilling to cope with the welter of uncomfortable memories and thoughts any longer, Christine walked into the kitchen and put on the kettle to boil water; then she brought out the Melita and the filters and began spooning her special coffee blend into the upper half of the coffee maker.

But she could not shake the feeling of being increasingly at odds with herself. Always before, she had felt a growing excitement when her inner senses warned her that the end of an assignment was getting near and that success was almost within reach. But, for the past several days, this certainty had left her feeling uneasy. She could not put a finger on what, in fact, she was really feeling. At best she defined it as a sense that she had overlooked some fact, some element that could change the outcome of everything. A joker buried somewhere in the deck that was going to surface only when the final hand was dealt.

She tried to shrug it away as a case of eleventh-hour nerves, but her unease persisted. With surprise, she saw that her hand was shaking as she filled two large coffee mugs prior to going back to the bedroom to wake David.

What the hell, she decided, this is the last assignment for me. After this PalmerCo business is laid to rest, I'm going to take a desk job, no matter what they offer me to stay in the field.

It was a familiar thought: one that had occurred to her on almost every assignment.

But this time it was different. This time, she reflected, carrying the steaming coffee mugs down the hall towards the bedroom, she meant it.

This was her last assignment. She'd never been more certain of anything in her life.

FIVE

SUZANNE HAD arrived in Oakland on a Friday. She slept almost until noon the following day. When she had dressed and gone downstairs, she found the house apparently deserted. In Elenora's tidy kitchen, she quickly located instant coffee and brewed herself a cup. While she was waiting for it to cool, she heard her sister's voice, muffled, coming up through the floorboards. A moment later, Jomo answered her. The two of them were apparently in some basement area under the house.

Still carrying her cup of coffee, she went out into the sun-warmed morning.

On the side of the house she found a door open into the darkened basement space underneath. Suzanne could hear Elenora talking to Jomo inside. She set her coffee cup on the window ledge outside the door and called, "Elenora?"

It took a minute for her eyes to adjust from the bright sunlight outside to the gloom under the main floor of the building. She blinked several times before she could make out her sister and her nephew rummaging through some cardboard cartons in a far corner of the room.

The flooring was raw concrete and looked damp; the ceiling was nothing more than the underpinnings of the first floor above, thick with cobwebs and criss-crossed with water and sewage pipes and electrical conduits. A single lightbulb overhead gave little illumination; it was assisted by some daylight seeping in through x-shaped lattices over one or two waist-high openings. The place smelled moist and mildewy . . .

When she could see adequately, she made out some crates full of old books, a rotting green sofa, odd bits of broken furniture, and a car fender. Apparently Elenora, engrossed in sorting through the contents of several boxes, had not heard her come in. She called more loudly, "Elenora," and tapped at the same time on the doorpost.

This time her sister heard her and looked up, saying, "Hello, Susie. I wondered how long you were going to sleep." She started toward Suzanne, rubbing her soiled hands carelessly on her paint-spattered slacks, saying, "Somebody could probably tell the whole history of our family from the crap that's accumulated down here."

"There sure seems to be a lot stuck in here," said Suzanne, with another doubtful glance around the area. "Are you cleaning it all out?"

Elenora laughed. "Oh, no—this is just my same old sorry attempt to get the place neatened up. I'm only pitching out stuff I'm absolutely *sure* I'm never going to need. I just want to clear enough space to move down the old purple chair in the upstairs hall; I'm getting a little tired climbing over it." She wiped her forehead and said, "Time for a little break, I think." She sat down on a sturdy-looking wooden crate and breathed a sigh of pleasure. Then she half-turned and yelled back toward the basement door, "Jomo; take a break. Finish that last beer in the icebox, if you want. We'll finish up in a few minutes." There was an answering "Okay" from inside. Then Jomo emerged from the shadowy space behind stacked debris. He smiled and said, "Morning, Aunt Sue, hope you slept well." Then he laughed and went past them. Both women remained silent for a moment, listening to his steps fading off along the narrow strip of concrete path.

Elenora fished a package of cigarettes out of her blouse pocket along with a yellow plastic lighter. She offered her sister a cigarette, but Suzanne merely gave a quick shake of her head.

"That's right, I forgot," said Elenora. "You're still a singer. You said in your letter you still sing at that place—what's its name—the one that makes me think of Duke Ellington."

"Club Indigo."

"Right." She took a thoughtful puff of her cigarette and looked at Suzanne with a sudden, serious look. "You know, all those years after— *well!* Anyhow, there's sure been a lot of times I've wanted to brag about my little sister who's a celebrity. But I was always too stubborn a bitch to mention your name all the time we were fighting."

"That's over now. But I'm afraid little sister isn't much of a celebrity. I sing Sunday through Wednesday—but they bring in the real names for the weekend. I'm not much more than 3-D muzak."

"Don't be putting yourself down so. I'm gonna be telling everyone what a great singer you are. A regular—what's the French word you used?"

"*Chanteuse.*"

"Yeah—I'll practice a little till I can say it right. Then I'm really gonna impress some of my friends."

"Won't they want to know why you never mentioned me before?"

"I'll say you're my long-lost sister. I'll say we're twins—like those stories you hear about, one twin findin' the other. I like that idea, 'cause it means I'm gonna seem younger and thinner, since we're twins. And no smart remarks about how it could just as easily mean you got older and fatter."

Suzanne smiled. "You're the one who said it, not me."

There was a sudden silence between them, neither one sure of just where to take the conversation next. Both had a lot they wanted to say, clearly—but both were being careful of what might prove, even yet, dangerous territory.

"Remember," said Suzanne, with a far-away

tone of voice, "Nana used to say in Bukawai twins were considered unlucky. There was a rule that twins born there were either killed or tossed into the jungle to be eaten by wild animals." She gave her sister a thin smile. "Maybe it's just as well we weren't twins."

"Yeah, well, even not bein' twins, our luck hasn't always been so great. Still, it's better now—for me—for both of us, I guess—"

Elenora glanced at her sister questioningly. But her sister did not add anything, so the older woman continued, "Now that you're here, let's forget that old business and just think about good luck." She ground out the end of her cigarette on the concrete flooring and lit another one. Suzanne saw there was something else on her mind, but it took a little while for her to get it into words. Finally, Elenora said, "You seem to be doin' a lot of thinkin' about Nana Charlotte, Susie. I'm not sure I understand."

"I'm not exactly sure *I* do, either. But I do think about her. She's even in my dreams sometimes. You know, I've never told anyone this, but I saw her the night she died. Hours before I got your telegram that simply said, 'Nana's gone,' she was in my apartment."

"Yeah, I've read about that kind of thing. I'm not saying I believe it, mind; but, if it did happen, it would mean that Nana considered you the most important person in her life. Or maybe she wanted you to finish some business for her. What did she say? What did she do?"

"She just stood there, in front of the door of

my apartment, like she'd just stepped through and shut the door behind her, while I was looking out the window. Only, I never heard the door open, and there was a deadbolt on the door that always makes a loud noise when you throw it. I never heard a sound. After she . . . went away . . . I found the lock was still in place."

"A ghost for sure. But didn't she *say* anything?"

Suzanne shook her head. "She just reached for me, and I saw blood at her nose and on her lips—"

Elenora nodded, her hands shaking slightly. Though she had had her lighter ready for several minutes, she made no move to light the waiting cigarette. "She hemorrhaged just before she went . . ." Her voice was little more than a whisper.

Suzanne was caught up in her own narrative now; she hardly seemed aware of her sister's presence. "I remember being real scared all of a sudden; I didn't want her to touch me. But she kept coming at me, and I kept backing away, until I felt myself come up against the window. Her hand was like a claw—I could see the veins bulging out across the back of her hand and arm—I could—" Suzanne licked her lips, which were suddenly dry, "see the color of her skin, how blotchy it had become. But I could see *through* it—like I was seeing two things at once: real, flesh-and-blood Nana and a horrible ghost at the same time. I remember I screamed out, 'Oh, Nana, you're *dead*, go away, leave me alone!' But she just kept reaching out to me. I turned to the window: I wanted to open it and yell for someone to come and help me. Then I felt her hand on my shoulder—warm and comforting and sharp and hurtful all at the same time. Then," she shrugged almost apologetically, "I fainted. A real cop-out ending to a ghost story, right?"

Elenora shrugged.

"I woke later, when the phone rang. It was Western Union with your telegram saying Nana was dead. She was gone—if she was ever there. That's when I found the locks all in place."

Elenora finally finished lighting her cigarette, and took a long, soothing drag before she said, "For a long time, before she died, Nana Chicory kept talking about how important it was for her to see you. But then, sudden-like, she stopped trying to get me to bring you out here. That's when she'd start saying things about how you and her were 'sharin' secrets through our blood.' Anyhow—I guess bein' so sick had finally made her lose her mind."

"Funny thing, though," said Suzanne. "It must have been just about that time I started dreaming about Nana. Almost every night—sometimes only about her, sometimes she'd just be a little piece of a bigger dream. Most of the time, I wouldn't remember what they were all about—only that she was in them. For a long time, after I saw her as a ghost, I tried to make myself believe I had had some kind of waking dream . . ."

Elenora looked at her sharply, asking, "And now? You sound like you might have another idea now."

"Now, I'm not so sure. More and more, I seem to feel her presence all around me—can almost feel her hand on my shoulder. And she's still in my dreams: she was in one I had on the bus ride out here."

"Now don't you go making a big deal out of your imaginings," Elenora said in a big-sisterly way. "You were probably thinking about the family all along. Nana's death just made you think about her most of all. Same way I'm guessin' that it was Nana's death made you write me and talk about makin' up things after all these years."

"Funny thing, I never really thought about it that way before. It just seemed the right thing to do—to come out, and see you and my nephew, and clean up . . . old business. But, now that you point it out, it all *does* seem to follow from Nana's death. If I didn't know better, I'd say she was controlling things from the spirit world."

Elenora stood up, suddenly saying, "Let's go get some lunch and stop this nonsense right now. Nana's gone to *someplace;* I hope she's happy—or at least not sufferin'. But she's got nothin' to do with any of us any longer. Any thinkin' along those lines is pure crazy."

"One thing, Elenora?"

"Yes?"

"That statue in the living-room window. The carving that belonged to Nana . . ."

"What about it?"

"Would you—would you let me have it?"

"That ugly ol' thing? You're welcome to it. Only, if I hear anymore of this talk about your dead granma coming back to haunt us, I'm gonna take it right back. Okay?"

Suzanne nodded quickly. "I really only want it because it makes me think of the good times I had—we had—growing up."

"We'll have more good times, now that you've come home. You'll see. This is just the start of what's going to happen for us."

After lunch, when she had returned to her room with Nana's Shango-cult carving, alone, Suzanne set the statue at the exact center of the topmost shelf of the bookcase, where it became immediately the most striking element of the room. She took out the brown envelope and placed it in the desk drawer. Finally, she repacked the remaining contents of the suitcase securely and relocked the case. Then she hid the suitcase at the very back of the room's single closet.

She had bought a map of San Francisco at the bus stop the day before; now she unfolded it and studied it until she had located the corner where Comstock Way met the Embarcadero, just a little south of San Francisco terminus of the Bay Bridge. It seemed to be extremely easy to reach by bus and foot.

When the plan for Monday had been formulated, she pulled out of her purse a clean razor blade still wrapped in its protective covering. She unwrapped it and, unhesitatingly, nicked the tip of her index finger. When she had squeezed out a single drop of deep red blood, she smeared it on the rounded base of the statue.

The wood seemed to sponge up the liquid with a thirsty eagerness. After a moment, there was only the faintest smudge to mark her symbolic offering. Nodding to herself, she refolded the razor blade into the paper and replaced it in her purse. The wound, she saw, seemed to have healed itself as soon as she had touched the wood of the statue.

On Monday, as the bus rattled over the bridge towards San Francisco, Suzanne felt excitement rising in her as she neared the end of her journey that seemed to have begun at three separate points: the death of the child, her discovery of David's wirephoto, and the death of her grandmother.

Death had begun it, death sustained it. Only death, several deaths, would bring things to the appointed ending.

Once again, she took the San Francisco map out of her purse and located Comstock Way again. With her fingernail she traced out the fine red line of the municipal transit line that would carry her to her destination.

A short distance from the stop she had selected as closest to PalmerCo headquarters, she found a little park sandwiched in between two rows of new steel-and-glass office buildings along the expensive-looking waterfront business district.

It was hot under the inadequate shelter of the

scanty shade trees. The benches, with their too-high backs and seats that were too wide and slats a fraction too far apart, seemed designed for people half-again as tall as she. Suzanne felt like a little girl sitting in an adult's chair. Into her mind drifted one of Nana Chicory's tales about the legendary giant Mwala tribesmen who were exclusive guards to the queens—descendents of Queen Naii—of Bukawai. Before the slavers came, and the old legitimacies vanished for a time.

People have grown smaller, she thought. *We've become tiny and wicked. The past was a larger place, a better place.* She herself felt tinier than an infant in the womb. She was swimming in fluids of events of which she only understood a part. The only thing that was firm in her mind was her determination to go through with whatever was demanded of her. She was the compass-point on which an infinity of causes and effects converged. At these moments—as in the strangest of her dreams—she seemed to have drifted outside her skin. She watched while someone else saw with her eyes, spoke with her voice, and understood all the fragmentary clues—clutter of dreampieces, emotions, happenings—that she (when she reclaimed her body) comprehended only hazily.

She stood up. She could feel the nearness of David. In the sunlight a dark filter seemed to have locked into place behind her eyes; the smell of the nearby waterfront brought the smell of decay along with the salt tang. Everywhere she saw signs of impending death: in the scents, the cry of gulls overhead, the chill that even the sunlight could not dispel. There might still be time to refuse the call, to leave undone that which existed as largely unformed ideas in her mind.

With a sigh, she shook herself free of these familiar doubts and continued resolutely on her way.

PalmerCo, International was headquartered in a five-story, brick-faced building with rows of high, deep-set windows on Comstock Way. It was set back from the street by a broad sweep of well-kept lawns. A border of waist-high hedges protected the lawns.

Suzanne stood for a moment at the foot of a broad flight of steps, looking up at the entranceway and the tidy facade of evenly matched rows of windows. Through the glass doors, partly obscured by reflection from the late-morning sun, Suzanne could see a number of people standing about and talking or walking through the expansive reception area.

A brass sign with raised lettering hung at eye level on the right beside the brass-trimmed doors. Suzanne read:

PALMERCO, INTERNATIONAL
SAN FRANCISCO-NEW YORK-NEW ORLEANS-
SANTO DOMINGO-FREETOWN-ACCRA-AJAPA

Ajapa. The capital of the little African nation of Bukawai. The once-upon-a-time home of her grandmothers. Just barely independent, but drowning in the blood of a civil war more devastating than anything seen in Zambia, Katanga, or Rhodesia. No quarter given: every day the newspapers were full of reports of ineffectual attempts by the United Nations to mediate. Accusations flew between Washington and Moscow, which jockeyed to maintain or create spheres of influence. Report after report told of the endless seesawing between the Central Government forces and the rebels under Col. Obitsebi.

And—Suzanne knew because her dreams had told her so—most responsibility for the bloodshed could be found right here at PalmerCo. Bukawai was in very real danger of being snuffed out—or, at the very least, of having its progressive and far-sighted Socialist Government exterminated by the right-wing insurgents. So far, the outcome still hung in the balance, but it wouldn't for long—not with money and arms channeled into the rebel forces by PalmerCo, International.

Bukawai would die in blood just as her infant son had been murdered, so many years before. And, in both, David Palmer's fine, white, bloodstained hands orchestrated the deaths, while they never actually touched his victims.

This was one of the things Nana Chicory told her repeatedly in her dreams—the one part she never forgot upon waking. And Nana would always end by saying, "Shango is a powerful god, protector and avenger of his children—no matter where the Bukawai people are scattered. When the need is greatest, when their blood cries out to heaven, he will spin a web more fine than Anansi the Spider, more deadly than the teeth of the ghost-hyena who punishes wrongdoers." Then dream-Nana's near-toothless mouth would twist into a smile that frightened Suzanne more than anything else in her dreams.

Suzanne pushed through into the air-conditioned cavern of PalmerCo headquarters. The reception area was flooded with light from randomly placed globular fixtures overhead. The polished wood floor was inlaid with a pattern of light and dark woods, suggesting a sunburst. Near the far wall, flanked by triple elevators on either side, was a reception desk. Suzanne approached the attractive Filipino woman wearing a featherweight phone headset.

"May I help you?" she asked Suzanne in clipped, professional tones.

"Is David Palmer in?"

The woman shook her head, studying Suzanne. She said, "Dr. Palmer's out of the office the rest of the day. You can leave a message with me, if you wish." She looked at Suzanne as if it was the most unlikely thing in the world for her to want to, let alone *expect* to, see the head of PalmerCo.

Needle and splinter, whispered Nana Chicory's voice far back in Suzanne's mind. *I share with you Shango's gift to your grandmothers before me.*

"Miss, did you wish to leave a message?" the receptionist prompted, disconcerted by Suzanne's staring silence.

Something like a distant memory floated into

Suzanne's mind. She had the peculiar sensation of remembering something she had never known before. It was like sharing the consciousness of someone else.

"If you don't want to leave a message..." The receptionist was growing annoyed.

In the front of her brain, Suzanne imagined a bone needle of the sort she had once seen Nana Chicory hold out to her, though she could not recall the context. She let the imagined needle float out of her mind, past her eyes, to hover—visible only in her mind's eye—in the air in front of the receptionist. When the other women opened her mouth to demand that Suzanne answer her, the latter imagined the needle suddenly plunging down, impaling the woman's tongue.

At imagined impact of sharpened bone and flesh, a suddenpain, like a white-hot wire, lanced through Suzanne's head.

The woman, looking up at her, blinked in surprise, then blinked again. But the question she had been about to ask, died unformed.

Suzanne, resisting the screaming pain that ran like a skewer from her forehead to the back of her head, forced herself to imagine a wooden splinter, filed to a dagger-like point. Fighting the pain which was forcing her to breathe rapidly, Suzanne mentally drove the splinter into the woman's forehead, just between her eyes.

This time, the woman only blinked once; the flicker of her eyelids was in perfect sync with Suzanne's just-audible gasp. Now a line of fiery thread ran from temple to temple. She could almost see a painfully bright seam across her vision. She could feel sweat gathering on her forehead; she had her hands pressed against the smooth sides of the desk to support herself.

"Now," she said, speaking with an effort. "Which floor is David Palmer's office on?"

Blink-blink. When the woman spoke, it was as if she was answering with difficulty from a great distance. There was an astonished tone in her voice, as if nothing could surprise her more than the fact that she was speaking. "His offices are on three. But you can't get up there—"

Suzanne's eyes flickered to the uniformed security officers—a man and a woman—who were chatting near the row of elevator doors. They paid no attention to persons exiting, but they screened everyone for a clip-on badge with photo or a hand-held pass of some sort. To the receptionist, Suzanne said, quietly and evenly, "I need a pass."

Blink. "Yes." The receptionist's hand moved uncertainly to open a drawer at the desk. She paused.

Suzanne imagined the splinter driving a fraction of an inch deeper into the other woman's mind. The wires in her own mind burned achingly.

The receptionist withdrew a brown-and-white pass and handed it to Suzanne. "Just show this to the guard," she explained in a dreamy-distant voice.

"Thank you," said Suzanne. She walked toward the elevators as rapidly and steadily as the throbbing of her head would allow. The guard, seeing the strain on her face, asked her if she was all right.

"Just a headache—I'll be fine." He merely glanced at her pass, nodded, and turned his attention elsewhere.

Almost as soon as she punched the elevator call, the doors opened to disgorge a noisy group of people. Suzanne got right in and jabbed the "Door Close" button, preventing anyone from sharing the elevator.

The moment the doors shut and she felt the faint upward motion, Suzanne let the pictures of the needle and splinter dissolve. Somehow she knew that she was releasing the woman—but that the receptionist would not remember their conversation; she would not, in fact, remember that Suzanne had been in the building at all.

Suzanne slumped against the wall of the elevator. The pain in her head subsided only gradually, leaving her feeling weak and dizzy when the doors slid open on the third floor. She stepped out into an informal waiting area with thick-cushioned brown leather chairs grouped around a free-form coffee table. The place was lit by recessed track lighting overhead.

Hallways ran off in either direction; she could hear the sounds of typewriters humming away down the left hallway. A discreet sign indicated the Director's office was down to her left.

Most of the doors were closed; Suzanne guessed that most of the people were out to lunch, since it was nearing noon.

At the end of the corridor on the right was a spacious office, open, but empty. A name plate of embossed bronze beside the doorway read, Christine Lee, Assistant to the Director.

The office was sunny and neat and filled with growing plants. The wall behind a handsome teakwood desk was lined with floor-to-ceiling shelves covered with books, files, and the ubiquitous plants. Two comfortable-looking chairs were set against the wall on the left facing the window, which showed an expanse of blue sky and buildings.

She stepped across the hall to the entrance of the other huge office, which also stood open and empty. The name plate here read simply, David Palmer, Director.

The walls facing east and south were entirely window, giving a double vista of the Bay, the arch of the bridge, and the city of Oakland and its surrounding hills. The Director's massive glass-and-chrome desk was parallel to the eastern windows with four expensive-looking black leather-and-chrome chairs facing it.

Suzanne hovered on the threshold, her eyes taking in the thick lime-green carpet, the lightly patterned beige drapes, the recessed track lighting. For a moment she imagined David sitting at his high-backed leather chair, drawing on his cigarette and making decisions offhandedly that would decide the fate of thousands of Africans half a world away. The last refuge of the man who had fled her threats and anguish half a lifetime ago.

Well, David, Suzane thought to herself

bitterly, *things are finally going to catch up with you. And how are you going to deal with me? I won't be gotten rid of as easily as one of those papers on your desk waiting for you to sign and drop into the "Outgoing" basket for some secretary to dispose of.*

Her eyes were fixed on the empty leather chair as she addressed her mental remarks to the absent Director. She was unaware of anyone else's presence until a pleasantly professional female voice asked from just behind her, "May I help you? Were you hoping to see the Director?"

Turning abruptly, Suzanne confronted a trim, young-looking black woman in a neatly tailored suit. She was regarding Suzanne with an expression that hovered precisely between official politeness and frank surprise at discovering the other woman on the verge of taking a step into the Director's office.

Suzanne quickly stepped back fully into the hall outside.

The woman waited a moment before saying, with just a hint of coolness, "The Director is away right now. I'm his assistant, Miss Lee: all appointments are made through me. If you wish to set up an appointment . . ." There was something in the woman's face, in the look she was giving Susanne, that the latter could not quite fathom. But she guessed that the meaning would—sooner or later—reveal itself. For the moment, the woman was an inconvenience to be disposed of without delay.

She imagined (though every nerve in her body

screamed out against it) the bone needle. It semed to hover waveringly in the air in front of her eyes; it drifted with agonizing slowness toward the face of the other woman who was clearly waiting for her to explain herself more fully.

With a blaze of agony that threatened to split her skull fore to aft, Suzanne willed the dream-needle into the other woman's mouth, felt the impact with such intensity that she was astonished, even in the midst of her pain, that the woman's injured tongue didn't gush sudden blood. But the woman only stared at her, eyes *blink-blinking*, with a look of passive confusion. Miss Lee moved her lips experimentally, but made no sound; a glaze of unfocused fear filmed her eyes. She took a hesitant step back away from Suzanne. Suzanne knew that—no matter the cost in pain to herself—she would have to follow through. But, this time, some inner voice warned her, an altered—not completely erased—memory would be much more useful to her.

Crossed, white-hot wires seared her brain. She imagined the grey matter sizzling and charring inside her skull. But she summoned the dream-splinter into her field of vision, then rammed it forward.

The other woman resisted instinctively, as though she had some counterforce. It was impossible, Suzanne knew, but, for a moment, she suspected the younger woman of having some *vodu* of her own. Suzanne's energy faltered; the other woman half-raised her hands in vague protest. If anyone appeared, if her concentration faltered for a moment, Suzanne knew the whole enterprise would fail.

Feeling the muscles cording in her neck, leaning toward the young black woman like a serpent arching toward a bird or mouse it hoped to swallow, she ignored her shrieking nerves, to draw out of the flesh and blood of her being her last reserves of strength. In her mind's eye she saw the imagined splinter slam partway into the sweat-dampened forehead only inches from her own now. She felt skin and bone resisting, as if the dream-instrument were real—not a *vodu* power, unseen, intangible.

The woman groaned through her still-sealed lips; she writhed as though the sharp fragment of wood had actually been driven physically into her frontal lobe. Again, Suzanne half-expected to see a sudden gout of blood on the unmarred skin. But, like the receptionist, Christine—once the momentary discomfort passed—gazed at Suzanne with a passive expression.

Down the hall the elevator door opened; two Chinese women, laughing together and talking loudly, stepped out, then walked down the opposite hallway. Suzanne, glancing past her captive's shoulder, saw them disappear into an office doorway.

Keeping the picture of the half-embedded spike clear in her mind, Suzanne said, speaking with effort, since the pain in her own head was threatening to rip her skull apart, "You remember—Christine—we're—old friends."

"I don't remember that." Her voice was

barely a whisper. There was the lightest edge of defiance.

Suzanne, her own pain lending force to her words, said, "You remember—you're a liar if you say you don't remember me. I'm a very good friend of yours."

"I donnnnn—I donnnnn—" Suzanne was astonished at the strength and determination with which the younger woman resisted her *vodu*. Christine was even trying to shake her head.

Suzanne re-focused, slipping the splinter in a fraction deeper; she was amazed at the woman's resistance—and just as wonderstruck at her own ability to remain in control even while her brain seemed to be burning white phosphorus behind her eyes.

"Donnn—" Christine protested.

But Suzanne said, "You do. Now you remember. Show me that you remember."

After a moment, a little sigh came from the other woman; her eyes blinked once at Suzanne. Again. Dully she said, "I remember, now. You are my friend."

Suzanne nodded, feeling her whole being in danger of being sucked into the cauldron of seething agony inside her head.

Christine Lee swiveled halfway around as the phone in her office began ringing. In a voice closer to normal, she said, "Pardon me a moment. Why don't you come in and sit a minute if you like?" She began walking toward her desk with the fluid gait of someone in a dream.

Suzanne followed the woman into the latter's office. Ms. Lee, still standing up, answered the phone. She talked briefly with the other party, then she put the phone on hold and left the office. Suzanne watched her cross into the Director's office. After a moment, she returned with a file and sat down behind her desk while she read some information into the phone. Then the other party rang off, and she replaced the phone in its cradle.

"Excuse me one more minute," she said in a faraway tone of voice. Rising, she explained, "I want to return this file and lock up the Director's office." She pulled out a large key ring from the lower desk drawer and went back across the hall.

When she could no longer see the other woman, Suzanne quickly moved to the desk and opened the brown leather address book beside the phone. Under "P" she found the entry she was looking for:

David Palmer
#14 Balboa Crescent
Chetwynd
Private Line: 555-1157

Suzanne scribbled the information hastily on a Phone-Memo pad and thrust it into her purse. She was just about to close the drawer, when she spotted a small metallic gold rectangle with a note slipped under the rubber band around it.

The handwriting was jarringly familiar. The note read simply, "Chris—Please get glass repaired—D."

With a quick glance to determine Christine was still in the office across the hall, Suzanne, with trembling fingers, unwrapped the rubber band.

It was a small, fold-over photograph frame with two photographs in it. She immediately recognized the faces of David's children. There was a diagonal crack in the glass over the girl's image, presumably the reason David had asked for repair work.

Hearing a faint sound from across the hall, Suzanne hastily dropped the photo holder into her purse.

Ms. Lee came quietly back, talking vaguely about how some temporary help had garbled her filing system and left her hours of work ahead correcting their errors. She had the making-small-talk tone of someone whose mind is, in reality, miles away.

Suzanne watched as the woman settled into her swivel chair. Christine regarded Suzanne with barely repressed curiosity. The effort of keeping control over the resistant woman was causing Suzanne agony. She knew she would have to let things ease back to normal. *Almost normal.*

Suzanne's voice sounded as old as she felt—older than the oldest ancestors her grandmother had told her ruled in Africa at the dawn of time. She said, in a whisper almost inaudible to herself, "You'll remember me as your friend from now on, won't you?"

She watched rebellion flare into the woman's eyes, then die away just as quickly. "Yes," the other woman answered dutifully.

"And you will do nothing—*nothing*—to stop me doing whatever I have to do?"

"No," Christine echoed.

With the last of her failing strength, Suzanne envisioned the splinter working free of the other woman's flesh. But, before she had withdrawn the dream-splinter all the way, she suddenly shook her head violently side-to-side. In her mind she heard the tip of the wooden fragment snap off with an ugly, cruel sound that made her gasp. The other woman seemed oblivious of what Suzanne was doing to her mind: leaving a little bit of false memory, residual control there. At the same time, some inner voice warned Suzanne that, by the supernatural laws governing this form of *vodu*, her newfound powers were diminished a little, because she had been forced to make this handsome young black woman her unwitting ally.

Christine Lee was looking around her office in mild disorientation. The only element in her world that seemed as it should was the presence of Suzanne. The *vodu* was holding.

Her brain churning like molten lava, Suzanne extended a hand to the young woman, testing the change as she said in her rasping voice, "Thank you so much for your help. Perhaps I'll stop by again if I'm up this way."

"I'd like that very much." Christine's words had the emotionlessness of phrases learned by rote.

Suzanne turned to leave the office; everything appeared in a throbbing red wash of pain.

Halfway to the door, she was stopped by Christine's murmured question, "Will we?"

Leaning her hand on the doorjamb to support herself, because the misery was threatening to engulf her, Suzanne without turning around asked, "Will we what?"

"Meet again. I have to know: will we meet again?" Her voice registered fear and something else that sounded to Suzanne's own, increasingly fuddled, fire-lanced brain, almost like *eagerness*.

She said, "I don't see how we can help seeing each other. Our life-threads seem to have become entangled: neither of us has any choice any more."

"Oh," said the unseen woman, the single, soft word managing to suggest utter incomprehension and full understanding.

Suzanne hurried away down the hall before anything else could be said.

The sun was beginning to set by the time Suzanne returned home. The terrible ache in her head had subsided during the bus ride back from the PalmerCo offices, but a feeling of being drained to her soul persisted. There was a heavy silence over her sister's house. Apparently neither Elenora, who worked in a department store downtown, nor Jomo, who worked part-time at a Stop-'n-Shop and who seemed to have unlimited amounts of friends and things to do in any event, was around.

Suzanne let herself in the front door with the key Elenora had given her. She climbed the inside stairs slowly, noting that the purple armchair was gone from the upstairs hall—probably moved down to the basement by Jomo in response to his mother's steady nagging. With each step, Suzanne's increasing weariness grew.

As she placed her hand on the knob of her own bedroom door, Elenora's cat, Dubonnet, appeared suddenly, rubbing its orange fur against her leg and whining.

She pulled back, startled; then she nudged the cat away with the side of her shoe, saying, "Go away. There's nothing for you here."

Dubonnet persisted. "Scat! Shoo!" she hissed jabbing at the creature with her toe. But when she pushed the door open, Dubonnet shot through, nearly throwing her off balance. "Get out!" she yelled into the gathering shadows inside. The cat, momentarily invisible, answered her with a defiant yowl.

She left the door open behind her, hoping the cat would retreat as quickly as it had entered. "Come on, kitty-kitty-kitty," she coaxed.

The cat whined again; she discovered him beneath the room's single chair, eyeing her spitefully.

She bent over and made a grab for the cat. Her hand almost touched its fur, but she lunged too quickly. She grabbed the animal's leg, but it only screeched and slashed at her with its claws, raking the backs of both her hands.

Suzanne pulled back with a cry, as the creature skittered across the room and onto her bed, hissing and arching its back.

"Get out, you devil!" she yelled, starting toward the bed. Dubonnet anticipated her, darting sideways and leaping outward, scrambling for purchase on the edge of the bookcase.

"No—NO!" Suzanne yelled as the cat ran the length of the top shelf, toppling the Shango-cult statue onto the rug before she could catch it.

The cat momentarily forgotten, Suzanne knelt beside the statue and lifted it from the floor. One wooden blade of the axe-headress had been snapped off completely. A large chip had been gouged out of the carving's base.

Moaning at the bad luck this augured, Suzanne picked up the wooden figure and cradled it in her arms, crooning to it the way one might comfort an injured child. She stood up, picking up the broken blade and the dark bit of stained hardwood. She set the injured ancestor figure on the bed, with the broken pieces beside it.

The cat was now crouched under the spindle-legged desk. It was breathing heavily, watching her with hate-filled eyes.

Suzanne smiled back, fixing those eyes with her own.

Moving quickly, she closed the bedroom door.

The cat whined uneasily.

"Poor kitty. *Nice* kitty," Suzanne murmured soothingly, as she opened her purse and took out a light-weight, ripple-edged knife. She had, for years, carried this always in New York. It had twice scared away would-be juvenile muggers.

She kept up a stream of soothing words, but

the bloody pieces into the garbage bag and used a rubber band to twist it shut.

A little cleanser from under the sink left the counter as unblemished as new. The bloodstains on the rug (the excess mopped up with Kleenex she flushed down the toilet) were nearly unnoticeable against the deep coffee color. Then she removed the little gold picture frames from her purse and drew the single, straight-backed chair close to the little desk and sat down; it only took her a moment to work the two pictures free of their frames. Suzanne set them beside each other on the ragged green blotter. Daughter. Son.

The pictures of the two Palmer children were polaroid snaps, each of them waring a hurry-up-so-I-can-get-back-to-what-I'm-doing expression. Amy was seated on an ornamental garden bench beside a bush flecked with red blossoms; Kirk stood with hands on hips, squinting slightly in the sunshine of a sandy strip of beach.

With her fingertips, she lined the photographs up just so. Then she reopened her purse and drew out the knife she had so recently used.

With the tip of the blade, she nudged the edges of the pictures. The last pale sunlight gently touched the blade, revealing smudged fingerprints all along its length.

She put the knifepoint under the girl's polaroid chin and pushed. The blade slipped through the paper with the tiniest sound. She pressed harder and felt it go through the blotter to sink into the soft wood of the desk until something in her voice disquieted the cat. Dubonnet bolted under the bed.

Dropping to her hands and knees Suzanne located the cat curled protestingly into the furthest corner, where the walls joined. It was trapped rather neatly, and it sensed its predicament.

She hissed, "Sweet kitty," and jabbed repeatedly at the cat. It clawed and screamed as the serrated blade sliced into its paws and legs.

Frantically, it launched itself at her arm, taking advantage of her sudden backward scramble to make a desperate rush for the bedroom door. The screech when it found the door shut pulled Suzanne right after it. Dubonnet tried to break past her, heading for the opposite corner, but she was ready, kicking him ferociously against the doorjamb. The animal clawed at her legs frantically, drawing blood. Then she kicked harder, catching the animal with her shoe, slamming him against the wall.

The cat shook its head dazedly side to side, staggering to its feet like a drunk.

Before it could regather its senses, Suzanne jabbed again-again-again until the blood-soaked pile of orange fur lay unwhimpering on the dark brown bedroom carpet.

She picked the distasteful thing up and carried it into the bathroom. She set the carcass on the narrow marble counter and quickly dealt with Dubonnet with the efficiency with which she would carve up a whole chicken. From the black-and-gold decorated waste basket, she took the little black vinyl liner. Then she swept meeting resistance at some deeper layer. To Suzanne, it felt the same way she imagined a knife slipping through skin into muscle and bone felt.

She pulled the blade free and then began systematically hacking the girl's likeness to pieces, her hand jerking *upanddown-upanddown* with increasing rapidity and force. She slashed at the picture, feeling the brown hatred—like fouled vase water—welling up inside of her as it found some release. She looked across her fisted, pumping knife hand and caught her reflection faintly in the uncurtained window glass; she had the momentary impression that her own image was nodding back at her in approval. Only, it was an aged, years-from-now Suzanne contemplating her. Or had she really grown that old? she wondered. So old she looked like Nana Chicory? When she glanced down at the ruined picture, she discovered that she had gouged a hole through the green felt blotter and deep into the wood underneath.

The two photographs she sliced up with surgical precision, quartering each, then methodically subdividing them into tiny fragments. While she was doing this, she looked again at her reflection. The old woman—herself, her grandmother, a stranger all at once—watched her with sad, compassionate eyes. They nodded to each other in slow, near-mournful agreement.

Then, in a swift motion, she swept the

remains of the picture into the desk drawer and dropped the knife in after them. She shut the drawer rapidly, silently.

Rising, she gathered the injured statue into her lap, and stroked the wood, while she sat on the edge of her bed, rocking it like an infant.

SIX

CHRISTINE LEE sat in the Leather Unicorn restaurant, nursing a Cinzano and waiting for Harry Metzger, who was running late, as usual. She had never quite understood the concept of an agency liaison person who handled his assignments—like their present information exchange and update—with such a casual disregard for the niceties of punctuality. Harry often seemed so offhand about timing, and so continually unsurprised by what she had to report, that Christine would find herself, after one of their dinners together, wondering why she was bothering with her end of the investigation at all. But, then, it was her job—and an awful lot of it was routine.

Oh, well, Christine rationalized, waving away the waiter in his crisp white shirt and black leather chaps, there were benefits to this particular restaurant in San Francisco's Castro area. She took a certain pleasure in gazing at all the handsome men filling a majority of the tables in cozy twosomes or drifting by the window arm-in-arm with other handsome men.

Even if she couldn't touch, she still liked looking.

She saw Harry before he saw her, waving to him just as the maitre d' turned and pointed to her booth at the back of the long room. He threaded his way through intervening tables, unwrapping the knitted scarf he always seemed to wear, winter or summer.

"Sorry I was late, it was—"

"The traffic. It's *always* the traffic. Why not start five minutes early?"

He shrugged, and murmured thanks to the waiter who delivered his drink. After a long swallow, he set the glass down on the tablecloth in front of him, and asked, "What have you got to report?" He added, "Give me everything, refresh my memory."

She said, "The big picture is beginning to shape up, but I need real facts—names, dates, amounts—the hard copy. I think, by now, we have a pretty fair idea of what's going on."

He nodded, and took another sip of his scotch-over.

Christine continued, "There are pretty clearly two levels at work here. PalmerCo's legitimate involvements in construction, mining, so forth in and around Bukawai's capital at Ajapa. At the same time, there are a lot of indicators—and a lot of guesswork on my part—that Palmer's group is involved with a number of casinos and smuggling operations also centered on that city. The connections are obvious on the surface. PalmerCo, International built the Royal Ajapa Casino and the Gold Coast Hotel and Gaming Complex, both of which do a huge business in separating tourists from their dollars, francs, Deutsche marks, etc.

"In addition, Ajapa in general and a lot of PalmerCo investments in particular seem to be a pipeline for goods in and money out—as well as little extras like dope, which finds its way west to the U.S. and Canada. The constant flow of PalmerCo personnel and equipment east-to-west and back again is probably the main artery for this *sub-rosa* business.

"When Premier N'dala's Government took control last year, they began a program of civil reform that had, as one of its goals, the nationalization of outside corporations and a clean-up campaign to purge the country of large-scale corruption and purge Ajapa of its unofficial title as West Africa's Vice Capital.

"Needless to say, this two-pronged assault hit PalmerCo where it hurt—both legally and illegally. There's some indication that PalmerCo actually was responsible for Colonel Obitsebi's initial rebellion against the legitimate N'dala Government, but nothing I've come up with so far confirms or denies this. Still, the fact is, the Obitsebi challenge has only been able to continue because of arms and money most likely supplied through the 'concerned but non-involved' PalmerCo." She paused to order another Cinzano before continuing.

"The civil war has prevented Premier N'dala from implementing his threatened phasing-out of crime and overseas financial influence; at the same time, there seems every likelihood that

Colonel Obitsebi has given guarantees somewhere along the line that PalmerCo's investments will remain untampered with if his junta prevails.

"In short, this bloody civil war seems to be largely the produce of David Palmer's fevered brain, and . . .

"Well," she shrugged, "it all comes back to the same old problem, the money. Most of it is on deposit in Swiss and other foreign banks. We can't get a read-out on it. We're sure that PalmerCo owns interest in a number of these banks, but I haven't been able to get to the information. With these kinds of connections, they don't even have to (unless there's a real need) transfer any hard cash. In a lot of crucial transactions, nothing more than letters of credit changes hands. And believe me, it's not just Palmer who's involved. I'll give you odds a fair share of respectable U.S. bankers are lending full cooperation to these various projects. And making a bundle."

"Tell me about it," Harry said, shaking his head, and signaling the waiter for a refill. "When push comes to shove, nobody's going to rock a multi-million-dollar boat that might set off a financial panic. There's a helluva lot riding on those bets at the Royal Ajapa Casino."

Christine set her own glass on the table and tapped it thoughtfully with a silver painted nail. "As for monies coming back into the U.S., to PalmerCo, the laundering is done in the Caribbean. PalmerCo has a variety of primary and subsidiary connections in places like Barbados,

Trinidad, Bimini, Nassau, Virgin Islands, and Martinique. Jesus, these are the old homes of voodoo—places where the devil walked. Now the devil has another name: organized crime. The 'Hoodoo Sea' is becoming the 'Hoodlum Sea.' "

"You're getting off the subject," Harry said.

"Sorry." Christine smiled. "It gets to me, that's all. Must be something to do with my roots."

"We were discussing laundries," he said.

"As near as I can tell," she said, "the focus is the Caribbean Commerce Bank, which is a subsidiary of the World-Wide Credit Bank in Switzerland. I've been able to determine that PalmerCo has a large number of financial deals on the books with C.C.B. I'm pretty sure that money is moving out of U.S. operations and Bukawai through C.C.B. to be deposited in numbered accounts in Switzerland for secret-money banking.

"On the other hand," she continued, this time attracting the waiter's attention herself, "monies to keep Obitsebi in operation are flowing through the same channels—with PalmerCo personnel as 'bagmen' and 'bagwomen' carrying the money to Ajapa, using the Caribbean-Swiss connection to back up letters of credit, and so forth."

Harry looked at her a long time, before giving her a half-smile and asking softly, "What can you give me in the way of hard facts—not surmise—*hard facts?*"

"At the moment?"

"Right now."

"Shit is what I can give you. The man covers his ass real carefully."

"What are the chances of getting me some concrete facts?"

"Iffy—" He started to protest, but she silenced him with a raised hand. "But we'll get him. This case is especially important to me."

Something in her voice puzzled him. He said, "What's making this case more important to you than any others we've worked on?"

She shrugged. "I can't put it into words, Harry, it just—*feels*—more important. Something in my gut."

This time, he shrugged. Then he said, "Something in *my* gut says I'm hungry. Let's order dinner. If I have another drink without any food, I'm going to slide right under the table."

When Harry had paid the bill, he insisted on accompanying her to her car with an old-fashioned nicety Christine would have found intolerable in most men. She put up with it in Harry because it was an automatic, uncalculated response, not an attitude with him.

When they reached her car two blocks away, she gave him a swift, friendly kiss and slid into the driver's seat of her sporty little Isuzu sedan.

"Lock your door," Harry warned as she rolled down her window partway.

"Yes, Mother," she laughed, and nudged the door lock down with her elbow. She always did this—the same way she routinely glanced into the back seat of the car before getting in to be sure no one was waiting to surprise her. All her years of training were now second nature to her.

She waved one last time to Harry, and pulled away from the curb. As she drove she found herself thinking about the old friend of hers who had turned up in David's office that afternoon. For some weird reason, she could not remember the name of the middle-aged black woman who remained an obscurely troublesome presence in Christine's mind. Yet, she had been . . . an old family friend? A friend of her sister's?

A sudden stab of pain threatened to split her head in two. For a moment, the woman was forgotten. Then, as the pain subsided a little, Christine thought. She's just about my mother's age. She must have been my mother's friend. She remembered now. The woman was a friend of her mother's when she had been growing up in the Western Addition. But the answer was only somewhat satisfactory: the nagging reality was, she could not—no matter how hard she tried—remember a single detail of that friendship. Something in her head (which was tormenting her again) told her the friendship had existed. But now, Christine's thought seesawed between easy acceptance of the woman's connection with her life and a frustrating inability to believe it. *I can't even remember her name,* she thought. *Fine way for someone with my training to act.*

It's almost as if my mind shut down for a few

minutes—just about the time I was talking with her, Christine reflected. *I'll probably never see her again, since she was only there to—*Again, she had the uncomfortable feeling of a gap in her recollection of the afternoon, since she now recalled, *I never even found out why she was there. Coincidence? Was she looking for me? For David? For someone else?*

She tried dismissing the trivial matter from her mind, but kept coming back to it, the way she might keep scratching a small insect bite. And the more she peristed in worrying the thought, the more her headache grew.

Christine was still thinking about the enigmatic woman, between flashes of pain, as she let herself into her apartment. Immediately she discovered not only the hall light (which she always left on) burning, but the steel-and-frosted glass floor lamp beside her leather recliner chair.

She instinctively backed through the still-open door, planning a fast exit to call the police, when David Palmer suddenly appeared in the living-room entranceway. He was shoeless and had his white shirt unbuttoned halfway to his navel. "I let myself in," he said unnecessarily, "and made myself a drink. Want one?"

"No," she said. "Jesus, you startled me. I thought you were going to be in San Jose overnight." She slipped off her coat, hanging it in the narrow closet beside the front door. She forgot her thoughts of a few moments earlier.

"No business tonight," he said, padding the

rest of the way across the thick cream-colored carpet to settle contentedly into the recliner. He put his head back, closed his eyes, then opened them again to take a swig of his scotch before he continued. "You. Tonight."

"Nice of you to let me know," she said. "Suppose I had spent the night out?" She sat down on the couch opposite him.

He gave her a thin smile. "Then we'd have a *lot* to talk about tomorrow." The threat, though vague, was unmistakable. "But," he said amiably, "here you are and here I am and everything's fine." He closed his eyes again and settled back, lightly holding his drink glass balanced on the wide chair arm.

Christine leaned forward to take one of her infrequent cigarettes from the lead-glass cigarette box on her coffee table. She lit it using the heavy matching lighter. She asked, "How did it go today?"

He waved the question aside. "The usual bullshit. Nothing important."

"So, who did you see?"

"Some computer firms—about upgrading our programs and equipment here."

She could tell from his tone of voice he was keeping something from her. He knew very little about computers, beyond his ability to read a print-out. Surely he would have sent one of his staff to do a preliminary look at new equipment. She made a mental note to do some nosing around in the next few days, but she knew better than to push David. Then he reached for her, and the subject was closed.

After their lovemaking, which was short and passionless, Christine drifted off quickly into a deep sleep. David, however, found himself tossing and turning, sleeping only in short stretches. What sleep he was able to find was plagued with a jumble of half-recollected dreams. He was haunted, through several of the dream fragments, by the face of a vaguely familiar black woman, middle-aged, who came to him, naked in a moonlit grove of trees. Her heavy breasts and thighs gleamed as if they were oiled, picking up a glow from the unseen moon, filtering in drops and splashes of light through the trees overhead. She was carrying pictures of his son and daughter in a gold frame just like David kept on his desk in his office. When she drew closer, he saw that a crack in the glass ran diagonally across Amy's face—just like his own frame that he had knocked off his desk last week.

As he watched, he became aware that there was a second, slighter figure behind her where the trees grew thickest and the shadow was deepset. He strained to see, but he could not tell the sex of the shadowed figure.

Then his gaze was forced back to the woman in front of him. She held out the damaged gold frame to him, and he saw that it was no longer the familiar gold frame, but the decapitated head of a cat, its opened eyes dull yellow in the moonlight. Blood from the stump of its neck had slathered the woman's hands and wrists; there were also daubings of gore on her forehead and just below her eyes, he saw to his disgust.

David, she whispered only once, then began to laugh raucously, and the dead cat's head let out a cry that was something between a shriek of terror and an almost-sexual yowl of animal desire.

In terror, he turned to run, and inexplicably found himself following a convuluted path through a dense jungle. He was naked now, and thorns and nettles stung him. Around him he could hear birds shrilling, insects chittering, animal bellowing or pushing noisily through the underbrush. It seemed to him that he had been following this path forever, and that he was fated to follow it into infinity.

But the trail suddenly opened out into a clearing. A stillness fell across the forest around him the moment he stepped onto the matted grass and mold of the glade.

At the far edge of the perfectly circular open space, the very woman he had tried to escape sat hunkered down. She was bare-breasted, but wore a skirt of plaited leaves. Upon her knees was a hollowed-out calabash.

He approached her and called her name, feeling a tremendous desire stirring in him. Looking down, he discovered his erect member had assumed Priapian proportions, betraying his nakedness. He called to her with some vague idea of apologizing for his nakedness and shamelessness. And with a desire for her. But she merely smiled and shook her head.

Then, she motioned him over to her, never

changing her position. When he stood in front of her, hovering over her, she held up the hollow gourd to him filled with calabash seeds the size of marbles. She rattled it impatiently at him, until he understood that he was to take them out. This he did, and she said quickly, "If you can throw these successfully into here"—and she held up the empty gourd to him by way of illustration, "from across the clearing, I will marry you."

Her voice, David noted, both was and was not familiar. She cast her eyes once on his sex, smiled again and in an obscene manner, and waved him toward the point where the trail entered the glade.

Once in position, David saw how hopeless the logistics appeared. But he gamely tossed the three seeds *one-two-three* in the direction of the gourd and, as if by magic, they landed *one-two-three* dead in the center of the calabash with three tiny, hollow sounds that followed hard upon one another.

With the swagger of a hero, David started across the clearing; opposite him, the woman climbed to her feet, carelessly tossing the shell and seeds aside.

She held out her arms to him; her breasts were firm, lifting out toward him. "Take possession of what you have earned," she invited.

Spurred by a desire that seemed to surface the very air around him, David sprinted across the clearing.

With a laugh, the woman pulled him into her

arms, and they sank down into the soft, warm grass.

Then she laughed again, a frightening guttural sound that made David draw back suddenly to find the woman was gone and that he was embracing the body of a young black man. The boy's skin felt chill and wet, his eyes were closed, the jeans were covered with dark mildew stains as though they had lain in the damp undergrowth a long time. To all intents, David was embracing a corpse.

With a cry of revulsion, he released the body and scrambled to his feet, backing away from the silent shape.

And then, terrifyingly, eyes popped open. David found himself staring into dead eyes within the blank face. The man's eyelids now looked as livid as if they had been burned with acid. The pupils were half-hidden, the eyes were rolled back into the head. And yet, David could feel them watching him, with an intensity that burned like acid itself.

Then the man's head seemed to *float* upward in an impossible way, tthe man's back levering into an upright position with the mechanical—*inhuman*—smoothness of a machine. *Or,* David thought, fascinated and repelled at the same time, *like a snake, moving into position, getting ready to strike.* Instinctively, he tried to draw further back, but some undeniable command in his head—barely distinguishable from his own thoughts—held him rigidly in place.

When the man was sitting up, the stench that

clung around the pale, bloodless-looking being was almost more than David could handle. He felt his stomach heave. Frozen splotches of moonlight mottled the livid face and chest in front of him.

And then, most frightening of all, the man—the *thing*—was speaking to him. He listened to the broken noises coming from its throat, that sounded as if the throat were swollen and sandpaper dry, and (his head swimming) heard as though from a vast distance, "I'm so thirsty and hungry." The sandpaper tongue moved uselessly over sandpaper lips.

Something in the look, in the words, hit David with raw terror.

From somewhere behind him he heard a half-forgotten half-familiar woman's laugh. The jungle around him was clotted darkness out of which hundred of eyes were watching. But David could not take his eyes off the dead eyes in front of him.

Against every impulse of his consciousness, the wordless command forced him to take one step, then another, towards the lank, nightmare figure that stood up. Waiting for him.

The creature's arm stretched out to him. David saw the fingers tipped with nails chipped to razor-sharp points. A blackened tongue like a slice of rotten meat flickered out over dry, fissured lips and yellowed teeth.

Suddenly the right hand snaked out to grip David's throat. While he struggled ineffectually against the superhuman grip, the creature spoke again. "I'm thirsty," it rasped, and there was something obscenely plaintive in the voice. "I'm hungry for life, because they've left me none of it. I'm hungry and thirsty for life, and you have so much of it in you . . ."

But now there was nothing between him and the onrushing, deadlines of those eyes, of the cracked sandpaper lips, the listless tongue, the hunger that roared out of the blind eyes that somehow managed to fix greedily on him. The hands like claws locked behind David's head, pulling him unwillingly forward into an obscene parody of a lover's kiss. The creature's face buried itself in his neck.

From near and far and all around him came the sound of the woman's laugh.

Then it was drowned out by hideous chewing and sucking noises and a blaze of pain so excruciating that—

His screams woke himself and Christine up. She held him tightly until his trembling stopped. "You had a nightmare, baby, that's all," she kept repeating over and over. But while the details of his dream had fled with his waking, the terror it had produced in him clung to him even more solidly than Christine's arms. He sensed that he had been within a hair's breath of dying in his dreamworld—and that would have meant never waking up, would have meant spending all eternity within the confines of that unremembered, but still terrifying, nightmare.

SEVEN

It was Nana Chicory who guided Suzanne through the next necessary steps of her training. The old woman came to her granddaughter in a dream, crossing the gray wastes between that distant place and the threshold of sleep where Suzanne waited, eager and afraid, for her aged mentor.

Shortly after she had entered the deepest, dream-haunted sleep, Suzanne saw Charlotte approaching her, stepping from ridge to ridge of gray silk with the effortless rhythms of a much younger woman. Suzanne herself felt frozen in place, unable to do more than wait impatiently for the older woman to reach her side.

But Nana Chicory paused some distance away, forcing them to shout to each other across the uncertain, hazed distance.

"I can come no closer, yet," the shade of the old woman explained.

Suzanne merely nodded.

Without preamble, the crone began, "Those who would take the most powerful magic into themselves must first show the *orishas* their willingness to make great sacrifices to claim such power."

Dream-Suzanne nodded as if she already knew what her ancestor was going to tell her.

"In the homeland, in Bukawai, you would be required to present the *orishas* the skull of the person you most deeply love among the living. This alone will entitle you to safety and success in wielding the power Shango would place in you—and which you so deeply desire to possess.

"The skull means a death. The *orishas* demand the death of the one most deeply loved by you: sister, mother, brother, father, child, loyal friend—whoever means the most in your life must be slain by you. Only then will you be able to claim in full the powers the *orishas* wish to give you in order to carry out their wishes and the commands of your own heart. These are one, as the power that will let you fulfill both is one."

"But who? . . ." she asked.

"The one living whom you most love," the old woman replied obdurately.

"Who?" she asked again.

But the old woman's lips curled into a brutal smile. She said, "There is another value in killing one you greatly love. Once you have done this, no other death you may cause will ever bring to you the horror you feel when you kill the one you love."

"Who is it?" Suzanne in her dream demanded.

But the old woman was already hastening

back to the gray boundaries of the dream. Her last words, shouted over her shoulder to her granddaughter, were "You know. As soon as I spoke the great one's wishes, you knew."

Then she was gone, swallowed up in the eager fogs, boiling at the edge of Suzanne's dream-consciousness.

But the old woman was right, Suzanne realized, laying hold of those thoughts she must carry out of her dream into the day. She knew exactly whom her grandmother was speaking of . . .

When she had drawn all the drapes in her bedroom and set her dressing chair lightly against the door, Elenora began undressing. In the full-length mirror beside her chinese-red bureau, she watched herself luxuriate in the feel of slipping out of garment after garment, baring her warm, deep-hued skin to the faintly chill, slightly erotic feel of the air in the room.

She shrugged out of the pale-pink silk blouse, slid her calf-length grey skirt softly over her hips to let it fall in a heap around her ankles. Her bra she tossed carelessly across the zippered boots she had, a moment before, kicked into the corner behind the bedroom door. She ran her hands over her breasts several times, feeling the nipples stiffen, responding to the touch of her fingers and the electric feeling hovering in the air.

Elenora pushed her panties partway down her thighs, then cupped her hands, gently massaging her vulva, letting the tip of her middle right finger enter a little deeper than the others, testing the wetness gathering there. Her breathing became deeper, more relaxed; she smiled at her image in the mirror. Abruptly she shoved the panties all the way down her legs, stepping free of the mounded clothing.

She paused to study her reflection one last time. Then she crossed the little hall to the bathroom and flicked on the lights. The familiar clutter of her morning *toilette* was still scattered across the basin; one of the bath towels had fallen off the towel rack and lay in a soggy bundle near the bathtub. This she kicked out of the way as she leaned over and began to run the water in the bathtub.

As the tub filled noisily, she took the little bag she had on the edge of the basin earlier and opened it. The single package of double-edged razor blades and the drug-store sales receipt fell into the basin in her suddenly shaking hands. *What was there to be nervous about?* she wondered; then recalled that she had wanted to explain herself, her fears, to the bored young black girl behind the drugstore sales counter. But she could say nothing, did not really have any idea why it seemed so important to tell the stranger anything. So she had—nearly dropping her purse, her hands were trembling so—paid for the little package, then waited while the girl carefully counted out her change and handed the little brown bag back to her.

When their fingertips had touched, for just the briefest moment, she felt the strength to say what had to be said. Only, the pure hell of it was: Elenora had not the faintest idea what she wanted to say. So, in the end, the girl had asked her if she was all right, and she had mumbled an "of course" and had left the store, her purchase tucked safely into her purse.

The tub was nearly full. Elenora turned the tap off and climbed in, having set the still unopened razor blades on the edge of the tub.

She slid down into the hot water, savoring the feel of it, the way it relaxed muscles in her lower back aggravated by a day of coping with demanding curstomers. She leaned back, breathing deeply of the steam rising up in clouds towards the pale-green bathroom ceiling. Here and there she could just make out tiny stains, mildew perhaps, speckling the ceiling. She had often meant to try scrubbing them out with some heavy-duty cleaner, or maybe asking Jomo to repaint the whole bathroom. After all, it hadn't been painted in almost ten years. She closed her eyes and leaned her head back on the folded towels she had set under her neck.

She made a mental note to talk to Jomo about the repainting after dinner. He didn't do that much around the house, he could at least repaint the bathroom ceiling.

She let her eyes drift open again. The bathroom was filling with steam. Perspiration was beading on her forehead and running in trickles down the sides of her face.

Sudden fear took hold of her; she had the feeling that someone else was in the room with her. She had left the bathroom door ajar to let some of the steam escape into the bedroom outside. She could see a portion of the other room; her warning sense told her someone was standing *there*, just beyond the half-open door.

But she could see enough, by sitting up and leaning forward, to be sure there was no one in the other room. And she reminded herself of the chair leaning against the outer door. There was no way anyone could get in without her being aware.

Unless someone had gotten in before she had come home from work. Unless he was waiting for her, had been hidden all the time she had been undressing and drawing her bath . . .

Stop that! she told herself. *That's foolishness: there's nothing to be afraid of. You're alone and there's nothing to be afraid of.*

Somehow the realization of just how alone she was in the house terrified her most of all. Then she grew impatient at her own timorousness. *What is the matter with me?* she wondered. She had been feeling on edge for days, since just before Suzanne's arrival—but that was only natural, after so many years, after all that had gone down between them. There was nothing to be afraid of, to be worried about: she and Suzanne were getting along all right, and Suzanne was making an effort to get along with her son. *Everything is fine*, she told herself. But she couldn't completely rid herself of the foolish impression that someone was watching her. On impulse she glanced up at the little window halfway up the wall above the tub; fading daylight illuminated the window set high above the pathway running through the skimpy flowerbeds at the side of the house and connecting sidewalk and backyard. The window was closed; even if there *were* some toehold for a voyeur to have his nose pressed to the glass, he couldn't see anything through its rippled glass. And the simple fact was that the window was two floors above ground level on the blank side of the building. No balconies, no fire escape on that side at all. *There is nothing to be afraid of.*

She leaned back one more time and tried to relax, but the steaming water now seemed incapable of easing the growing tension in her.

She sat up partway and reached for the little plastic-wrapped package, splitting it open with her thumbnail. She withdrew the first blue-metal, paper-thin blade and studied the way the light caught it. She flexed it thoughtfully between her fingertips, careful not to cut herself.

There is nothing to be afraid of.

She slipped her left arm below the surface of the gray, soap-foamed bathwater and, in the warm liquid, began rapidly making one-two-three-four-five long slits from the edge of her palm halfway to her elbow. Unmindful of the suddenly crimson water, she held the blade in her left hand and, immersing her right arm, made the same number of swift incisions with the blade. Then she dropped the blade onto the tub edge, near the package of unused razor blades, noting with curiosity more than any other emotion the way her blood and bathwater dripped from her fingertips, running in unreal-looking crimson rivulets back into the pink bathwater.

With both her arms sunk at her sides in the warm water, there was no pain; there was little sensation at all. She leaned her head back and stared at the ceiling because the staining water disturbed her in a way she could not articulate to herself.

There is nothing to be afraid of.

She was getting weak; she could feel some pain; she had an overwhelming sense of something being radically wrong. Like when she tried to talk to the salesperson in the pharmacy to tell her . . . to tell her . . .

What was I going to tell her?

She forced herself to examine her mind, to seek out the answer. *I was going to tell her . . . Yes, now I remember: I was going to say, I don't want to buy those things; I have no use for those. Please! Don't sell them to me.*

But the girl had taken her money and handed her the brown package and she had come home to her bath.

There is nothing to be afraid of.

It was growing steamier in the room; there seemed to be a haze growing behind her eyes, making the stains on the ceiling seem to dance.

Must tell Jomo about those spots . . . get him to paint and—

She struggled into a sitting position, nearly slipping down the back of the tub. Scarlet water swirled around her knees, lapped at her waist.

Oh Jesus Oh my God what's happening what has happened?

She half hoisted herself unsteadily to her feet, narrowly avoiding a fall, clinging with her damaged arms to the side of the tub. She slipped over the edge onto the bathmat. There was blood all over the side of the tub—all over her. She hit the floor with a soft, wet thump. She wondered if anyone was downstairs to hear, to come help. She tried to call, but her voice was less than a whisper. *I'm not allowed to call; I shouldn't be trying to get away,* she thought.

Lightheaded, terrified of blacking out, she began crawling toward the bathroom door, tantalizingly ajar, leaving streamers and pools of watery blood behind her. She was so dizzy now she had to force herself each inch of the way.

There is nothing to be afraid of, some voice near the surface of her awareness reminded soothingly.

But a deeper, more urgent voice—her own—screamed inside her head, *Why is this happening to me? I don't want this to happen.*

In the end, however, the blackness took over; she was too weak to reach the bathroom door, too helpless even to ever reach the hall door and pull it open a precious inch or two to call for help in the hope that someone was downstairs or that someone outside the house might hear her. And even that was futile because she was not allowed, for all her terrifying fear of what was happening, to make a sound on her own behalf. The only thing that was left to her was her own interior voice that just kept protesting, *Why is this happening to me?*

One of her hands was under her stomach; she could feel the hot blood pumping out against her bare, damp skin, soaking into the carpet. Her fear grew; it seemed to make her blood pump faster; she almost felt like something had taken control of her body, making the blood circulate faster, hastening her death—

And then she knew that even if she found the strength to crawl out into the bedroom, she would not dare open the hall door, because someone was just on the other side, now, she was sure, someone who knew what was happening to her, someone who wanted it to happen, was *making* it happen to her.

And death was infinitely less fearful than confronting that *presence*.

And because she no longer had any hope, she ceased even protesting, though the blood continued seeping out of her long after she had stopped caring forever.

On the other side of the closed door, Suzanne hung as though her own hands were melded to the wood and paint of Elenora's bedroom door.

In a way, she felt like a Christ-figure upon a crucifix, hanging suspended, committed for all eternity to a course of action upon which her own fate—and the outcome of countless larger issues—was suspended.

She felt her sister dying, inches away, just beyond the closed door, but she was no more able to help Elenora than her sister was able to do anything to help herself.

Splinter and needle, Suzanne knew, robbed

her sister of her will, even of her ability to cry out.

The door felt warm under Suzanne's hands; she felt her sister dying, her life seeping away out of her cruelly violated flesh, blood-price to the Shango-*orisha*.

There was a kind of comfort for Suzanne in the certainty that what Nana Chicory had promised in her dream would always be true: nothing, ever, could anguish her more than the death of her sister—so long estranged, suddenly become friend again, now lost to her until they met in that uncertain place from which Nana Chicory reached out to her dreams and from which the power of Shango himself poured into her to each degree that she proved herself a worthy vessel of his potency.

Suzanne had dropped to her knees now; the palms of her hands were still pressed hungrily against the wood of the door. Now she was drawing power hungrily from the event beyond the door—even as she had earlier poured the self-destructive impulse into her sister's unsuspecting, unresisting mind.

She leaned the side of her face, wet with tears, against the door. There was no longer any sound of movement; she felt, just beyond the panel, a chill void, pulling inward. She wondered that the walls of the room didn't collapse in on themselves, to be swallowed into the infinite, lightless maw she imagined filled the space just beyond the frail barrier of painted wood. She thought of it as the mouth of one of Nana Chicory's *orishas*, demanding flesh and blood from this world in order to manifest itself here in return.

She climbed to her feet, trembling, and reached for the door knob—then jerked her hand back as if the old-fashioned glass handle had suddenly become electrified. The facets seemed to burn with an intensity beyond any possible refraction from the hall light above her. It was a warning to her, she decided, not to enter the room where the power of the *orisha* was manifest in such a way.

Suzanne backed away, unable to take her eyes off the door handle, which suddenly flared into a white blaze, then kaleidescoped through infinite, eye-searing shades of purple and green.

Only when she had backed as far as her bedroom, was she able to turn away. Slipping into the darkened room, she thankfully closed the door behind her.

Jomo, returning late from partying, would find Elenora in the morning.

She would stay in her room, pretending to sleep, until her nephew must inevitably rouse her. Then she would arise, indulge her deeply genuine grief with Elenora's son, arrange for a proper burial for her sister—and take charge of the household, letting Elenora's survivors play out the parts the *orisha* had decreed.

EIGHT

Two nights after Elenora's funeral, after the long service in the neighborhood Baptist church; after the sermon extolling her virtues as wife, mother, and sister; after the endless hymn-singing; after the graveside service, the tearful embraces of friends and church-members; after the long ride back in the limousine Suzanne had insisted upon; after spending a stifling afternoon under the puzzled, fearful, vaguely hostile gaze of Jomo, whose eyes ran through quicksilver emotional changes while his body remained listlessly propped against a pew or the folding chair at gravesite or the ribbed gray cushions of the limousine; after a return to the silent house where emotional neighbor-women brought an array of foods, offered more hugs, dabbed their eyes and closed the front door behind them . . .

After all the grief and confusion Suzanne took Jomo to dinner at a little restaurant near the house of mourning on Manningtree Lane. She invited her nephew, explaining that she was worried about him becoming too wrapped up in thoughts of death and guilt over whatever drove his mother to do what she had done. And Jomo seemed eager enough to share her company for the time, at least.

Seated in the restaurant, Suzanne studied the menu perfunctorily. She ordered herself a chicken dinner and a pot of tea. Jomo, seeming only half present, ordered a hamburger and coffee. They sat at a free table near the back of the cafe.

When she had finished her salad, she noticed Jomo looking at her with a curious intensity. She read in his look a sudden mingling of fear and a deeper recognition—as if he sensed some kinship, some hidden bond between them. And she knew it involved both fear and curiosity on his part.

She met his eyes steadily with her own. She asked, "Why are you looking at me that way?"

"What way?"

"Like I'm some sort of weird exhibit you've come across in a museum, something you're not really sure is human."

He laughed too quickly, too sharply in response; then he said, "But you *are*. *Too weird*, I mean. You're the aunt I hardly knew existed—the one my crazy old greatgrandmother talked about all the time she was living with us. When she was really out of it, I heard her say, 'Suzanne is the one. That's the way it's got to be. Suzanne has got to come home and finish what I ain't been able to.' I never did understand what she was talking about. And I don't think she knew she was talking to me. I think she believed she was talking to someone else completely." He held his untasted hamburger midway between his plate and mouth, asking suddenly, "Do you have any idea what she was talking about?"

"I was three thousand miles away," Suzanne said evenly, forcing herself to meet his eyes dead on. "She was delirious. Your question is foolish."

After a moment, he dropped his eyes to his sandwich, concentrated on taking a bite and chewing it carefully. "Yeah," he said, through a mouthful of bread and meat. "It was a dumb question."

But she knew his unformed suspicions had not truly been laid to rest.

"Anyhow," said Jomo finally, "that's what the old lady said."

Poking with a fork at her own plate, Suzanne asked, "So what do you think of me—honestly?"

Unexpectedly, her nephew smiled. "You're sure not a little old lady auntie, for sure."

"Thank you for that. I still don't feel like any old lady." She drained off the last of her tea and said, "Would you get me some more hot water?"

While Jomo was gone, Suzanne gathered her thoughts together, sifting out the most important elements.

Jomo was going to play an important part in the unfolding design; but it would require a tremendous effort on her part to win him *utterly* to her service, body and soul. Her distaste for what she would soon have to do—for what she would have to begin *this night*—was overridden by her certainty that what she did had to be done; that she was simply the vessel that would carry a divine blood vengeance to its final, inevitable, *necessary* climax.

And yet, and yet—the ghost of her old self (before she had surrendered that self to the *orisha* and gained herself powers of *vodu* and *obi* in return) protested the enmeshing of her nephew in the complex working-out of a hazily grasped web more many-stranded than any devised by Ananasi, the spider-divinity. Like the most wonderful of Ananasi's legendary webs, the strands of what Suzanne had become, what she was doing, wove together heaven and earth with cables of infinite subtlety, yet inflexible strength.

Jomo returned, carrying a cup brimful of scalding water. Some of the liquid spilled onto the greasy blue-and-white tiles of the tabletop when he set down her mug. She regarded him, anguished that one so young had to bear the burden she was shortly going to give him. She forced herself to remember she was no longer who and what she had been. She was the vessel of a god—and human feelings had no place in her heart. She should only feel the indwelling of the *orisha*.

"You almost done?" her nephew asked. She sensed her staring was making him uncomfortable, impatient to be away.

She nodded, but she made no move to leave. Instead, filled with a deep hunger, she finished her chicken, attacking the little pile of bones, sucking each clean of any bit of meat that she had missed. *Like a ghoul,* Suzanne thought, *dining on the bones of a tiny child.* The uncomfortable image of herself played over and over in her mind.

"It's getting a little late," Jomo prompted, growing more impatient.

"It sure is," she said, glancing at her own wristwatch. She let the false note of lightness mask the tension that had suddenly settled cloudlike over her, putting every muscle and nerve on alert.

Jomo made a show of digging in his pocket for money to pay the bill, but she laid a hand gently over his and said, "No way—this one's on me."

He shrugged, but made no protest. They rose, pausing to pay at the register beside the door.

They walked part of the way home in silence, Suzanne following her own threads of thought; Jomo seemingly having exhausted his supply of small talk. As they passed the empty lot, weed-and-tree choked, that marked the entrance to Manningtree Lane, Suzanne said, "Come with me. I want to show you something."

He started to protest, but she grabbed his hand and pulled him toward the thick copse of trees at the center of the expensive, shadowy area. Too surprised by her actions to protest, Jomo followed.

There was a little clearing at the heart of the trees. Oval-shaped, it found its natural focus in the thick bole of an ancient oak that spread thick branches overhead, twisting them into the foliage of the lesser trees. One thick, gnarled root, the wood polished to a gem-like sheen by others who had used it for a seat, provided a place for Suzanne to sit. Jomo hovered over her uncertainly, while she pulled a small, flat bottle out of her purse.

She held it out to him. "It's rum," she said, "a traditional drink of our ancestors from the Caribbean. It's also," she said off-handedly, "my one vice. Share it with me. In memory of your mother—my sister."

Jomo shrugged and accepted the bottle, holding it a little away from him, angled into a patch of moonlight so he could real the label. "Bacardi," he said. "Good stuff."

The bottle was three quarters full; he unscrewed the top and took a swig, swallowing it down with a loud gulp.

He made a face. "Tastes a little funny—like licorice or something else." He looked at her suspiciously. "You put anything in it?" Then, seeing her look of ready denial, he laughed and said, "I'd better take another taste. Just to be sure it's okay." He took another long, loud swallow, handing the bottle down to her and wiping his mouth. "Aren't you having any?" he asked.

"Not just now," she said, screwing the cap back on the bottle and setting it carefully beside her feet, so it leaned against the base of the oak.

Jomo started to say something, then stopped in mid-sentence, apparently confused. He passed his hand several times in front of his face, as though brushing away cobwebs. He tried again to speak, but only managed to lick his lips, as though they were suddenly very dry. Finally, he dropped his hands to his sides and stood watching Suzanne with a vacant expression; his eyes seemed focused on some far distant point in the night sky.

Still in the shelter of the tree, Suzanne stood, her hand resting lightly, possessively on its trunk. She shed her jacket, and the silky fabric of her pale-green blouse glowed in the diffused moonlight with cool chartruse fire. Her eyes, staring into Jomo's, burned white-hot around black irises that pulled on his still-resistant consciousness like twin black holes, the ghosts of stars, that could suck him into a universe of dead suns and nonbeings. . . .

Jomo shook his head stupidly, trying to free his mind of the disturbing, confusing images that suddenly filled him full of terror.

"Now," she said, retrieving the bottle and opening it, "you have another drink." She whispered in a voice that sounded gentle, but her unblinking eyes that never left his seemed snake-cold, threatening.

He wiped his mouth with the back of his left hand, gripping the bottle firmly with his right.

She began to unbutton her blouse, watching him all the time; and he took several more swigs of the rum as his eyes followed her fingers unfastening the row of delicate, lime-colored buttons. She pulled her blouse free of her belt; opening the front to reveal her full dark breasts gleaming in the moonlight, heavy, the nipples taut; letting the silky material slide off her shoulders and to the ground so that it lay like a pool of green water at her feet.

He watched passively, only responding when she urged him, "Take another drink." He obeyed, tipping the bottle to his lips. A great distance, an unfathomable barrier seemed to separate them.

All the while she watched him, like a spider watching a winged insect hover closer and closer to its fatal net.

She removed the bottle from Jomo's suddenly numbed fingers.

"Sleep awhile," she said, and the burning liquor, the warmth of the night, her words engulfed him, smothered her, wrapped him in a cocoon of deadly solicitude. Somewhere deep inside his mind he had a vision of a spider hastily, yet meticulously, spinning a trapped fly into a mummy of threads. Then this impression was overwhelmed with the message—seeming to bubble up from his own subconscious—that it was good to be inside, lost in an interior place of cloying darkness and sweet noncaring. . . .

He dropped slowly to his knees, then fell to his side on the ground. He curled himself into a fetal position, unmindful of the wet grass and stones beneath his left shoulder. He was aware before he fell into a thick sleep, only of Suzanne's eyes burning down at him, like twin moons mimicking the moon he could just barely glimpse through the tangled webbing of the oak tree overhead. . . .

He awoke briefly from a drug-like trance to see his aunt kneeling in front of the tree, the bottle of rum, uncorked, held out to the tree-hole as if she were offering it a drink. She was muttering something—it sounded a little like French, and then again, it sounded like no language the boy had ever heard before.

He noted how her back, shining with sweat as though it were oiled, tapered down to a slender waist, then broadened into heavy, sensuous hips, resting on the backs of her legs as she half-sat, half-knelt before the tree.

In a loud voice, she cried out something that sounded like "Shango! Shango!" Then she poured out the bottle of rum across the roots of the tree. He wanted to say something to protest the waste of good liquor, but he found himself, instead, falling asleep with the helpless down-rush of a man blacking out....

The second time he came to, he found himself lying on his back, uncomfortable on the cool, stony earth, because his shirt was gone. He moved his right hand slightly and felt the material of his shirt, which lay in a careless bundle beside his head. He sensed that *she* had removed his shirt, though what *she* wanted of him, he could not guess.

His throat burned; he pulled his thoughts together enough to remember that she had poured away the rum, and that she had been chanting, naked, at the base of the oak tree.

He tried to call for her, but the only sound

that emerged from his throat was a half-strangled rasp.

Jomo let his head fall to one side, looking at the edge of the seemingly deserted clearing. He saw the moon had sunk low into the topmost branches of the surrounding trees.

And then he saw something dark standing in the shadows, and something shining. The dark shape moved; by the time he realized in his sleep-drugged state that the shining thing was the blade of a carving knife, it had already sliced once into his windpipe and once into his stomach and was thrusting at him a third time.

Don't do no more, please God, he wanted to plead, but only gurgling came from his ruined throat. His bowels gave way; he could feel urine soaking his jeans.

The terrifying pain slammed everything into sharp focus: he saw every shade of moonlight on every leaf of the oak tree; he saw his aunt's face, half in moonlight, half in shadow. Her eyes glittered with cold snake-like intensity, and her mouth was twisted into a grimace that was almost a grin. Each stroke of the blade moved with the rapid efficiency of a well-tended piston, as she jerked the knife into position yet again—

He rolled onto his side, only to feel her blade slip into his back—but he knew it wasn't necessary. He was finished. He was dying. He was drowning in his own blood and fear. He was losing control of everything. He was losing it all: blood . . . consciousness . . . life. He couldn't even move his head to see the face of the woman who had done this thing to him. He could see the toes of a pair of naked brown feet. That was the last thing he saw before he lost all control. The light was hazing; he could no longer even see her toes clearly.

He moved his fingers, trying to hang onto something, trying to retain some hold on something to slow the process of dying; but it was all going, going

gggggggg——

Suzanne rolled the still-warm body onto its back and made a final, quick slash across the throat of the boy whose sightless eyes stared past her own into some unimaginable place. There was little blood from his last wound. Even so, she was able to smear enough on her hands to daub at the base of the tree, where the thick roots joined the trunk.

Then she laid the bloody knife across the end of the V and poured the dregs of the rum-bottle over it, washing a little of the gore away. She held her hands out to the tree, breathing deeply of the night and the sweet cloying smell of rum. Then she began to chant over and over.

"Shango!"

"Faitre, Maitre, L'Afrique Bukawai, qui retti en ciel:

"Ce ou minn, Shango moi vley."

From time to time she paused, listening; once she half-turned, thinking she heard a footfall behind her. But there was only night and stillness.

And then she felt fingertips no heavier than dried grass on her left shoulder. She smell of rum was hidden in a rush of fragrant herbs, a familiar, rasping whisper told her, "Don' turn 'round, chile—I can't let you see me this way. *He* don' allow it. Jus' close your eyes and put out your hand."

Suzanne did as she was told. The ghostly fingers left her shoulder; a moment later she felt them press something into her hand. Then she heard a brief cry, "Ah Bo Bo!" dying away from her ear, and she knew it was safe to open her eyes.

She looked down at her hand, found in it a spike of ebon wood that felt diamond-hard and a curved needle made of bone or ivory. Slowly she rose from her knees and turned toward the corpse, lying palely in the center of the clearing.

Now she would find out just how much of the power of the god lay within her grasp.

Much later she returned to the silent house; the lonely porch light she and her nephew left was still burning.

She and the silent figure that followed her walked along the little path at the side of the house. It was so quiet she could hear her own breathing—the only sound disturbing the nearly absolute silence.

From her purse she took the basement key and unlatched the door; she pushed it open quickly, smelling mildew and dampness that was exhaled from the darkness inside.

Unhesitatingly, she stepped into the dark, and the silent figure followed her.

When she emerged, to lock the door, she was alone.

A weariness filled her as she climbed the steps to the front porch.

Without turning on any lights inside the house, she went down the silent hall to the kitchen. There she turned on the light. With only the briefest glance at the carelessly scattered dishes—a reminder of the everyday life the house would never again know—she went to the sink and began to wash off the knife blade she carried. When she was satisfied no speck of blood remained caught between the serrations, she wiped it dry and carefully replaced it in its drawer. Then she wiped her hands on the same towel with its cherry red-rooster design.

Then she went up to her room, and sat on the foot of her bed. She listened for a time, hearing only the sounds of the house settling into the last hours before dawn.

For an even longer time she looked across at the face of the Shango-cult figure. She finally fell asleep, while the warmth of the room wrapped itself around her with a clinging sultriness like the last moments before a thundershower.

NINE

Late the next morning, Suzanne rode the #83 bus to the stop in Marin nearest her destination. The day was windy but clear. There were only the vaguest clouds in the east, and they seemed likely to be blown away by early afternoon.

She was wearing a light sweater; but she took it off and carried it on her arm as soon as she got off the bus and looked around the old-fashioned square, faced with brick and stone shop fronts, that was the heart of the suburb of Chetwynd. She stopped at a service station to get her bearings and discovered the street where the Palmers lived was only a half-mile away, nestled in the rolling hills that cupped the township. Eagerly, she began walking. She paused to consult her map from time to time. Satisfied, she walked about twenty minutes, turned to her left on Balboa Road, and began the steep climb up toward Balboa Court.

Number 75 Balboa Court was an expansive, white, two-story Ranch-style house approached by a sharply upsloping lawn ending in a series of garden terraces. At the far end of the garden, she could see a Japanese gardener pruning a cluster of rose bushes; his truck was parked in the driveway just past the roses. The separate garage had three doors, all tightly closed. A waist-high hedge, neatly trimmed, separated the property from the road. A white brick path and flight of brick steps divided the garden in half. The house was shaded by two immense live oak trees in front; a cluster of dark green fir trees, towering above the two-story house, grew behind it. The shutters, window-trim, and front door were painted a dark green; to Suzanne the house looked expensive, comfortable, smug.

She paused a moment, letting her hand run absently over the mailbox perched on the old-fashioned white post. Then she opened the low gate and, latching it carefully behind her, started up the path.

She knew that David would not be home; she could feel his absence with a certainty she had come to accept without questioning. But even if he were present, he probably would not recognize her on a quick glance: she knew too clearly the changes nearly twenty years had made in her. She was no longer the sensuous, eager, passionate young woman with the desperate need for love he had once loved (and hated) so much; there were only the faintest reminders of that fullsome young black woman who had once boasted she was going to become the greatest blues singer since Billie Holliday and Bessie Smith.

The gardener glanced at her, then returned

his attention to the rose bushes; but she could feel his eyes still on her.

She rang the bell. She heard running inside; someone called, "I'll get it!" The front door was jerked open, and she found herself face to face with David's daughter. The newspaper picture, she realized, didn't do the girl justice. She was pretty—had the eyes been a little greener, the mouth shaped differently, she would qualify as a raving beauty. Her name, Suzanne knew, was Amy.

"Yes?" the girl demanded impatiently, almost petulantly. Clearly she had been expecting someone.

"Hello, I'm a friend of Christine Lee's. Mr. Palmer's assistant? She suggested I call on Mr. Palmer's family."

The girl softened slightly, but she made no move to open the front door further to invite her in.

Glancing past the girl's head, Suzanne could see a hallway covered with thick, cream-colored carpet. An antique grandfather's clock stood against the opposite wall beside a small beveled mirror in an antique gold frame. She caught a faint, lemony smell of furniture polish and the fragrance of Amy's perfume. She couldn't recall the name of the scent but she knew it was expensive.

"I am Amy Palmer. What, exactly, did you want to see us about, Mrs. . . ."

"Andrews. Elenora Andrews. And it's 'Miss,' not 'Mrs.'—or 'Miz,' if you prefer." She laughed softly.

"What do you want, Miss Andrews?" Amy asked, clearly not amused.

"Well, Miss Lee—Christine—indicated I should speak to you. About my group?"

Amy sighed. "If Christine sent you, well, I can give you a few moments. Let's go into the living room."

She led them along the hall into a vast, sunken living room. Then she invited the other woman to sit beside her on a pea-green brocade couch—the material only a shade more intense than the color of the girl's eyes. Amy sat uneasily on the edge of the couch, rubbing her hands together, hoping that her visitor would get right to the point.

Suzanne let her eyes roam around for a moment. She noted the porcelain figurines on the end tables, the original oils on the walls, the heavy, immaculate curtains. Sunlight slanted in through drawn blinds, making a warm patch near her foot; unobtrusively, she slid her foot into it, savoring the warmth.

A good-looking boy about sixteen entered the room, saying, "Amy, I'm going over to see Frank."

The boy. David's other son. The one named Kirk. Suzanne caught her breath. His hair was much darker than the photograph indicated; he was a disquieting echo of his father. But the boy's good looks were innocent of the egotism and sensuality that had already begun to corrupt his father's features when Suzanne had known him.

He looked at Suzanne. His eyes were, like his sister's, aquamarine—not the wonderful blue of his father's. Kirk shot Amy a questioning look, which she answered with just a faint shake of the head and momentary tightening of the lips. Then he was gone.

Amy returned her attention to her caller. "Now, Miss Andrews—"

Suzanne snapped open her purse and pulled out the orange-and-white pamphlet she had been handed by two black women that morning while she had been waiting for the bus in Oakland.

She said, "Miss Palmer, Jesus has moved me to appeal to you to support the work of the New Bethel Church of Christ Imminent. Miss Palmer, are you aware of the work we are doing and the work we need to do to alert the world to the coming of the Savior?"

Amy Palmer's expressive face flashed resentment at being subjected to another in what was manifestly an endless line of such appeals.

Ten minutes later, Suzanne was let out with a chilly "good day" and a twenty-five-dollar check made out to the New Bethel Church of Christ Imminent.

As she walked back down into town to catch the #83 bus to take her back to San Francisco and her connection back to Oakland, she crumpled the check into a ball and tossed it down a storm drain.

During the return ride, she thought of David's children, fixing their living selves in her mind, focusing on Amy's condescension and careless beauty, Kirk's resentful green eyes.

But she was mostly thinking of their absent father, who had once been her lover.

She and David had met during her third year in New York. At the time she was working in the secretarial pool of a large brokerage house making use of the skills she had had the foresight to learn during high school. She had finally begun getting some regular singing jobs at some of the smaller Harlem clubs, but the breakthrough had been her steady work at La Chambre, a small after hours club on West 125th Street.

Since the trouble with Elenora, her family had become as remote as the West Coast. She kept up a fitful correspondence with her mother, always feeling that the latter was maintaining contact out of a sense of duty—not through any deep-set affection. Every one of her mother's letters contained an implicit charge that Suzanne's conduct in what her mother persisted in referring to as "that Benny business" had hurt them all so deeply that she must assume responsibility for all misfortunes the family went through: her mother's depression, her continued layoffs, her growing conviction that the family was "under a curse."

The only one she ever wanted to hear from— Nana Chicory, her father's mother—never wrote to her, never asked that some words be enclosed in Thelma's complaining letters to her daughter. Charlotte seemed to have forgotten her entirely, once she moved away. And that was the hardest thing to bear, because, all the time she had been growing up, young Suzanne had loved her grandmother best, had made a constant show of her love for the old woman.

Suzanne had dutifully read each of her mother's complaining, accusing letters once, and had faithfully consigned each to a wastebasket after that single read. Suzanne had ignored her mother's ramblings, often indecipherable fault-finding about Elenora's becoming a "tramp" and "forgetting her mother as bad as you," her mother-in-law's "craziness and becoming a burden to me," her husband getting himself killed at a construction site leaving her to bring up her family alone. And there was endless pleading for Suzanne to come home, to send money, to send her a ticket to New York.

More than anything else, Thelma Raine's last letters had traced out, in erratic scrawls and feverish word-pictures, her certainty, no longer a mere suspicion, that her family—the women of three generations—had become tangled up in a web of supernatural machinations that seemed to Suzanne, at the time, compounded of equal parts *vodu*, paranoia, and an inability to sort out dreams from reality.

Her last letter, dated the afternoon of the day she died, read:

> Nana don't want to tell
> Elenora don't want to see
> I'm afraid because I *know*—
> Susie, you be a good girl
> Don't ever come home

There's nothing but bad things waiting for you here.
>Your Mama, who loves you very much

Later that night, while her daughter was out with the man she was to marry, and her aged mother-in-law slept in the small bedroom that had once been a sun porch, Thelma Raine killed herself by downing several bottles of aspirin and locking herself in her room.

Elenora had called Suzanne the day after the incident, reporting the facts tersely, clearly keeping her own emotions tightly in check. She had made it clear that there was little need—and less desire—for Suzanne to fly out from New York. It was to be a brief funeral, embellished only with a few words from Reverend Hosea Cartland (son of old Reverend Amos Cartland, who had argued so long and uselessly with Nana Chicory years before when the old woman had first moved into her son's house from her home in New Orleans), and a quick interment. Not even those friends of the family and Elenora's fellow church-members who had requested permission to attend were invited. Elenora told her sister this in two brief phone calls.

Suzanne had pleaded her poor financial status as reason for not attending the memorial service. Elenora had made it clear that she neither believed her sister nor much cared.

Suzanne had wired flowers, and wished her mother peace in wherever the dead went to:

Christian heaven or the place Nana Chicory talked about, where the dead kept their earthly personalities in a land ruled over by tribal gods. She wrote a final note to Elenora, that went unanswered, and returned her energies to her daily routine and, most especially, to her singing.

Then, surprisingly, two weeks after she mailed her final note to Elenora, with an enclosed greeting to Nana Chicory, a note arrived from the old woman. Charlotte had written it herself: Suzanne immediately recognized the labored, childish block letters, in thick green ink. Startled, Suzanne had hesitated a long time before opening the letter to discover what, after all this time, Charlotte wanted to communicate.

The message was short—more disturbing in what it did not say but rather suggested than in the actual words (which were upsetting enough in themselves):

> Your mothers blood was first hers dont be last this family be marked with blood power and curse and you be at the heart of it soon your Nana do what she can but you be the one with maybe one other Im not sure yet and maybe wont be but Nana be there for you then when you be what you got to be just the same she was there when you growing up and so you wait but dont be afraid because what happens is just beginning and it got a long way to go but I be there with you at the end of what you just see beginning.

It was signed with the little drawing of the chicory but the old woman had always used to sign anything, drawing or rare letter, since Suzanne had first come to know her.

She had scrawled a hasty note to her grandmother asking for clarification of the confusing, obscurely threatening jumble of words.

Suzanne received no answer. She wrote a second, longer letter. This also went unanswered.

In the end she convinced herself that Nana was going senile (Elenora had broadly hinted at this during her final phone call, referring to her repeatedly as "poor old thing"). Suzanne had thrown out the troublesome note and soon was caught up fully in the criss-cross rhythms of her daytime and nighttime careers.

Though primarily a person who kept to herself, Suzanne had become friendly with Reed Hendryx and Nora, his woman. Reed played piano at La Chambre, both as backup to vocalists like herself and as, in Suzanne's opinion, a first-rate jazz stylist himself. Nora was a self-styled "sometime singer" who once in a while filled in at the club, or joined Reed for a number or two during his solo performances. But Nora took little—and her music, least of all—seriously. It was a pastime with her, something to do now and then. For the most part she was content to live on the money and drugs Reed brought home—and to let the world slide by as smoothly as Reed's seemingly effortless reworking of an old Duke Ellington number.

They had helped her get her first apartment on 127th Street, in the same building they were living in. They had the apartment immediately below hers. At first she had been stand-offish because of her natural shyness, her fear of getting caught up in the casual use of dope, and, most forcefully, because Reed and Nora reminded her uncomfortably of the whole unpleasant business of Elenora, Benny (who had also been a musician), and herself. But there was something in her, and something in them, that made them natural candidates for friendship. And, in time, she let her friendship with Reed and Nora happen.

It was through Reed and Nora that she first met David Palmer. It was near Christmastime nearly twenty years before. Her friends had persuaded her to attend a "Karamu" feast climaxing the week-long Kwanza festival in Harlem recalling the traditional African celebration marking the time when the first crops are ready to be harvested.

This particular event was held in the basement of the Afro-American Church of the Word Incarnate near the Harlem Performance Center. Reed had managed to coerce Suzanne into singing some of his songs adapting the blues poems of the poet Henry Dumas, whom he had just discovered.

She still remembered the huge, mostly unadorned church basement, filled with laughing, shouting, jostling people—the long, sagging, folding tables covered with bright paper tableclothes and laden with chitterlings, ham hocks, pork chops, spare ribs, cornbread, grits, fried chicken, fried porgie, collard greens, black-eyed peas, candied yams, bread pudding, peach cobbler, sweet potato pie—more prepared food than Suzanne had ever seen in one place. She had eaten herself silly, drunk red and white wine until she grew giddy, and wondered how she would ever get through the numbers she had promised to perform later in the evening.

David Palmer was one of the special invited guests. Reed pointed him out as one of the up-and-coming young politicos come to speak on behalf of Howard Wexler—who was seeking part of the Harlem vote. Suzanne had noticed the tall, well-built, handsome white man with the ice-blue eyes from the first. She had been unable to get up enough nerve to speak to him until they both reached for the same napkin-wrapped knife and fork at dinner. Their eyes shared information lightning fast even while they murmured needless apologies and politely laughed at each other.

"Are you alone?" he asked, touching her hand deliberately this time.

"With friends," she answered, trying to sound casual but not trusting her alcohol-fuzzed voice to carry it off. She made a show of looking for Reed and Nora, but the only clue to their whereabouts was a flash of deep red from a knot of people across the room that *might* have been Reed's *dashiki*. "I seem to have lost 'em," she confessed after a moment.

"Well, I've managed to shake my group. I'm

tired of talking politics—which is also spelled 'back scratching.' "

"I've got to sit down a minute—whoohee! that wine is really setting my head spinning. You, uh, want to sit with me? If we can find someplace to light," she added doubtfully, glancing around the crowded auditorium. People seemed to be sitting everywhere, on the stage in front of the dusty-looking green velour curtains, on the steps leading up to it, on scattered folding chairs, some even perched fitfully on the corners of the already dangerously overloaded serving tables.

But he had taken her elbow and steered her directly to a far corner, where two elderly women had just gotten up to begin the long trek to the powder room on the other side of the hall. There they balanced the paper plates of "Karamu" foods on their knees and ate greedily, while David told her of his work with Wexler and she told him a little about her job as secretary and a lot about her ambitions as a singer. She felt foolish, conspicuous, flattered, uneasy to be sitting beside one of the very few white men in the room, to feel the amusement and resentment that came in alternating currents from the watchful eyes of the people who passed near them. Some of the resentment she felt directed at her white companion, some at her for blatant "collaboration." Some seemed to come from men who were jealous of the good-looking ofay's seemingly easy attraction for a black woman; more seemed to flow from women who resented her making a contact they had hoped to make. All of it rose and fell, came and went, on rolling waves of loud talk, louder laughter, and the restless background noise of a large crowd.

Sometimes she was able to talk in a normal voice, more often she had to shout to make sure she was heard. He never seemed to have to raise his voice to make himself heard. When he went to fetch more wine for himself, she refused his offer of more for her. She was already unsure of how she was going to perform: but now it mattered—something she read in his eyes *made* it matter—that she give a first-rate performance.

He returned and they talked freely, like old friends, like new lovers, until someone Suzanne vaguely recognized as a rising black politician who was also connected with the highly influential Afro-American Church of the Word Incarnate, which was hosting this feast, came up, tapped David on the shoulder, whispered to him a moment.

"Sorry, duty calls. My speech?" He shrugged; then, pushing his empty paper plate and wine tumbler under his folding chair, he took her hand, squeezed it, and said, "Meet me afterwards. Will you?"

And she had nodded. Had he really had any doubts she wanted the chance to be alone with him? Or was he just playing up to the romantic notions she had confided in him—like never wanting things in a relationship to be taken for granted? It didn't matter, she realized: she wanted him, was fantasizing him in bed with her, his body pressing deliciously down on her as she opened hungrily to him . . .

She listened to his whole speech—an appeal for political support from the Harlem wards—but understood little through her desire-and-alcohol-fueled haze except her determination to have him tonight, as soon as it could be decently arranged.

When the long-winded "speechifying" was done, and David had been swallowed alive by a gaggle of Harlem influentials, all eager to find out the particulars of what Wexler was *really* offering them, a handsome, middle-aged woman took over the microphone and said, "All right! We've *had* the commercials, now let's get down to having some *entertainment!*"

Ragged applause and shouts filled the smoky, restless auditorium.

The speaker made calming gestures with her hand and, when the roar had died away to an acceptable hum, she said, "The first on our *very special* program is Suzanne Raine. Some of you may have heard her sing at La Chambre and a few other places, and you *know* what a treat it's gonna be. The rest of you just sit back, finish up that *good food*, and let yourselves in for some fine singing. Suzanne?" Here the woman held her hand out to Suzanne, motioning her onstage. Amid a smattering of applause and a few shouted oh-yeah's, she made her way into the smoky spotlight in front of the dusty curtain. The woman leaned back to the microphone and added, "I almost forgot: Suzanne's gonna be accompanied by Mr. Reed Hendryx on the piano. Then she withdrew to the right side of the stage, applauding for Reed and Suzanne.

When Reed had taken his place at the little piano downstage, he made a few experimental runs on the keys, then hesitated, watching Suzanne. She took a deep breath, let her vision expand for a moment over the sea of expectant brown-black faces, then gathered her awareness into the protective blue-white-hazy bubble of spotlight and began to sing the first of the songs she and the pianist had decided on weeks before, Reed's musical setting of Dumas's poem *Keep the Faith Blues*. As she sang the opening lines, she made the lyrics carry an emotional meaning beyond what they already powerfully expressed:

> They say if you ain't go no faith
>   you keep the blues all the time
> If you ain't go no faith, you keep the
>   blues most all the time
> Must be the reason I'm almost 'bout to lose
>   my mind.

She lost herself momentarily in the song, then reemerged into blue-white awareness playing off of Reed's easy accompaniment. She let her eyes stray down to the front row of standing men and several older women sitting on folding chairs that had been dragged forward for them. Dead center, she spotted David, his arms folded, his head nodding in time to Reed's playing, his glittering eyes like blue ice chips focused tightly on her. She felt a sudden desirous *hollowness* in the whole of her—a need to be filled by him. And from her own wanting, she built a powerful new emotional framework to stretch the limits of her voice, of the lyrics, so that even Reed momentarily swiveled his head from his syncopated bobbing over his keys to stare at her in appreciative surprise—though he continued matching her notes, improvising as brilliantly from his own talent as she was from her own heady mixture of emotional charges. The entire audience was caught up in the experience as she sang,

> Yes the world gone crazy, they can talk
>   about God is dead
> Yes the world is gone crazy, some say
>   worship the Devil instead
>
> Well, I'm keeping my own faith, people
> Can't let religion
>   bust open my head

The applause was testimony to the power of her song. While she floated on the wave-after-wave of it buoying her up, her joy was mixed with a regretful certainty that she would never achieve the same mixture of lyric, music, emotion again. But, looking down at David, who seemed to be personally leading the applause, she felt it didn't matter: they were fused in the moment of music, elation, shared desire.

She suddenly crossed to Reed, abandoned in hasty whispers their planned performance of *Harlem Mosaic*, and demanded that he accompany her with the unscheduled *Play Ebony Play Ivory*. He started to protest, then gave it up when he saw that she was determined to have her way. So he began to play the crescendoing notes of the song, while she sang to David and each member of the intoxicated audience believed she was singing personally to her or him.

>   play my people
>   all my people who breathe
>   the breath of earth
>   all my people who are keys and chords . . .
>
>   now touch
>   and hear and see
>   let your lungs scream
>   til they explode
>   till blood subsides
>   and flesh vibrates . . .
>
>   make chords that speak
>   play long play soft
>   play ebony play ivory
>   play ebony
>   play ivory

White man, black woman, they moved together like the interwining themes of Reed's music—Suzanne's bed their stage and their bodies the instrument. They had left the auditorium after the last applause for Suzanne had faded; they lingered only long enough for her to whisper an explanation to Nora, then hurried out into the chilly, hungry dark to find a cab.

Their urgency more than anything else decided them on Suzanne's apartment. Like eager children they had tumbled themselves across her purple-and-green bedspread and laid claim to each other's body.

She was amazed, dismayed, ecstatic over her sudden involvement. Thankfully, it happened so fast that all her inner voices were too slow to stop her eager capitulation. But then, she realized, she never had a chance at all.

David touched every emotion and played on every longing she had ever acknowledged and seemed to open new recesses of her being that had been (up to this moment) hidden from her. He had insinuated himself into her very being; she had felt her life rearranging itself at that minute; for the first time she gave someone else the central role. And she found that things she had resisted so long she took to herself with damn-the-consequences eagerness.

He had awakened her to sex beyond the fumblings of high schoolers, beyond the casual embraces of the men who sometimes hung around La Chambre and made her fool herself for a few minutes into believing she had found something that mattered; he uncovered the passionate woman in her she had up to now rejected as foolish and dangerous. Amused and delighted to find her such an eager pupil, he had playfully, skillfully, indefatigably aroused her to the pleasures of her body and the hungers that only a male body—his body—could satisfy in her.

The feel of his tongue probing her mouth, his hands gently kneading her breasts, the helpless/delicious physical longing to open herself wide and pull the whole of him deeply/deeper into her—these facts conspired to silence, for a time, the outraged voices within her—mother, sister, grandmother—and banish them, lock them away, in the recesses of her mind. She was never fully at peace with herself even in their most satisfying moments together, but she was closer to happiness than she had ever been in her life and that was enough. As long as she and David were in the first throes of passion, the precarious truce held.

And—as something all along, something in her deeper even than her dreams had warned—her lover proved too human, too changeable early on; there were subtle, unmistakable alterations in their relationship as swiftly time wore on.

And those disturbing inner voices were never truly silent. When the passion subsided a bit, when she could catch her breath and see this man as a man and not as a thousand delicious assaults on her senses, then she became painfully aware of the locked-away voiced growing louder and more persistent.

The doubts would trouble her most at night, when David was asleep beside her and she was alone in her head with only the sound of his breathing, the ticking of the bedside clock, and the on/off flicker of the all-night neon sign across the street playing on the drawn window shade. Then she heard the interior warnings. *He only wants a white man's pleasure in your black woman's body—never you; you're only a side attraction; there's nothin' permanent gonna come of this. You're a fool of a daughter, sister, granchile.*

And then she missed her period, the blood did not flow; and—half denying, half praying—she felt the child beginning to grow in her, like the fulfillment of a wish someone has been too eager for to risk speaking even in her heart.

David's gradual emotional defection seemed less important to her with each passing day. As the baby grew beneath her heart she was able mentally to let her lover drift into a more supporting role in her life. She could not let him go entirely; she still felt a real—though lessened—hunger for sex with him and, for a time, she and the baby would need him in very practical ways. He owed them well-being: he had, in having his male way, brought them both truly into being. There would come a time, she decided, when she would reward him for his double-begetting and the attentions she would continue to demand by letting him go easily when she and the child could manage alone. Because, all unexpectedly and undeniably, the child laid hold of the heart of her life.

When he at first suggested—then insisted upon—an abortion, she had resisted at first with rational arguments, then anger, and finally the feral protectiveness of a lioness whose cub is threatened. In the end, unable to face off her uncompromising determination to have the baby, he backed off, threatened to leave her, but continued to come back to her stifling apartment with the doggedness of a man who refuses to leave until it is on his own terms.

She could almost taste the violence he kept contained, but poorly concealed, in himself. He wanted her, he wanted nothing to do with her child-to-be. She sensed he regarded the baby as a rival for her love and a threat to his career. A child—his child—gave Suzanne a hold over the man that neither one of them could deny.

Until that time, she had her own duty to the child to keep him satisfied enough so that he would stay around. And there was still enough sexual energy between them for her to please him, pleasure him, bring his mind around to every other issue but the impending birth.

But when David's sometimes-impassioned gropings became too rough, when she was far enough into her pregnancy to be aware of what his insistence might do to the child inside, then she refused him. But she hid the sudden distaste that had begun growing in her in her fifth month, a feeling that made her loathe his embraces with almost the same power that she had once felt drawing her to him.

Now she read too often in David's eyes a kind of panic. While she sensed in the growing child her own movement toward total freedom, he was reacting like a man feeling the fatal pull of an undertow dragging him down and down to drown.

She bore his rages for the sake of the child; she was relieved to learn that he was finding plenty of satisfaction with other women. She left herself suspended in a warm calm, a feeling of completeness, which she imagined must be like the child inside her dreaming its way toward birth, protected and nourished by her own flesh and blood.

By the sixth month she had given up even occasional appearances at La Chambre; she kept on at her secretarial job a little longer, and then got David to give her the money necessary to supplement her meager savings. After that, she stayed most of the time in her apartment, or took long walks in the warming spring weather, feeling unafraid—protected even—as if she were surrounded by watchful spirits. She walked and dreamed and planned for the baby, what the child would be and do. Though his father was white, she wanted him steeped in his own black beingness. From his father, she decided, he would take a hard-edged savyy, a knowledge of how to organize people around his ideas, an ambition that would reflect (and ultimately surpass) his father's own still-forming ambition. But *she* would provide him a full sense of who he was and what he must do to become what he would become.

His final identity she could only grasp in outline: a mixture of Frederick Douglass, George Washington Carver, Nat Turner—with a balancing mix of Langston Hughes, Richard Wright, Eubie Blake, Henry Dumas. He would be hard and gentle, pragmatic and compassionate; he would be the compendium of all his black (and, to a lesser degree, white) ancestors;

and he would be totally his own person.

Her son.

So she walked, tirelessly—her unseen guardians keeping her from harm in the often dangerous streets. She lingered for a time under the marquee of the Apollo Theatre, which had showcased the early careers of Bessie Smith, Ella Fitzgerald, Louis Armstrong, and Cab Calloway . . . returned frequently to study the compelling WPA murals executed by Aaron Douglass inside the Countee Cullen Branch of the New York Public Library . . . lingered by the massive Italian marble baptismal font of the stained-glass and peach-colored interior of the Abyssinian Baptist Church . . . wandered past the high-rise apartment buildings of Sugar Hill and the neatly trimmed hedges and highly polished brass door knockers of Striver's Row . . . treated herself to a chocolate malted under the tin ceilings and still functional ceiling fans at Thomforde's Confectionery.

Each day was a voyage of exploration and discovery; each day had a different complexion because she was one day nearer to holding her son in her arms.

Yet, when the baby began to arrive, one week ahead of schedule (she had no doubt that he was responding to her eagerness for them to meet face-to-face) it was Nora who helped her pack an overnight case, while Reed phoned for a taxi. She had not seen David for two days.

They arrived at the hospital in the nick of time; the baby arrived with only a minimum of pain. Still doped-up, she hungrily held the tiny Nathan Frederick (she had decided on the name months before) yelling, squirming, freshly swabbed, skin the color of rich cafe au lait, and perfect in every detail; and she remembered her grandmother once saying, while Suzanne was still a little girl herself, "If you have a boychile —as I b'lieve you will—love the happiness you find early on, because there's gonna be a grief to follow."

But there was no way she could envision, or would allow, any worry to cloud her joy. She "loved her happiness" and dismissed any thoughts of sorrow.

When she brought the baby back to the apartment, she was bursting with confidence that she could build around this Nathan the life she had begun mentally outlining during her walks before his birth. The child was proof against the disquieting voices inside her head, of which the most persistent was that of Nana Chicory, intruding upon her dreams, rasping at her that she was a fool, that the time of change and suffering was coming, that there would soon be a complexity of duties for her to perform. And behind the old woman was sheeted blood: blood that flowed in curtains, thin as gauze, copious as a Niagara Falls.

Then Suzanne had always managed to escape the old woman by screaming herself awake in the tangle of her sweat-soaked sheets.

In the end, however, Nina Chicory's voice, heard half in dream, half in memory, had been right. *There's gonna be a grief to follow.*

The child had entered her life with surprisingly little pain. Nathan's death—violent and soul-shattering—had left her with pain enough to span a thousand meaningless lifetimes.

TEN

IN HER own apartment, Christine awoke from two abortive attempts to sleep. Both times she had dozed off, then soon began dreaming. The first time she had been walking down a forest trail beneath avenues of trees whose massive branches interlocked overhead, shutting out sun or moon; the second time, she had been walking down a street she vaguely recognized as a street she had driven by when visiting friends in Oakland several weeks before. The dream forest had been silent, brooding; the dream street silent also, the windows of the houses boarded up, the doors shut firmly against her.

In both dreams she had become aware of someone following her; her dream self grew terribly afraid of the footfall rattling pebbles, breaking a twig—or making a hollow sound that echoed on the blank facades hemming her in.

Unwilling at first to look back, she had begun running, feeling nightmarish resistance that kept her from making any real forward progress, that forced her finally to turn and confront her pursuer.

Each time, it was only an old woman Christine discovered, limping with arthritic slowness toward her. The woman wore a black skirt and blouse that hung limply on her body as if there were little more than skeleton underneath; the shoes on her feet seemed loose as though several sizes too large. Wisps of white hair escaped from under a green and purple kerchief wrapped around her head. She leaned heavily on a knobby cane of ebony that clicked on the ground in time with the sound of her footsteps.

She seemed harmless enough, yet Christine dreaming found her a terrible threat. She watched in terror—now rooted to the spot, incapable of any movement to escape—as the old woman hobbled very close, finally pausing only a few steps away. When the crone spoke, her voice was like the sound of dead leaves stirred by a wind. "Who are you?" she asked Christine.

"Christine," she replied, her own voice barely a whisper.

"Who *are* you?" the old woman demanded, stamping the end of her cane impatiently on the ground.

"Myself. I am myself," Christine said, recognizing (in her dream) that this was the wrong answer, but unable to supply any other.

"Girl, I'm askin' *now*. Who are you?"

"I don't know," Christine answered, meaning, *I don't know what you want from me.* But the old woman took another meaning, and answered, "I'll tell you who you are. You are your mothers and grandmothers, you are your sisters and your daughters and ancestors. You are the first Queen Naii and you are the last barren girl child. You are *Os Pretos Velhos* remembered and made to live again through the power of Shango."

"I don't understand," Christine protested.

"Then see, then see, then see," the old woman said, striking her cane more loudly on the ground with each word. And each dream changed suddenly: the forest glade had become filled with a mass of black men, women, and children being hauled out of nearby huts at rifle point by other black men in sweat-stained, haphazard army fatigues.

A man appeared, dressed as a commander. She heard the horrified cries of "Obitsebi! Obitsebi!" from the circle of people.

They were forced into a circle by commands in an unfamiliar language, snapped out by a short black man, broadchested, barrel-bellied, with gold epaulettes and a row of tarnished stars across his military cap. The glade was filled with the shrieks and cries and pleas of terrified men, women, and children, who milled around like cattle. All this Christine witnessed as a disembodied observer.

At a command from the leader submachine guns suddenly appeared at ready in the hands of a dozen soldiers. A second shouted order started them spraying the writhing circle of screaming people, who tried to escape not outward into the deadly crossfire, but into the circle, tightening the knot struggling toward the center, crawling over each other, slipping in blood, the dying crawling over the dead, the wounded crying for help or mercy until there was only the sound of machine gun bursts, ripping open the bodies that still twitched. There was blood everywhere, the smell of it—cloying, acrid, metallic, sweet—everywhere—

Christine woke up screaming.

In the second dream the house facades melted, ran together, then flowed upward, forming an arch. With the inexplicable logic of dreams she found herself part of huddled crowds of blacks in the near pitch darkness of a ship's hold. She could feel the side-to-side motion of the vessel, could hear the slap of waves against the wooden hull even over the sobbing and whispering and moaning of the thickly massed people chained together, the ends of the chains secured with massive locks to immense iron rings embedded in the wooden walls. A child cried, someone whimpered, she could hear what was clearly a muttered prayer in an alien language. Christine, both a part of, and not a part of, the densely packed humanity, felt the stifling air, the raw fear, the despair that was the worst of all—so tangible she could taste the poison of it: a mixture of bile, sweat, salt water, *blood*. The yawning space, as crowded as it was, gave her sudden terrifying claustrophobia. She felt the need to get out, get away, blot the scene from her memory.

And then she saw, standing a little ways away, the old woman. Her left hand rested lightly, as in benediction, on the head of a young mother suckling a tiny girl-child at her breast and crooning a strange lullaby to the infant. The aged black woman leaned heavily on her cane with her right hand; more of her white hair had escaped the kerchief. It seemed to glow white hot, framing her wrinkled face with the halo of white fire. The young mother seemed unaware of the old woman's touch; she gave all of her attention to her baby.

"Help me get out of here," Christine called to her.

The old woman stared across at her, fixing her eyes on Christine, but saying nothing.

"Please," Christine pleaded, "I *have* to get out of here."

This time the woman nodded, but still she said nothing.

"Please—who are these people?"

"*Os Prestos Velhos,*" responded the other, pronouncing each word carefully, as though to assure Christine would remember. "*Os Pretos Velhos,*" she said again.

"*Os Pretos Velhos,*" Christine repeated carefully, as if it were the magic formula to release her from her nightmare.

Then the old woman began to fade, melting into the fetid air of this nightmare hold; and Christine was suddenly terrified that she would be forever trapped in this airless, sunless, stinking prison. She began to scream, as though it would summon the old woman back, as though it would give her release, "*Os Pretos Velhos! Os—*"

"*—Pretos Velhos,*" she was in the middle of shouting when the sound of her own voice awoke her from the second nightmare and returned her to the familiar—though still fear-charged—air of her own apartment bedroom.

She fumbled on the bedside lamp and sat up, shivering, though the room seemed warm almost to the point of stuffiness. Pulling on her robe, she walked out into the living room, putting on the overhead light, glancing nervously into the darkened kitchen as though she expected the old woman to materialize there, following Christine out of her dreams.

When her trembling subsided, she became acutely aware of just how close the apartment had become. Sliding the glass door open as far as it would go, she stepped out onto the balcony, lit by an unexpectedly bright moon in an almost tropically warm night.

She replayed those parts of her dreams that she could remember over and over in her mind while she leaned on the concrete coping looking out over a city that (to judge from the number of lights on so late at night) was resting uneasily (dreaming stranger things than she had? Christine wondered) under the hothouse night.

The phone ringing startled her out of her reverie; she quickly crossed to answer it, noting that it was after two—wondering who could be calling her now.

She picked up the phone, saying rapidly, "Hello? Hello?"

No answer—the silence on the other end of the line was absolute—she could not even detect the ghost of breathing. After a moment, there was a faint click—then the buzz of a disconnected line.

She was halfway back to the balcony, when the phone rang again. Wearily, she picked it up, listening carefully after a curt greeting that went unanswered. This time, far down the wire, she heard something that may have been static—or might have been the faintest of faint whispers.

It went dead again.

This time she remained perched on the arm of the black naugahyde chair beside the phone. After a few minutes, the phone rang a third time. This time she picked it up carefully, saying nothing. Out of the silence on the other end of the line floated a staccato string of whispered words, "You. Are. They. Are." Then the voice seemed to die away, so that she was not afterward certain that she really heard the final three words—"*Os. Pretos. Velhos.*" Then the line was finally, irrevocably, silent, leaving Christine only the echo in her mind of a whispered voice that sounded like dried leaves whirled in a rising wind.

The next day Christine found the words *Os Pretos Velhos* playing over and over in her mind like the tag end of a too-popular song or a bit of nursery rhyme. She did not believe anything more extraordinary was happening than that she was remembering some phrase she had heard sometime in the past, but it piqued her curiosity. Why had her subconscious latched onto the words in the first place? And why had it thrown them up to her in a dream at this particular moment?

So she worried it, saying it out loud, writing it out phonetically and staring at the variations she had scrawled across a yellow legal tablet. When all her efforts yielded up nothing, she attempted to forget it—only to find the words becoming a chant running *dum/dum/dum/dum/dum* faster and more persistently through her mind like a mental tape-loop that she guessed would only stop repeating itself when she found some sort of explanation.

She decided this obsession was a sign of the strain she was under, trying to piece together PalmerCo's international adventures, play mistress to the most important man in the corporation, and still hang onto some shreds of belief in what she was doing—and (even more tenuous) some integrity, some conviction that she was more than the "company" (even when the "company" was really the government) whore.

No wonder she felt she might be cracking, Christine thought bitterly to herself as she went through the motions of boiling down a sheaf of reports from a South American mining operation into a precis for David—no wonder I'm losing it. I'm all things to all people, and

I'm beginning to feel like I'm all over the map, even more than PalmerCo.

Enough! she warned herself. Promise yourself a long rest when this assignment is over, and hang on there, girl!

Sitting at her desk, she closed her eyes and ground the heels of her palms into her eyes, finding relief in the pressure. For a moment her mind was as darkly blank as a moonless, tideless ocean, then—

Os Pretos Velhos began threading its way through her consciousness, filling the momentary void behind her shut eyes.

With a sigh, she began flipping through the rollodex on her desk, until she found the card for the general information number of the San Francisco Public Library.

As always, the person who answered was helpful, though she was not able to shed any light herself. She put Christine on hold while she (presumably) picked her co-workers' brains for clues.

After a short wait, the young woman returned and said, "One of the assistants here is a real bug on the occult—he's found a book that mentions it several times. It has something to do with spiritualism in South America. The book can't be checked out—it's a reserve book—but I can put it on hold for you."

Christine had the book put aside. Thanking the woman, she rang off, then looked at her watch. Nothing she was involved with had any pressing deadline. She phoned down to the switchboard, informing them she would be gone on an extended lunch; then she telephoned a cab, gathered up her sweater and purse, and left.

The taxi left her off at the main entrance to the San Francisco Library at Civic Center. Listening to the rapid clatter of her shoes on the steps, Christine realized that something deep in her—something she was not conscious of—was urging her to solve the riddle of the strange dream-words.

Inside, it took her only a few moments to locate the proper reserve desk, to discover that the woman who had helped her over the phone was at lunch, but that the book—with scraps of paper in it marking key references—was waiting for her. A young black man handed her an oversize volume, rebound in blue-green standard library binding, and directed her to the reading room.

Seated at the long wooden table, she opened to the title page and read:

Three Hundred Years of
Indigienous Afro-American Sects,
Cults, and Religions
1650-1950
Thaddeus L. Merryweather, Ph.D., Th.D.,
L.L.D., D.D.

Guided by the thoughtfully placed bookmarks, Christine found the core of material she sought and began to read rapidly:

The Shango-Naii Cult

This curious blend of West African religion, Caribbean *vudu (voodoo)*, and Brazilian spirit religions thrived in the American South from the early eighteenth century until its abrupt and violent extinction in 1938. Yet another variant of the *obi (obeah)* and *vudu (voodoo)* schools of sorcery infused with *orisha (spirit)* worship from Africa and *macumba* sorcery from Brazil, the cult is symbolized by the wedding of the god Shango, the familiar West African divinity of storms, with Queen Naii, the legendary ruler of the territory now known as Bukawai Free State.

Apparently the cult originated in the large concentration of black African slaves from the Bukawai region who found themselves translated to Louisiana plantations—especially in the parishes immediately surrounding New Orleans.

The central belief of its adherents was the conviction that in their midst was a descendant of Queen Naii (always a female) who embodied certain powers granted by the thundergod to the first Queen Naii for establishing his cult as dominant among her people's pantheon of gods.

The exact identity of this woman, who was *mambo (priestess)* of the religion, was always kept a secret. Rumors were circulated that assured that any cultist who revealed her identity to a white person or to anyone outside their ranks was subject to death at the hands of the *houngans (priests)*, who could conjure powerful magic against their enemies. The exact nature of such executions varied in the telling: black magic that wasted the victim at a distance, or a more direct method in which the victim was seized and bound, placed in a boat, and towed into a lake, river, or bayou, where a cut was made behind the left ear and a fast-acting poison rubbed into the wound. Then the victim, perhaps already dead, was cast overboard. There are even more fantastic stories that tell of *houngans* creating a *zombi* to carry the sinner into the swamps, where both would disappear forever. In any event, the threats of reprisals, added to several documented disappearances, served to keep the cult one of the most secret until long after Reconstruction.

Then, in 1890, a black woman named Catherine La Cour, who worked as a seamstress in New Orleans, announced that she was *mambo* of the Shango-Naii cult, true descendant of that first Queen Naii, and that her ancestress had come to her in a series of dreams telling her to reveal what was hidden and bring new honor and worshippers to Shango.

Her announcement touched off a wave of violent reactions: she was denouced in some quarters as a self-serving liar, a madwoman, or, most telling, as a traitor who was revealing what was never meant to be heard by more than a select few. On the other hand, she was eagerly proclaimed *mambo* by an even wider number of voices.

When the furor subsided, Catherine was indisputably high priestess of the cult, the spiritual—perhaps blood—descendant of Queen Naii and direct link to powerful African gods, foremost among them Shango.

The key to her personal power was the ability to contact the *orishas* by letting her body—and the bodies of the most influential *houngans* who served her—be entered by spirits called *Os Pretos Velhos, the Old Black Slaves*, spirits of the first slaves from Africa who were the direct line of communication with the old African divinities. It was said that the *orishas* themselves could not enter a mortal body without causing it to explode from the concentration of power. Catherine was also said to have the spirits of her own dead relatives and those of *criancas*, children who died before the age of five, at her command.

Though she had no formal schooling, Catherine was able to read and write with amazing facility. This she always credited to the instruction of *Os Pretos Velhos*, who guided her every step. She gave frequent courses during which she instructed the faithful on honoring the old gods and ways, respecting their own blackness, and resisting white attempts to keep them as economic and social inferiors—slaves in fact, if not in name. She would often meet with—or debate—noted white political or religious leaders. The reports that have survived indicate that Catherine—guided, as she always insisted, by the Old Black Slaves—consistently bested her opponents.

She became the most loved—and feared—woman in New Orleans since Marie Laveau, the so-called "Voodoo Queen of New Orleans." There are stories that Marie and Catherine met before the former's death in 1897—and an equal number of claims that they never met, maintaining discreet distance and silence in a kind of friendly rivalry.

A tremendous *homfort* (place of worship) was built, at Catherine's express instructions, across the Mississippi River from New Orleans in Jefferson Parish, where she would preach and conduct her services, though she insisted on living in New Orleans.

Her daughter, by an undisclosed father, Cecile La Cour, was born in 1904. She early on manifested the same sharp intelligence, charisma, and—if reports can be believed—*vudu* powers as her mother. She also inherited her mother's passionate twin loyalties in Africa and to the black descendants of Africa in this country.

When Catherine died in 1922, Cecile slipped comfortably, and without challenge, into the role of *mambo* of the Shango-Naii cult. She carried on her mother's work, preaching in the *homfort*, living in New Orleans, doing all that she could to challenge the white establishment and urge blacks to appropriate their rightful place in this country, while never forgetting the ancestral gods of Bukawai.

The problem that arose grew out of Cecile's direct challenge to growing Mafioso power in New Orleans which had, by the 1930s—as in all major American cities—established a major foothold in the city, through drugs, extortion, all the familiar tactics.

But when they tried to bring the black community "into line," they found a powerful opponent in Cecile, who, with all the power of her own skills and whatever "spirits" she could call down, denounced the crime bosses and urged her people—and even those blacks not directly affiliated with her cult—to stand firm and resist all attempts to let the Mafioso corrupt and destroy them in yet another manifestation of white insidiousness.

So strong was her resistance, and so unified was the black response to her summons, that even some whites began to rally to her campaign to run the criminals out of town. Among the black community it was rumored that she and her *houngans* planned a "big magic" against the mafioso that would drive them out with *vudu* power.

The Mafia bosses, however, exerted their own particular brand of power. One afternoon in March 1938, during a healing ceremony, while Cecile was summoning the spirits and power of the Old Black Slaves, six masked men appeared in the *homfort* and began blasting away with shotguns. Cecile was killed instantly when blasts severed her spine and sheared away half her head. Thirteen other people were also killed, including two children.

The public outcry was so great from both black and white communities that, the very day Cecile was buried, amid the hysterical tears of thousands, six Mafiosi "hit men" were apprehended, charged with the *homfort* murders, and placed under arrest in a Jefferson Parish prison pending trial.

That same night a crowd largely—but by no means exclusively—composed of Negroes stormed the prison. Reporters later described the sound of the crowd as "the roar of a thunderstorm growing closer and closer."

While the accused men huddled in their cells, and the police officers stood aside, helpless in the face of the crowd, a giant Negro, using a sledge hammer, shattered the wooden doors of the prison in a few blows. Later rumors said that this was a *zombi*, the body of a man who had died some days before and who had been resurrected and infused with superhuman powers by those of Cecile's *houngans* who had survived the *homfort* massacre.

Once inside, the machete-wielding rioters dragged the six accused men into the main room. There the blades flashed swiftly, mercilessly, crushing skulls and ripping away bowels. When the six lay in a blood-clotted heap on the floor, the rest of the people surged forward with a great cry and further chopped the bodies into pieces or tore them to shreds with their bare hands. It is said that nothing, beyond their blood on the floor, was left of the six accused murderers when a rescue force, hastily composed of police and state militia, reached the prison and drove off the mob with several volleys of rifle shots.

In the aftermath, because of the attack on the

police station and murders of six men accused —but never convicted—of the murder of Cecile La Cour, the Shango-Naii cult was discredited and, at the instigation of several public officials (most rumored to be in the pay of the Mafiosi), was finally outlawed.

There is an interesting footnote in this.

Though Cecile died childless, one month after the raid of the prison, several hundred people around the city reported having dreams in which Cecile La Cour appeared to them and told them that a girl child lived whom she had selected as her "spiritual daughter" and as "spiritual daughter of powerful Queen Naii"—a child who would absorb into herself the power of the Old Black Slaves, all the dead *mambos* (including, presumably, Catherine and Cecile), and who would at some unspecified time in the future manifest the power to Shango, and all the gods of ancient Bukawai, against "those white folk who had angered her so greviously."

To date, the truth or falseness of that particular dream-prediction (itself one of the most remarkable cases of "mass hysteria" on record —if nothing greater) remains to be discovered.

Closing the book thoughtfully, Christine glanced at her watch. It was after two. She had no idea how the time had rushed by. She had been caught up in the repellent and fascinating stories of Catherine and Cecile. Parts of what she had read had touched her mind and there set off deeper resonances, especially the business about the Mafioso confrontation and the notion of these black women standing so uncompromisingly in the face of white corruption. But, for all she had read, and though she now understood the meaning now of the words "Os

Pretos Velhos," she was no nearer remembering where she might have heard them before—or imagining why she recalled them *now*. What could stories of the ghosts of eighteenth-century slaves mean to her, in San Francisco, today?

None of it made any sense. Still, as she returned the book to the reserve desk, Christine could not rid herself of the gut-deep conviction that there was a message in all of it, if only she could be clever enough to decipher it. Elements of the narrative—especially the references to Bukawai—had leapt out at her; but her feelings of disquiet were more vague, as if she had been shown something of importance, but had not been able to make herself *understand*.

The same young black clerk was at the desk. As he accepted back the heavy book, he said, "If you're interested in African religions and that sort of thing, you might be interested in the exhibit of central African art—mostly from Bukawai—on the third floor of the library."

Startled by the coincidence, Christine nodded wordlessly while he gave her directions to the exhibit wing.

A discreet sign at the entrance to the exhibit room announced:

ANCIENT ART OF BUKAWAI—RARE
TREASURES FROM THE WEST AFRICAN NATION

There were only two or three people wandering about the large room, lined with display cases, wall hangings, and black-and-white photographic enlargements of Bukawai's people, land, handiwork. A solitary guard, a middle-aged black man with a neatly-cropped salt-and-pepper afro on which his cap sat somewhat uncertainly, smiled at her.

Almost immediately, Christine found several things to interest her.

The first was a series of copper plates, hammered into bas-relief and telling a story of a lengendary Queen of Bukawai. According to the information on a placard underneath the series of nine panels, the artisans had been imported from distant lands, because such metal-works was not indigenous to Bukawai. But the tale was so important that one ruling Queen wanted it preserved into immortality in the best way available to her.

Christine studied the plates several moments. She recognized the recurring figure of two younger women, perhaps twin sisters, and the stylized figure of an old woman. But, beyond this, the complex symbols of lightning, ram's heads, and others defeated her attempt at deciphering the panels.

She gave up and began to read the story typed on a card beside the panel sequence.

> Many, many years ago, that Queen Naii who was the fourth ruler of Bukawai to bear the name gave birth to twin girls who were very beautiful and well-formed. In her innermost chamber, that Naii looked with pride and horror at the children. For though the children seemed perfect in every way, the birth of twins

was considered a bad omen for the land—a thing unnatural and monstrous.

Now that Naii knew that when the birth was made known, she would be driven from her throne and country, because the arrival of twins—to any woman of any station—was thought to pollute the land and was sure to cause bad luck. The twins would be killed straightaway. Then the countryside would have to be purified. All half-burnt firewood, cooked food, and water in vessels would have to be thrown away. Only after three purifying rains would the tribal elders select another Queen to rule in the banished Queen's stead.

Fearing the loss of her throne, that Naii summoned her old nurse and midwife, Nana Alake, and told her to take one child (that Nana was to make the fatal decision), carry it into bush, slay the child, and bury the body. This the Nana did exactly as her Queen commanded. When she returned, the Queen wept for a time, then told the old woman to go out and proclaim the birth of a young daughter, who would one day succeed her on the throne and rule Bukawai. This Nana Alake did, and the Queen's secret remained hidden from the people and, in time, was as forgotten as the dead child's bones moldering under the roots of an immense mahogany tree.

Years passed, and the daughter came to the throne, when her mother the Queen followed her old maidservant Nana Alake to the land of the dead.

But, all during her mother's reign, the fortunes of Bukawai had been going badly. When the young Queen took the throne, they were beset by warriors from two neighboring countries who pillaged the land, carried off crops, and made slaves of the Queen's subjects. The people of Bukawai, sure that the god Shango had turned his face from the land, refused to rally behind her and defend the land. Soon there were rumors that an enemy army was marching on the royal city itself.

In despair, the young Naii went alone into the woods to a certain mahogany tree a wise woman told her contained a spirit who might act as messenger for her to Shango, returning his protection to Bukawai.

But when she reached the clearing in front of the mahogany, she found a beautiful young woman sitting on the roots of the tree, waiting for her. Immediately the young woman rose, embraced the Queen, and kissed her on the forehead, explaining, "I was born in a distant village, on the day your sister died. The spirit of that unhappy girl-baby entered my parents' home and was born again as their child. But I have always known who I was—and, in dreams, an old woman called Nana Alake, who says she is atoning for her part in slaying me, has instructed me to visit this place every day, until the Queen, who is my sister in spirit, should meet me here. And now this has come to pass."

And after they walked awhile, the Queen came to understand her mother's wickedness and to embrace her spirit-sister, who now inhabited another body. Then they talked of the danger to Bukawai from the invading armies.

Together the young women, whose beauty caused all who saw them pass to wonder and comment, returned to the royal compound. There they took down from behind the throne the crossed axes of Shango, made a razor-edged iron worked with gold figures of a ram's head and lightning—Shango's symbols—and, thus armed, went out to rouse the people.

No one could resist the summons of the

warrior women; they rallied behind Naii and her sister, who divided their forces into two battalions, each woman leading one. After two days of ferocious fighting, they forced their enemy to flee, recapturing all the lands and goods the invaders had stolen, and returning to the royal city victorious.

There was a great feast in celebration of the victory. At the feast, Naii rose, silenced the room, and introduced her sister to the throng. At first there was some muttering about the advisability of permitting twins—whether of the flesh, or of the spirit—to remain in the land. But the glow of victory turned opinion in favor of the young ruler and the one she claimed as her sister. The crowd cheered both women.

Then Naii and her sister-in-spirit returned the axes to the wall above the throne. Afterward, Naii ruled for many years with her sister as paramount adviser; and Bukawai enjoyed peace and prosperity. When Old Man Death called the two sisters home, they were buried in the same grave, beneath the ancient mahogany tree. The Queen's daughter ascended the throne, and ordered the tale recounted on scrolls of beaten copper, for which artisans and materials were brought from distant lands.

From that time on, twins, no longer considered omens of ill-fortune, have been held in high regard in Bukawai.

Christine finished reading and, in a reflective mood, continued along to the next case.

Here were some smaller artifacts—wood carvings, beadwork, reed and bone flutes. But what caught her eye were a half-dozen pale, rounded stones, veined with green and purple. The identifying label indicated they had once decorated an altar in Bukawai dedicated to

Shango. They were called "thunderstones," and were said to fall from the sky during heavy storms.

In the last case, on a background of black velvet, lay a massive, twin-bladed axe. It was made of some base metal heavily overlaid with gold. But the opposing parenthetical curves of the finely honed blades had a grimly functional look to them. The handle, of gracefully shaped ebony, was embellished with intertwining braids of gold. Upon both blades were ram's heads with lightning zig-zags spewing from the beasts' jaws.

Christine found a small information placard at one corner of the case. It told her that this was a "thunder-axe" used in rituals by the Queens of Bukawai. She was further advised that the people of Bukawai considered the god Shango their special protector and once worshipped him with elaborate, largely forgotten rites. The noise of thunder was often compared to the bellowing of a ram—which animal was always held sacred to Shango. Thunderbolts were referred to as Shango's own "thunder-axes"; the "thunder-axes" carried by the priestess-queens of Bukawai were symbolic of Shango's divine power.

"Beautiful, isn't it?" said a soft voice behind her.

Christine turned to confront the strange woman whose name she could not remember, but whom she recalled as an old family friend. The latter wore an old-fashioned long black skirt, and a maroon blouse and bandana. As soon as Christine's eyes settled on the older woman's face, she felt a sudden flash of pain behind her eyes, threatening to split her brain in two. She was immediately torn between a compulsive need to be courteous to this woman and, at the same time, a gut-wrenching desire to get away from the woman, the museum, the history that pressed her in on all sides.

As if she read Christine's mind, the older woman smiled and laid her hand gently on Christine's arm.

By the time they stepped out into the late afternoon sunlight, Christine's headache had subsided to a relentless throbbing that plagued her all the time her companion talked. Christine's awareness of everything seemed to compress into that knot of pain; she answered her companion's comments and questions automatically as they walked along the tree-shaded paths. Once or twice she wondered why the majority of the woman's endless questions were about David Palmer and his family, but then the pain would intensify and such thoughts would slide away. She felt so distracted, she felt unable to protest the woman's incessant questioning, or remark on the strange coincidence that brought them to the library exhibit on the same day, or even ask her her name.

But she noticed her companion also seemed increasingly unwell; Christine had the puzzling impression that the other woman was experiencing the same near-migraine headache as she.

Her inquisitor stopped abruptly, placing a

hand to her head, wiping away the sweat that had gathered there. She was breathing heavily. Christine saw her hands were shaking, and she seemed unsteady on her feet.

"Are you all right?" she asked, feeling her own discomfort ebbing to a manageable level. "Do you want to sit down?" She glanced around for someplace to sit.

"No, I'll be fine, I've just—I should go," the other woman said. "I've got my bus to catch."

"I'll walk with you—" Christine began, still feeling an unwilling compulsion to put herself at her companion's disposal.

"No—I won't hear of it. You—enjoy your day." Then she was gone, hurrying down the path toward Market Street and the main bus lines.

Christine, like a person coming slowly awake after a heavy sleep, watched the dwindling black-and-maroon-clothed figure and noticed with relief that her headache was now completely gone. She took a deep breath of the sun-warmed, green-scented air and began looking for a taxi to take her back to PalmerCo, realizing she would have to work late to make up for all the time she had lost on what seemed to her, at the moment, the wildest of wild-goose chases.

ELEVEN

THE PHONE rang just as Amy Palmer was gathering up a stack of books and notebooks off the table by the front door of Rho Tau Delta sorority house.

From the living room came the murmur of voices gathered around the huge open fireplace. Her nose wrinkled slightly at the thought of the boring house sisters and their braggart male grad friends settling down for coffee and a discussion of the state of the economy and international politics. Amy had excused herself right after dinner over Sarah Breslin's protest that Amy owed it to herself "to become politically aware and involved."

Janet Sharpe, holding the silver tray which she had been carrying to the kitchen, answered the phone on her way.

Amy, trying to decide if she needed all the books on the hall table, heard Janet say, "Amy? One moment, I'll check." She put her hand over the mouthpiece and held the phone out.

Already very late because dinner had dragged on so long, Amy whispered, "Who is it?"

Her friend shrugged and murmured, "Some woman. I don't recognize the voice."

Amy shook her head and gestured toward the door.

Janet nodded and removed her hand, saying, "I'm sorry, Amy has already left. No . . . no, we don't expect her back until late." She glanced at the books Amy was fussing with and said, "She's gone to the library on campus, and she usually stays until it closes. If you want to leave a message—" Clearly the caller did not. "Well, then, I suggest you phone her sometime tomorrow. Good night."

Janet continued on her way toward the kitchen swinging the tray casually in her right hand.

With a sigh, Amy conceded, picked up all the books, and opened the front door. She hoped her study companions had not given up on her and left for coffee at one of the Telegraph Avenue shops near the campus.

It was only a short walk down hill to the campus from sorority row.

A late fog was settling over the Berkeley Hills, but it had not yet reached the fringes of the campus—though she sensed that it would soon enough. By the time she walked through Sather Gate just inside the south entrance to the university grounds, she noted that the damp fog had not yet chilled the air. It was actually pleasant out as she walked toward the library in the middle of the campus.

She passed few late-evening strollers; but the

grounds seemed more deserted than usual.

When she reached the doors of the library, she realized the last thing she wanted to do was read up on the Bloomsbury Group. What she really wanted was to go listen to some good jazz or take in some really rotten movie.

Duty called; she pushed through the glass doors and into the lighted entry way. Karin Wade was waiting for her. "Where are Dave and Tony?" Amy asked.

Karin shrugged. "They said they'd come by a little later. They wanted to check the timing on Tony's car first." She led Amy toward a fairly unpopulated table.

Amy had been studying for about an hour, when something prompted her to look up and glance across to the reading table opposite.

A young black man, looking as scruffy as the worst Telegraph Avenue street person, sat with a book open in front of him. His hands hung limply in his lap, he was paying no attention to his book: his eyes were locked on hers. For just a moment she held his gaze, but something in his eyes chilled her, forcing her to look away. They seemed so cold and blank, like the eyes of someone who was not quite right in the head. And his white tee-shirt, under a filthy, unbuttoned denim jacket, was stained and moist-looking, as though the man—she guessed he was about her own age—was sweating heavily in the cool, air-conditioned room. His eyes were like a snake's eyes. She had the terrifying feeling that, if she looked into them a second longer, she would be hypnotized, trapped, made to go over and speak to him and maybe let him touch her—

She forced her attention back to Virginia Woolf and rejected the horror-story images she was playing with. He was probably just high on something, spacing out. But after reading the same paragraph over several times without registering a word, Amy found she couldn't get the man out of her awareness.

She took another look.

The guy was gone. His book still lay flat open on the table in front of the empty chair. She wondered if he had just gone to the restroom; but when, after several minutes, he failed to reappear, she decided he really had gone and promptly forgot him.

She had just returned to Bloomsbury when Karin said, "Here come Dave and Tony. With no books. I've got a feeling study time is over and party time is here. And, God! Am I ready for it."

"Me, too," said Amy. "This place is beginning to get to me." She closed the cover of *The Death of the Moth and Other Essays*. "Goodbye, Virginia," she added. "Hello, beer and pizza."

As it turned out, there was considerably more beer than pizza.

Because it was Thursday, and her earliest Friday class was not until 10:30, Amy wasn't concerned about staying out late.

The four—Amy, Karin, Tony, and Dave—left the pizza parlor to walk the two blocks to

Dave's northside apartment for an after-the-beer beer.

They arrived just together enough to fall apart again over a six-pack of Olympia and Patti Smith's recording of "Because the Night."

Amy sat in a wicker chair, the cushion of which was threatening momentarily to drop through the sagging seat and onto the floor. Sipping her beer, she felt very tired; she glanced at Karin, perched on a hassock, and saw that her friend was wilting also. Tony had passed out on the couch, snoring loudly. David was sitting on the floor, stroking his red-gold beard and singing "Beast of Burden" along with Mick Jagger—just as he had been doing for almost fifteen minutes now. He would pick up the needle at the end of each play and (miraculously, Amy thought, considering how blitzed he was) find the right groove to start the song over again. She decided that, if she had to listen to that offensive song one more time, she was going to slam the needle across the record and eliminate side one completely.

She stood up to leave; Karin got unsteadily to her feet also. Tony continued to snore. David said, somewhat laboriously, "If I could stand up, I'd walk with you."

Karin told him, "Don't worry: we'll be fine. You better not drink any more, though. You won't be worth shit tomorrow morning."

But he wasn't listening; he was moving the stereo needle to start up "Beast of Burden" again.

Amy said, "Let's go now! If I hear that song one more time—" She grabbed Karin's arm and steered her toward the door. She managed to slam it behind them, cutting off Mick Jagger's "I'll never be—"

As they walked down Euclid Avenue back toward the campus, she had the momentary impression that the weird black man from the library was standing in an alley beside the brightly lit Bazooka Burgers all-night cafe across the street. She couldn't be sure because neon glare contrasted so much with the shadow she could only be sure a man was hunched there. *Letting your imagination run away with you,* she warned herself. But she began to walk faster, causing Karin to complain, "Slow down a minute. We're not jogging, are we?"

"It's late—I'm tired," she explained.

"I'm glad my apartment is only a block away." Karin shivered in the cold wind which was bringing fog in ragged gusts from the west.

Amy suddenly wished that Karin would walk with her across campus to her sorority. Then she dismissed the idea as idiotic jitters. What was she afraid of? she wondered. Probably too much beer and the late hour were making her nervous. Sorority row was only a ten-minute walk across the University grounds. There were lights, people still walking around—there probably wasn't a safer place in Berkeley at the moment, she reassured herself.

She and Karin separated at the corner of Euclid and Hearst, Karin turning west, while

Amy headed south towards Sproul Plaza, Sather Gate, and Telegraph Avenue beyond.

The path by the Earth Science building was almost deserted. Two people still huddled together on an ornamental bench near the entrance. The fog had closed in with amazing rapidity; the moldy, unpleasant smell of it filled her nostrils. Other buildings loomed darkly above her, locked tight. In the shelter of the concrete portico a single cigarette glowed like a coal—like a red eye watching her. The glare was reflected by the glass facade behind the solitary smoker. Unconsciously, Amy began to walk faster.

Just as she passed closest to the darkened entranceway, Amy felt a sudden urge to look again. She saw that a shadowy figure had detached itself from the shadows, heading toward her on the intersecting footpath. Though the fog and poor light and beer made positive identification impossible, she felt a frightening certainty that it was the man from the library following her.

She began walking faster—on one level annoyed with herself that she was giving in to such irrational fear, but unable to escape the demands of the fear itself.

She hesitated a moment to consider taking a different route—cutting through the trees and benches down behind Dwinelle Hall and heading west toward Shattuck Avenue, but those paths were even less likely to be traveled so late at night. She continued hurrying straight ahead, afraid to look behind and confirm her terrifying suspicions that she was being followed.

Her clogs (she cursed the impulse that caused her to wear them this night) made staccato sounds on the lonely concrete pathway. She felt incredibly isolated in the thickening fog; the pressure of it seemed to combat the overhead lights into ineffectual pallid bubbles.

She was panting as she hurried up the slope toward the darkened library and the cluster of lamps on the crest of the hill in front of the building.

Amy was almost to the top when she discovered the figure of a slender, middle-aged black woman sitting on a stone bench beneath one lamppost. She wore a dark brown coat with a red scarf tied around her head. Her hands were encased in light gloves; she had them folded primly over the top of her purse, which sat on her lap. Her face was an ebony oval in the lamplight. The whites of her wide eyes and row of even teeth revealed by her grin stood out in contrast to features that seemed sliced from deep shadow. She shifted around on the bench to face the approaching girl. She looked vaguely familiar, but Amy could not place her.

The woman called out to her, "Amy Palmer!"

Startled, the younger woman paused and said, "Yes?"

"We met not long ago at your parents' home. I'm a friend of Christine Lee."

Now she remembered: the religious fanatic she had given a check to on her last visit to her father's house.

On any other occasion, Amy would have resented the woman accosting her. Tonight she felt grateful for her presence. She finally dared to look back along the way she had just come.

No one was following her; she felt her fear subside as suddenly as it had arisen.

The woman rose from the bench and said, "I suffer from insomnia. I often take long walks at night. Would you mind if I walked with you a bit, since we both seem to be heading in the same general direction? I must have been wool-gathering; I hadn't seen how thick the fog was becoming. I'll tell you the truth: it makes me nervous." She gave a laugh.

"Yes," Amy fervently agreed. "The fog can do that sometimes."

They strolled along, Amy letting the older woman set the plodding pace. She paid no attention to the woman's dull chatter; she was simply grateful for the company.

No one else passed them along their foggy way. They were well past the library when the woman abruptly took her hand and started down a side path which curved along between Haviland Hall and the cyclone fence screening the tiny creek that ran across campus.

The girl started to pull back, but the woman was insistent. Her gloved hand held the younger woman in an unexpectedly strong grip.

"Please!" Amy protested, growing angry and impatient to get back to her sorority. "It's late and I have to get home. There are house rules—"

But the woman ignored her. "I just want to

show you what I found earlier," she explained, continuing to pull the reluctant girl down the narrow concrete walkway. Amy had just made up her mind to hit this Mrs. Whatever-her-name-was if need be when the woman announced, "There!" and pointed triumphantly at what seemed to be a compost heap. The top of the pile of clippings was strewn with quite nice-looking cut flowers, only slightly wilted, or in some cases seemingly freshly cut. Amy saw daisies, carnations, daffodils, plus sprays of ferns.

"I think they might have a hothouse around here," the woman said, "that these might be from some university experiment in botany. Wherever they come from," she said thoughtfully, "they're lovely, aren't they?" She added something in a whisper; at the same moment, she let go of Amy's hand.

"What did you say?" the younger woman asked. "I couldn't understand you."

"It was Spanish. I'm a singer. I was just recalling one of my favorite songs."

"Oh," said Amy, deciding the woman was definitely short a few marbles. "Well, I've got to get home. It was nice to see you again."

The woman didn't say anything, just smiled at her in a way that made the girl distinctly uncomfortable. As she started to turn away, the woman said, quite clearly, "Jomo."

Amy realized that he woman wasn't looking at her anymore. The girl followed her gaze—

The black man was standing, silently, on the path right behind her, his horrible eyes fixed on her. She had heard nothing; the woman's talk had hidden his approaching footsteps.

Instinctively she turned to run; but he grabbed her, slamming a damp hand over her mouth before she could cry out. She was nearly overwhelmed by a smell like rotting garbage. *Why is this happening?* she wondered; and disbelief made her think, *It can't really be happening to me: it's too crazy!* She fought, twisting from side to side in the man's embrace, but he was too strong. And now the woman was holding her too.

The woman was crazy; the girl could see it in her eyes now—eyes that held an irrational mixture of regret and pleasure. The woman's hair was a tangle of weedy blackness speckled with gray where her scarf had fallen back while Amy struggled. Her grip felt as strong—stronger than—her companion's.

The man remained curiously silent; Amy had the impression that he was waiting for direction from the woman. The stench of uncleanness—it was deeper than lack of washing—had the vileness of spoiled meat. Fighting back the vomit she felt rising in her throat, the girl renewed her struggle to pull her face free of the smothering, greasy hand. Through tears of fear and frustration she heard herself struggling to ask, "Why, Why?" Only a muffled sound, like the voice of someone underwater, seeped through the man's fingers that smelled of mold, decay, death.

But the woman apparently understood what she was trying to ask, because she answered, in a chillingly reasonable tone of voice, "The children always suffer because of the sins of the fathers."

Then she clenched her teeth and a hard look came to her face. She nodded once at the dark man.

The man's hands shifted abruptly to Amy's throat. In terror the girl arched away from his grip, but was unable to elude it. She threw her head desperately from side to side in frantic protest, but the woman was holding her too tightly and the man was too strong. While the woman's blood-veined eyes swallowed her alive, the man, with the sureness of a musician, added pressure, playing her down from dizziness to unconsciousness to—

The last thing Amy was aware of was her left foot kicking out violently, purposelessly. She felt her clog fly off to hit the pathway a moment later with a sharp, wooden sound. She tried to hold onto the sound; but the black silence she fought off resolutely filled her nostrils, throat, lungs, mind—like drownin—

Jomo, still supporting the girl's limp form, stood silently.

Suzanne had released her hold on the girl. Now she stood back a ways, breathing heavily—great ragged gasps—as though she had done the executing instead of him. She placed the gloved fingertips of both hands to her mouth as though embarrassed by her loud breathing, as if trying to stop it altogether. But her nostrils flared: she continued breathing noisily, unevenly. In the foggy stillness, it sounded almost as if she were sobbing.

Finally she took control of herself, and of the situation. She forced from her mind the unexpected shock she had felt at the moment of the girl's death—whose only crime was her parentage. But what the god decreed must be carried out. She ordered the silent man, "Put her behind that pile of cuttings." While Jomo did so, she walked up the path and kicked the single brown clog under a hedge. Then she opened her purse and pulled out a little paper bag of purple-and-green-veined pebbles. Selecting one, she dropped it on the cement path beside Amy's eyes, which were frozen open in horror. Impulsively, Suzanne leaned over and closed those eyes.

Then she jerked a thin silver chain from around the girl's bruised throat. She looked at the medallion: a woman's face surmounted by twining hair growing into the branches of a tree. She could not recall ever having seen a similar design. She wrapped the silver bauble and broken chain into some Kleenex and fastened it with rubber bands. She slipped the packet into a side pocket of her purse.

"Hurry, now—before someone finds us," Suzanne said. When he failed to move quickly enough, she grabbed his wrist, though the feel of the chill, moist skin made her shudder in spite of herself. Together they began walking rapidly down the path, towards the west entrance to the campus. Jomo loped along beside her, keeping pace just a fraction behind her. They didn't talk anymore; the fog swallowed the sounds of their footsteps. She watched her own breath emerge like puffs of smoke in the chilling mist. No breath-clouds marked his passage. This startled Suzanne: a small detail that made her realize how little she knew of the powers she was involved with.

They were outside the University grounds now, walking down University Avenue now, past rows of unlighted store windows. Just as they passed a hardware store window which was filled with an elaborate display of model railroads dimly visible under a single overhead light, two bronze Berkeley police cars sped up University Avenue toward the campus with their lights flashing and sirens and warning lights also at full pitch.

Jomo paid no attention to the commotion; he stood patiently, while, behind his reflection in the window glass, the toy train endlessly followed the sinuous curves of the figure-eight tracks. Suzanne was alarmed at their proximity to the campus. She had been startled by the sudden appearance of the police; there was no doubt in her mind that they were on their way to investigate the death of the girl. She was disturbed to realize that someone must have discovered the body only minutes after they had left it. Someone must have been just seconds from seeing them. She found it chilling to think that all her plans had been within a heartbeat of ruin.

She pulled on Jomo's arm, urging him, "Come

with me right now!" Another police car tore along the streets, lights flashing, but without a siren.

Jomo resumed his rhythmic pace a fraction behind her.

She had parked Jomo's battered Volkswagen on a side street blocks away from the campus. Her hands were shaking so that she nearly snapped the flimsy key off in the passenger door, unlocking it for the silent man. Her companion remained indifferent while she fumbled and cursed and prodded the antique lock. When she did finally pull the door open, he slid silently into the seat, leaving the door for her to close.

Suzanne said nothing during the drive back to Manningtree Lane. She felt the chill of the night wrapping itself around her bones, even though she turned the car heater as high as it would go. All the way home, her teeth chattered almost as loudly as the car rattled.

Jomo remained staring straight ahead through the windshield, indifferent to her, to the lights and people on the streets, to anything.

The house was silent as Suzanne let herself in; the night stillness pressed in on her as she stood alone in the hallway, pushing the door gently shut behind her. As if across some vast distance, she was aware of Jomo in repose, who was neither asleep nor awake, but merely *waiting*. For her, for what they had yet to do together.

After a mometary hesitation, she shook her head slightly. Then she walked across the dining room to the kitchen; she didn't turn on any lights, being content with the soft mingling of streetlights and moonlight seeping in through the half-drawn curtains and shades.

Humming Billie Holiday's "Strange Fruit" softly to herself, Suzanne put on water to boil. When she had prepared a cup of herbal tea for herself, she carried it through the dark, silent house upstairs to her own room.

She shut—and bolted—her own door. Then she flickered on the wall-mounted lamp over her tidily made bed. Suzanne peeled off her coat, hung it carefully in the closet, and sat down on the single chair and placed the cup of tea on the little desk in front of her. Lying on the desk was a slim green volume labeled, in faded gold stamping, *Folklore of Bukawai People;* it had fallen open to one of the sections she read most often. She had found the book years before in a little Harlem hole-in-the-wall gift shop.

Sipping tea, she reread the lines that were so familiar to her she could almost have recited them by heart:

> And the Queens of Bukawai ruled in wisdom and splendor, each glorious in royal jewelry, bearing the staff and ax of her power, a robe of rich purple and green cloth drawn over her shoulder—until the coming of the Portuguese, who brought strange weapons, a stranger god, and confusion. Then the protective walls of the Queen's enclosure were destroyed and the

Queen's counselors slain and the last Queen Naii led away into slavery.

But there is a saying among the Bukawai people that the spirit of Naii lives on in a distant land, the Spirit Mother gathers threads of circumstances, and Shango bides his time. And one day, soon or late, they will, together, weave a powerful magic when the Bukawai people need it most, and when the time of gathering threads has come to an end.

She set down her teacup and pressed the heels of her hands hard against her eyes, searching out, in the darkness behind her unseeing eyes, the threads running through her own life—trying, as she did so often these days, to pick out the full pattern of the events which had taken control of her life—and so many other lives.

There had come a time, not many years before she boarded the Greyhound bus for California, when Suzanne had foundered in despair so deep she doubted she could ever get outside it. The blackness had not receded as it had always done on other occasions; it had lingered, ingraining itself into the texture of her life. She knew that the darkness existed only in her mind; but she could not rid herself of the sense of a physical substance that actually filmed the windows, smothering the lights she left on around the clock, pressing against her eyes and mind relentlessly.

Frightened and unable to move from the apartment, she had phoned the club and her office to plead sick.

She sat by the window, and watched, as through a fog, the flow of foot traffic along 127th Street, three flights down.

Then late one Saturday afternoon, a sudden restlessness took possession of her; at the same moment the darkness around her seemed to subside somewhat.

Pulling on a bulky sweater over the housedress she had worn and slept in for three days, she fled the stale air of the apartment, walking rapidly east, then north, then further east on a bus into Spanish Harlem. She felt more *pulled* than aimless in her journey to the Spanish-speaking neighborhood she had visited only infrequently.

She walked down Park Avenue, aimlessly watching her twin, her reflection, in a variety of shop windows, perspiring in her sweater and enduring the stares of passersby who commented rudely on her disheveled appearance in laughter-punctuated Spanish.

At last Suzanne felt impelled to pause in front of a dusty store window; hand-painted red letters near the entrance identified it as *Bois Verna Botanica*. She looked into the eyes of her twin, saw only her own uncertainty reflected there, and, shrugging, pushed into the dim shop.

Inside, a heavy-set woman—apparently of West Indian descent, judging from the mahogany hue of her skin—was in conversation with a young, powerfully built man whose comparable skin tone and some quality of his features suggested kinship. Suzanne guessed he might be her son.

They stopped talking to watch her entrance. Then the woman asked, "What help you be needin' today?"

"None, right now—just looking."

The two resumed their conversation, speaking softly, as though afraid Suzanne would overhear. From time to time they glanced in her direction just long enough to assure themselves she wasn't shoplifting.

Not sure why she had come into this particular shop, Suzanne wandered up and down the narrow aisles, checking out the stock in desultory fashion—occasionally picking up and quickly replacing some dusty item or other.

She was in a magic shop—the stuff of black magic, white magic, *voodoo* filled the shelves and cabinets. Packets, boxes, jars of dried herbs and powders. Amulets. An open ceramic dish piled high with cactus leaves. Elixirs. Snake oil set in an elaborate spice rack. A creaking spinner rack filled with books on dream interpretation, palmistry, astrology, pamphlets on cures and curses. Collections of Haitian folktales, French books on *voodoo*, records of Haitian music.

In a small glass case set atop a much larger one filled with a jumble of *voodoo* dolls, icons, horseshoes, and rainbow-colored votive candles was a single statue: a tiny, ebony duplicate of the Shango-cult figure Suzanne had last seen on her grandmother's mantelpiece back in

California. The bare-breasted figure, bearing its double-blades-axe crest, seemed to stare back at her from behind the fingerprint-and-grime-smudged glass.

"Now you be needin' some help, maybe?" the shopkeeper asked. Suzanne started—the woman had come up and was standing right behind her.

Turning to look at the woman, she saw the man, leaning on his elbows, staring at her from the far side of the counter, beside the ancient cash register.

"How—how much for the little wood figure?" Suzanne asked.

"Fifteen dollars. A bargain. That be an antique. From Haiti or some-such."

Suzanne stared at the seated figurine, then nodded abruptly. "Yes, I'll take it." While the woman, smelling of musk and gentian, lifted away the front panel of glass and removed the statue, Suzanne nervously fumbled open her wallet, uncertain that she had enough to pay for the object. But she discovered a twenty-dollar bill sandwiched in between some singles. This she handed to the woman, who carried the currency across the store and handed it over to the man saying, "Toni, ring her up. Fifteen dollars plus tax."

"Want a bag for it?" the man asked, counting out her change.

She shook her head, taking the little carving and shoving it deep into the pocket of her sweater. Then she pushed her way out of the shop into the twilight, astonished to find that—

somehow—hours seemed to have slipped away while she was in the tiny *botanica*.

On one level, she was afraid to be out on the streets—largely unfamiliar streets—as night was falling. Still, she was not ready to return to her apartment. Uncertain, she reached into her sweater pocket and felt the hard, uneven warmth of the wood figure under her fingertips.

Her hand still in her pocket, she walked northwest across Madison, then down Fifth Avenue until she was across the street from Central Park. She walked a block or two further. Then, touching the figure in her pocket a final time, she crossed Fifth Avenue, just as the sun was setting, and walked recklessly into the Park.

She followed one of the curving paths in the general direction of Harlem Lake, but quickly became lost wandering deeper into the tree-heavy green landscape, against the tide of visitors leaving with the setting sun. Where a patch of grass separated a grove of trees from the footpath, Suzanne (after glancing around to be sure she was unobserved) left the trail and slipped quickly into the dark green shade of the massed branches.

Scattered beer cans, broken bottles, and food wrappers showed she was not the first to explore the interlocking clearings, screened from passersby. Deeper and deeper she went into the green and purple gloom, following some inner line of least resistance.

And then, she stepped wonderingly into a

silent clearing—like the cool, shadowed heart of the grove. The tree trunks formed a nearly perfect ring; the ground was covered with spongy dead matter. Here, she saw, there were no beer cans or other signs of intruders—she might have entered a jungle clearing where no human had preceeded her.

While she stood, savoring the coolness, drinking in the fragrances of living plants and decaying matter, she heard the sound of a twig snapping underfoot behind her; she spun around, looking back through the thickly massed trees in the direction she had come. But she saw no one.

The silence closed in on her again.

Fast-approaching night was making it difficult to see even the trees on the other side of the clearing. She felt wonderfully, *terrifyingly* alone. She let her fingers play over the carved surfaces of the Shango-cult figure in her sweater pocket.

Suzanne waited patiently, expectantly, feeling a power gathering in the dusk.

The pale, gleaming tree trunk to her immediate right began to ooze blood, then the leaves overhead started to drip it, hitting the leafy floor covering with a raspy sound. The ground began to ooze it, seeping through the organic carpeting, threatening to soak her shoes.

Again, she heard a sound behind her.

She turned around to see who had come to share this extraordinary moment with her, but the grove was still empty of any other human presence. Perhaps this was only happening in her mind, she thought. With mingled curiosity and repulsion, she leaned down and touched her fingertips to the seeping redness; when she held them up to her face, they were coated to the first joint. She made no move to clean off her hands, but waited for whatever would happen next.

She closed her eyes; all around her she could hear the blood cascading down the tree trunks, splashing from the leaves onto the ground.

She let her eyes flicker open, but the red twilight, the bloody rain from the trees all around, the redness that seemed to fill her brain, made it nearly impossible to see through the thickening red haze in which she now felt as helplessly embedded as an insect in amber.

When she heard the soft footfall just behind her, she was incapable of even turning to see who was there. It no longer mattered: she had decided that whatever was happening was going to play itself out, and she could do no more than play whatever part was assigned to her, without protest.

"Who?" she asked, her voice so faint she might only have thought the question—not really uttered it.

In answer, two muscular black arms encircled her shoulders, reaching under her unbuttoned sweater to cup her breasts through the silky-thin fabric of her housedress. She shifted suddenly, half in protest, half in pleasure; when she felt the pressure of the imprisoning arms tighten in response, she made no further movement. She smelled a cloying fragrance of mingled musk and gentian. Lips nuzzled her right ear, whispering something indecipherable. All around her was the sibilance of the dripping, flowing blood, hissing in the near darkness.

"Who?" she asked, but fingertips, smelling of incense, pressed against her lips, silencing her —but with a rough gentleness. The whisper at her ear cautioned her to silence. All around her the bloody rain, unseen now, continued to fall, but not a drop touched her. Everything was out of kilter: she felt herself frozen in a moment before some deep understanding.

Then, across the clearing, her familiar blackskirted form outlined with blood-tinted light, Nana Chicory appeared, carrying an infant in her arms. She was crooning softly to it, trying to hush its restless cries.

Suzanne recognized her child immediately— twisting to break free of the imprisoning arms that continued to hold her fast.

When Nana was several paces away, sheathed in an envelope of red firelight, she raised her head to look directly into her granddaughter's eyes. In the old familiar raspy voice, she said, "Your baby—your son." Suzanne could see the infant was wrapped in blood-stained swaddling clothes.

Even against the restraining hand, she managed to nod her head, feeling the tears start.

"There are others, longer dead than this chile —dead by many hands, dead by the same hand.

Their blood cries out to heaven. And one god will answer, according to his promise. But, first, he mus' be called with blood."

Blood echoed in chorus of ghostly voices that seemed to issue from the trees all around the little clearing. Suzanne was so startled by the multitude of unseen voices that she scarcely dared to breathe; the fingers holding her in silence relaxed a bit—but not enough to allow her to speak, even if she dared.

"The old ones," Nana said, nodding her head slightly. "You are their hope now."

The infant in her arms squalled; Suzanne writhed with the need to go to it. The arms held her prisoner, but the voice at her ear whispered, "See!"

The restive infant in the old woman's arms turned abruptly into a bleating goat which she dropped onto the ground, holding it tethered with a bit of rope grasped firmly in her hand. The unseen, unceasing rain sweated from the tree branches overhead, grew in tempo and volume, became the sound of drum beats, as if the hidden presences Suzanne sensed all around her were pounding out a rhythm that seemed the same beat as the blood she felt pounding at her temples, in her throat.

Nana Chicory, veiled in waves of glowing red, nodded in time to the drum music, then began to sing a song Suzanne remembered from her childhood, but which had—up till this moment —never made any sense. But now, as the old woman tied the loose end of the rope around her waist, then reached into the deep pockets of her skirt to pull out a hollowed-out gourd the size of a cupped hand and a knife with a serated edge a little larger than a bread knife, Suzanne understood the meaning in the half-sung, half-chanted words:

> Hand a' bowl, knife a' throat
> Rope a' tie me, hand a' bowl
> Hand a' bowl, blood a' night
> Shango come, come, knife a' throat.

The drumming exploded in intensity all around her. Nana stepped toward her, holding out the knife and gourd. Suzanne felt the arms drop away, releasing her—but she did not dare to turn and confront her captor, though she could feel the warmth of his breath on the back of her neck. Nana Chicory's eyes held her more completely helpless than the arms of the unseen other.

The old woman thrust the implements at her impatiently. Like a person in a dream, Suzanne reached for the knife, the gourd, and took them from the old woman.

"*Now!*" said the old woman, jerking the struggling goat so abruptly that its front hooves momentarily left the ground, then dropped back with a sudden *thunk!* "*Now!*" Nana Chicory ordered, motioning at Suzanne with her free hand.

She looked down at the terrified wide eyes of the beast, which tried hopelessly to twist free of the restraining tether.

Then it wasn't a goat's head she was looking at, but the head of a man: David Palmer, grotesquely fused to the goat body. The man's features melted, softened, became those of a young white boy and then a young white girl whose faces reminded her of David.

David's features returned, obscenely grafted onto the matted white hair of the goat's neck. The line of rope divided the pale human skin from the animal hair.

"Now-now-now!" Nana rasped, while the obscenely misplaced human mouth twisted into a scream. All around her, the voices urged,

> Hand a' bowl, blood a' night
> Shango come, come, knife a' throat.

"Now," ordered the male voice behind her, and she drew the blade of the knife swiftly across the half goat's throat, above the rope-line, watching the jagged edge of the knife bite deep into the soft white skin, tearing the cartilage, releasing the blood, while the face contorted and tried to scream.

She let the knife slip unheeded from her fingers to the ground; she put the hollow gourd to the wound, catching the blood of the dying animal (now wholly goat) in the vessel, while Nana Chicory held the head upright at the end of the taut rope.

Suzanne held the half-full gourd out to the old woman, but she shook her head and said, "Taste it."

With trembling hands, Suzanne raised the cup of thick, steaming blood to her lips, while Nana led the chorus of voices—men and women —in the cry:

Hand a' bowl, Shango come come
Blood a' night, Shango come come.

Unable to resist, she raised the gourd to her lips, and took a sip of the salty, thick blood. She nearly gagged, but forced herself to swallow it. She dropped the rest on the ground beside the knife.

Nana smiled and nodded; the light wrapped around the old woman began to fade, as though the dark night under the trees were drinking in the vision of the woman as surely as Suzanne had the goat's blood.

Before she had disappeared completely, the old woman cried, "Shango," and the voices, that seemed to fly away from her on all sides into the dark and now-silent trees, took up the name of the god and carried it away with them in tatters of sound rapidly lost in coherency, then hearing, all around her.

In a moment, she was alone in the clearing, into which only a little muted moonlight seeped.

Not quite alone. She could hear a faint breathing behind her. The smell of musk and gentian filled her nostrils. The hands that had so recently released her took her by the shoulders, and turned her around to confront a faceless figure, the shadow-image of a man. To her overwrought perception, it seemed she could see right through the man—through darkness to the moon-dappled trees behind. His arms, holding her, were man-solid, but the rest of him was insubstantial as a dream. She felt herself in the presence of a miracle. She whispered, "Shango," and the response was a booming laugh that filled the glade and threatened to shake the few stars she could see through the branches overhead.

Then, with the laughter continuing, the muscular arms pulled her close; and she felt, all at once, that she was a woman in the arms of her most beloved, a child pulled to her father, and a helpless bit of humanity in the terrifying, incomprehensible embrace of the divine.

Her body burned with desire; she screamed in terror—even as she surrendered to the embrace, she tried frantically to twist away— even as the goat-no-longer-goat tried to save itself from her sacrificial knife.

And then, she fainted.

The police, alerted by several children who had come exploring the glade early the following morning, found her collapsed on the ground the next morning. She was dazed; she was uncertain where—or even *who*—she was.

She was vaguely aware of being led through the maze of trees to the foot-path. Later, she was aware of being placed on a stretcher, and then raised into an ambulance, while dozens of wide-eyed children and adults—most of them black—looked on in silence.

Very much later, doctors in the hospital (the second one to which she was taken) talked to her about an assault, about the rape.

When she argued the details of what (she

knew) had really happened, they read her the police reports which detailed that no knife, no gourd, no sign of blood or animal had been found in the clearing. The little Shango-cult statue was no longer in her pocket.

When she pressed them further, they assured her that there was no such shop as *Bois Verna Bontanica* listed—certainly not in the city.

With impatient, professional kindness they explained that she had been assaulted—raped—and that this, together with other pressures, had brought her to the edge of a nervous breakdown. She was (they assured her) creating a fantasy to disguise her own inability to accept some too-painful facts of her life.

For a time she protested.

For a longer interval, she refused to have anything to do with the doctors or the other patients, locking herself into a space of silence and safety.

Finally, she decided to agree with their diagnosis. She began to give all the right answers; they were, by turns, relieved, pleased, proud of how well their treatments had worked.

She was pronounced cured, released, allowed to return to work. She had to find a new daytime job, but soon had her old job at Club Indigo back.

But she never—to herself—denied that something extraordinary had happened that night. Something that would forever change the course of her life. So she waited, she worked, and in time she came across the newspaper clipping that began to pull it all together for her.

Now, seated at the window of her dead sister's house, Suzanne, feeling sleep not yet ready to claim her, let other memories, too long buried, come clamoring into her consciousness.

TWELVE

Though Elenora was dead, her presence seemed to fill the room—the staleness like an exhalation from the grave.

Suzanne found her mind filling with memories of her older sister.

The summer Suzanne was nineteen and Elenora twenty-two, their mother had gone back to Detroit when her father, whom the girls had seen only a handful of times, had become senile and required constant care. There was also a question of some property the old man had and the likelihood of a fight with Thelma's half-sister and younger brother over how money matters were going to be settled.

Elenora and Suzanne had seen their mother off at the Oakland train depot. Thelma had been grim-faced, like a soldier off to the wars. She was determined to do her duty—and doubly determined not to let anything that was rightfully hers slip into the hands of the less-deserving.

She expected to be gone several weeks. Both girls were anxious for her to be on her way, so they could be on their own. Their mother, however, seemed to sense potential trouble in the girls' poorly concealed eagerness for the train to pull away. But her daughters gave all the right assurances that they would watch out for themselves, for the house, and look in frequently on Nana Chicory, who was still living in her own apartment.

As the train pulled away, Elenora said, "You wait for me here, I've got to call Benny."

Suzanne stood on the platform, smoking one of the infrequent cigarettes which were a private sign of her independence from her parents. But she was careful not to let herself harm her throat with more than two or three a week: her ambitions as a singer were beginning to crystallize, and she would not risk that for all the independence in the world.

Elenora returned as she was stubbing out the cigarette butt underfoot. "Benny is coming by tonight—after his last set." She was trying to sound casual, but Suzanne could see she was tensed for an argument.

She shrugged. Benny was a white musician, about thirty, who played local clubs when he could pick up side work. Elenora had met him at one of the clubs Suzanne had appeared at for "tips only."

Benny had been one of the trio (piano, drums—he was bass) the manager had thrown together as general backup for the "freebies" Monday through Thursday, and the various "names" (on-the-risers or has-beens) who played three sets each night Friday through

Sunday.

Suzanne thought of Benny as just adequate accompaniment. Benny, she sensed, thought Benny was God's gift to the world of jazz. To her annoyance, she saw Elenora buy into Benny's self-appreciation right from the first moment he had invited himself to their table, managed to down three "bourbon neat's," and snow Elenora—all before their next set began.

"Well?" Elenora said, the challenge in her voice unmistakable.

"Benny," Suzanne had responded, "is your problem. Just don't make him mine."

And, in silence, they had walked through the crowded, high-ceilinged waiting room and outside to where the family Studebaker was parked.

If Elenora had seen Benny and slept with him occasionally, things might have turned out differently.

But Benny, it turned out, was in the process of being (once again) evicted from his apartment for nonpayment of rent. And Elenora immediately invited him to stay in the half-empty house "for the time bein'."

Only, the "time bein'" turned out to be of increasingly indefinite duration. After a few days, Suzanne realized that Benny intended to stay with them until the return of their mother —still several weeks away—drove him out. She complained to Elenora several times, but was only told to "quit bein' such a jealous bitch!"

But with each passing day, the constant presence of Benny (who had lost his job at the club after an argument with the manager and who seemed little inclined to find new work) began to disturb Suzanne in a host of different ways.

She was working four or five evenings a week; Elenora had a steady job daytime as assistant bookkeeper for a San Francisco import firm. Benny hung around the house all day, playing records, practicing, waiting for Elenora's return so they could go to a show or dinner (always on Elenora) and then settle down to sex, while Suzanne left for the evening or shut herself into her room to listen to the radio or sleep.

But there was no real escape from Benny's presence. He was everywhere underfoot. Even when he disappeared during the late afternoons on private business, Suzanne was aware of the smell of him, his constant cigarettes, his bay-rum cologne, his sweat, and—this last she usually hated to admit—the persistent image of Benny sprawled across the living room couch in her father's pale-blue terrycloth robe while he listened to Charlie Parker on the old record player, while his thin, hairy legs dangled off the edge, his foot keeping time to the music and his sex lying limp and heavy against his pale thigh.

She stayed away from home as much as she could, regretting that her lack of money made it impossible for her to move to a place of her own, away from her mother and, more importantly, away from her sister and her lover.

Even now, so many years later, Suzanne was not sure why she had finally let the barrier of resentments and fear of the consequences simply collapse.

Elenora seemed unaware of the change; Benny, however, with his ability to sniff out anything of possible advantage to himself, quickly began coming on to her whenever Elenora was safely out of the house.

So that one Friday morning, after Elenora's departure, when Suzanne was sipping coffee in the kitchen in her green-silk kimono, when her reserves were nonexistent, Benny had come into the room, draped in her father's robe. He had not bothered to tie the front of it; his hairy chest and groin, his sex at half-mast, were on full display.

"Morning, Little Sister," he said, teasing her with the nickname she hated.

"Give me a break, Benny—I can't handle that been-around body so early in the morning." She tried to make her voice casual, disdainful.

It didn't work. They both knew she was no longer truly resisting him.

Benny's mouth, when he leaned over her to kiss her, and push his tongue past her briefly resistant lips, tasted of cinnamon-flavored mouthwash. He shoved his hand into her robe, grasping and kneading her right breast. Her own right hand reached up to take hold of his now fully erect member.

For a few moments the kitchen was filled with their half-muffled groans of increasingly urgent pleasure.

Then Benny had pulled her to her feet, letting her kimono slide carelessly to the kitchen floor, and had led her eagerly to her mother's bedroom and the bed that, up to now, had been the domain of her sister and Benny.

The day stretched languidly out in front of them; they had it all to themselves and their lovemaking.

As much as she took from Benny, and gave, Suzanne resented him—his rough handling, the smell of his unwashed hair, the cinnamon taste of Elenora's mouthwash filling her mouth, the knowledge that she was nothing more than an easy pleasure to him.

But Elenora had come back unexpectedly early, her face flushed with the fever she had been fighting off for days. She was pulling off her sweater as she came into the room, saying, "Honey, I was just feeling too bad to—"

Then she saw them.

They were tangled in the sheets of the big double bed, Suzanne sprawled alongside him, one of her hands on Benny's sex. Elenora had stood frozen between the bed and doorway while Benny, his face half-buried in a pillow, muttered, "Oh Jesus, oh, sweet Jesus oh—!" Suzanne, fascinated as if she were watching a slow-motion automobile crash, could only stare at her sister.

Then with a loud, indecipherable cry, Elenora had launched herself at the bed. She yanked Suzanne aside and almost off the bed; Benny suddenly rolled aside with an "oh, fuck!" He made no attempt to protect his bedmate from the pummeling Elenora was giving her. He simply lay across the bed, cupping his hands protectively over his diminished sex, as though he was afraid Elenora might attack it/him next.

But, for the moment, she concentrated her ferocity on her dazed sister. She hauled Suzanne to her feet and tried to push her out into the hall. When Suzanne pushed her away with unexpected fury, Elenora stood with her back against the closet door breathing in great, ragged gulps. Suzanne, feeling oddly removed from it all, saw what fools she and her sister were making out of themselves over a worthless man. She was furious with herself for letting herself be drawn into such a grotesque, sordid confrontation.

Benny still lay on the bed, one arm thrown across his eyes, his hand shielding his genitals. At first an exasperated "shit!" was his only comment on what had happened; then his anger grew and he yelled at Elenora, "Who the fuck do you think you are, bitch-cunt? What the fuck gives you the right—?"

Elenora spoke with exaggerated, rage-fueled clarity. "No one gives me the right. No one gives me anything. I took it." She was looking past Suzanne, directly at him.

"So great. So why don't you take your ass out of here?"

She didn't answer him, just turned on her heel and left the bedroom, slamming the door behind her. Suzanne heard her sister running along the uncarpeted hall, then downstairs. She listened for the sound of the front door slamming, but there was only silence, indicating Elenora had stayed in the house. Suzanne supposed she was downstairs crying.

She stared at Benny. "You'd better get out," she said to him. Suzanne knew that she was the bigger fool in this mess because Elenora, at least, could claim the faulty vision of a person in love. But Suzanne had no excuse: she had bought her way into this three-ring circus with her eyes wide open. "Get *out!*" she shouted.

But Benny just turned away from her in the bed to face the wall, lying on his side.

Suzanne had just taken a step towards him, her hand outstretched to grab his shoulder and haul him off the bed, if need be, when Elenora suddenly sallied into the bedroom, waving a double-pronged serving-fork crazily over her head. With a single "son-of-a-bitch!" she threw herself at the bed, at her lover's naked back. Some instinct warned Benny to twist about suddenly, so that the fork tines buried themselves in the back of his left calf.

He gave a shriek, and Elenora jerked back, leaving her weapon impaled in the screaming man's leg. Benny reached back and yanked the fork free, throwing it across the room, where it hit the wall and dropped to the floor. Then he pressed a wad of blanket against the wound, which Suzanne could see was bleeding profusely.

Elenora just stood over the bed looking down at Benny. Her mouth worked convulsively; her breath came in uneven gasps; her hands hung helplessly at her sides, clenching and unclenching. Tears of frustration and outrage poured unheeded down her face. But her anger was gone for the moment.

Benny was writhing around the bed, alternately screaming in pain or shouting abuse at Elenora.

Suzanne, who seemed suddenly forgotten by the other two, took hold of her sister, spun her around, and shoved her out of the door, telling her, "Go into the bathroom and wash your face; or go downstairs—go anywhere, but just get out of here for a few minutes." Elenora, moving with an infuriating, dreamy slowness—as though she were in shock—did what she was told without protest. Suzanne heard the bathroom door across the hall close with unexpected gentleness; a minute later she heard water running into the basin.

Benny lay moaning with a length of sheet twisted around his wounded calf. He had managed to get blood everywhere. To her question about how badly he was hurt, he only responded with a string of curses.

Suzanne, with a clearheadedness that astonished even her, went downstairs to the kitchen and pulled the single ice tray—impacted in several months' worth of accumulated frost—out of the tiny freezer compartment of the old refrigerator and wrapped it in a soiled dishtowel. She brought the stopgap ice pack back and handed it to Benny, ordering him, "Hold this against the cut; it should stop the bleeding and the pain." He accepted it without comment, setting it on the bed, unwinding the sheet, and laying his injured limb across it. He was completely naked now, alternately studying his injury and Suzanne's face. "Your sister," he said nastily, "is a complete fuck-up."

Not wishing to add to her problems with another argument, Suzanne merely shrugged.

Seeing his ugly, shriveled member amid this welter of blood and pain and self-pity, Suzanne felt almost sorry for the man. He was such a loser, she wondered how either she or her sister could have wanted him touching her, entering her. He was less than nothing: he was pathetic. Any woman who deluded herself about him was a fool. He aroused such revulsion in her, she could hardly bear to look at him at all without wanting to rake his stupid face with her nails.

"Jesus," said Benny, "I'm freezing." His teeth had begun to chatter.

"Then cover yourself up; you're probably in shock."

"Yeah," he said, pulling a blanket tightly around himself.

Suzanne moved to a chair across the room from the bed and sat down, watching, thinking. For a long time they sat in silence, the only sounds were his rapid breathing and the muffled splash of water into the bathroom basin. After a while, the water turned off, but the door remained closed.

Benny leaned forward and twisted his leg around on the ice pack to look at it. The bleeding had stopped; the skin was moistly white around two puncture wounds like a snake bite. "Shit," he said, more disgusted than angry.

He toyed with a tiny flap of skin on the edge of the larger hole.

"Don't poke at it; you'll start it bleeding again," Suzanne said; then she asked, "Can you wiggle your toes?"

Benny demonstrated that he could.

"Then," she continued, "you'd better pull yourself together and go let a doctor look at that." She didn't move from her chair. Somewhere at the back of her mind was a vague resentment, growing stronger, that Elenora hadn't finished what she had begun—had, instead, left things for Suzanne to sort out.

She pushed aside such thoughts and calculated the results of her sister's stupidity. Benny would undoubtedly go to the police; she was sure he would make whatever trouble for Elenora he could, exacting every bit of punishment (and money) he could from her. Once again she regretted that Elenora had not simply finished things. She felt that the world could hardly be accounted any poorer if he were . . . removed.

Benny tore off a piece of the sheet. His mouth was a tight line as he bandaged his leg and glanced through the open doorway at the closed bathroom door across the hall from time to time. When he had finished, he fished up a grimy pair of boxer shorts and a pair of slacks from the space between the bed and the wall and pulled them on. His shirt—one sleeve soaked with blood—he extracted from the tangled bedclothes. He sat unsteadily on the edge of the bed, drawing on his clothes with hands that had started to shake again. "Your sis—" he started.

But Suzanne cut him off abruptly. "Why don't you get out—go to the doctor or whatever. Leave us alone." She could imagine Elenora listening from inside the bathroom as she added, "There's nothing more for you here. Nothing."

He stood up, swaying slightly, and looked at his leg as if he was surprised to discover that it could support him. He limped across the room. When he reached the doorway, he paused with his hand on the lintel and said loudly to Suzanne, who was standing in the center of the living room, "You tell that homicidal bitch one thing for me." Here he looked at the closed door, clearly considering slamming his fist against it, then dismissed the idea with a gesture of contempt. "She hasn't seen the last of me. She hasn't heard the final word on this. You tell the cunt that!" Then he was gone, clumping downstairs, slamming the front door behind him.

Suzanne remained standing where she was until she was sure he wasn't coming back. Then she went and knocked on the bathroom door, saying, "He's gone. You come out." She knew Elenora would be listening, hiding until things were sorted out. Elenora had never been much good at facing the consequences of her emotions, whether anger or love.

There was a brief silence, then the lock turned with a click. Elenora, looking sick and weary, but calm, only the puffiness around her eyes betraying her inner distress, cautiously opened the door. After a minute she asked, "Now what?" Her voice was little more than a harsh whisper, uncannily like their grandmother's voice.

"The police will probably come around."

"What will you tell them?"

Suzanne gave a short, bitter laugh. "I'm going to tell them just what happened. That Benny started it by trying to rape me, and you were only trying to help me."

"But he didn't."

"Elenora! You have a witness. I'm your witness. And I know what I saw with my own eyes."

Suzanne made a motion to touch her sister's arm, but Elenora suddenly jerked away, snarling, "I know what *I* saw too! Maybe I should have jus' stabbed *you*."

Suzanne said evenly, with her angry contempt coming through clearly, "It's too late to think about that. And chances are, you wouldn't have done *that* one right either."

"This is all your fault, anyhow," Elenora said sullenly.

"Jesus, God—will you stop worrying about that crap and think about what's gonna happen when the police come?"

This time Suzanne's words seemed to cut through Elenora's anger. She grabbed Suzanne's upper arm with painful intensity, saying, "You don't really think the police gonna come?"

"Girl, will you get it into your head? You committed assault and battery, and that skinny white mother is gonna say it was with intent to kill."

"Well, it was—I was aiming for his back."

"Forget that. Forget you did anything but defend me when you found Benny trying to rape me."

"It won't work, Susie. The police are men—they'll probably be white. They'll get our asses for being black whores trying to hurt a white man."

"Well, aren't we? Just what you said? But that doesn't matter. We're going to *make* them believe what we're sayin'. Besides," she added as an afterthought, "we both know Benny uses drugs. I got friends at the club—"

"I can't—" Elenora was whining now. Suzanne had to keep her own growing impatience in check. Her sister's fear of police reprisals had, for the moment, pushed Suzanne's betrayal to the back of her mind.

"You're gonna have to. Now, come along with me downstairs. I'll fix us some coffee—and a shot of Mama's bourbon, and we'll talk about what we're gonna tell the police."

Her hand firmly around her sister's wrist, Suzanne led her downstairs. They had just entered the kitchen, Suzanne motioning Elenora to sit down at the table, still littered with the remains of breakfast, and bringing down the cannister of coffee from above the stove, when a voice from the back door said, "There's been trouble here—bad trouble."

Suzanne spun around, nearly dropping the

half-full coffee tin, recognizing the voice immediately.

"Why, Nana—this is a surprise! What makes you think there's anything wrong?" She glanced at Elenora who sat, her hands folded on the soiled tabletop, staring intently at a saucer of strawberry jam around which several flies had settled. Suzanne tried to make her own voice sound casual, but her hands were shaking so much under the old woman's searching look so that she couldn't pry up the yellow plastic lid.

"Don't be wastin' your breath lyin' to me. I had a seein'. And don't be doin' coffee. There's some my special tea up there in that jar. Fetch it down and we drink that. Be quick, girl."

Suzanne did as the old woman ordered, replacing the coffee tin and lifting down the jar of herb tea her mother kept against Nana's visits.

"Put on the water, then you tell me what you both done."

While the old kettle heated, Suzanne, knowing it was useless to lie, outlined events of the past two hours. Elenora, reduced to simply shaking her head, contributed nothing but a repeated, "What we going to do, Nana?" to which the old woman answered shortly, "Hush. What's to do is what I doin'."

When the whistling kettle distracted her, Charlotte measured out the aromatic herbs into a chipped ceramic teapot, let everything steep a few moments, then poured the two girls each a full cup and gave herself half a cup. She and Suzanne downed theirs quickly. Elenora, concentrating now on a little vase filled with dusty straw flowers on the wall opposite her, hardly touched her own tea, until her grandmother said, "You drink that all, then pour out what's left in the pot and drink that too. All."

Elenora nodded dully and lifted her cup, taking a healthy swallow, while the old woman nodded approvingly. "All. Your sister and me got one errand to do right now. Don't you be movin' from there."

Charlotte motioned Suzanne to follow her into the hall at the foot of the stairs. "Now," she said, her raspy voice suddenly urgent, "get me somethin' that white man been wearin'. Your sister cut him, so bring me another somethin' with his blood. *Be fast.*"

Suzanne, feeling as if the tea had taken away all her will power, hurried upstairs. From the laundry pile in the corner of her parent's room, she pulled out one of Benny's tee shirts, sweat-stained and pungent from overwear. From the bed she gathered up the bloodstained sheet, rolling these items together into a bundle which she thrust into the old woman's hands.

"Good, good," the old woman nodded. "Now you take care of your sister. That white man don' be botherin' you anymore. But—and you remember this, girl—" The old woman spoke fiercely, yet Suzanne detected a note of sadness in her words. "To buy you safe now will put a cost on you later. That be how such things go. My seein' weren't just' 'bout today—and I was seein' for lots time to be. Little parts—I don' know all that meanin'—but there was blood there. Maybe—" Here the old woman's voice dropped away to so faint a whisper that Suzanne had to lean close to understand her, close enough to smell the warm herb-tea smell that sweetened the old woman's breath. "Maybe this is the beginnin' of more things than any of us be able to dream."

Then she was gone, slipping out the front door with her bundle and closing it soundlessly behind her.

Suzanne returned to the kitchen.

"What should we do now?" Elenora said, settling down her empty tea cup.

"We wait."

"Well, then," Elenora said, seemingly sharing Suzanne's sudden sense of well-being that seemed compounded of the aftermath of their shock; their grandmother's tea; and an unspoken, shared sense that Nana had somehow taken a burden of action off them. "You might as well sit down."

Suzanne sat at the little table facing her. They sat, silently, until evening seeped into the kitchen. Each was lost in her own thoughts, suspended in time. Neither one moved to switch on the lights, even when they could no longer see each other clearly in the dusk.

But the phone never rang, the police never came to the door. Much later, by mutual, silent agreement, they went into the living room, leaving the light on in the hall but not putting on any living room lamps. They were content to sit in semi-darkness, aware of each other's presence, but isolated within the soothing shadows. In the end Elenora fell asleep on the couch and Suzanne dozed off upright in an armchair; they both slept fitfully until morning.

Suzanne's dreams, unrecalled in the morning except for an aftertaste of fear, were filled with strange, terrifying images and recurrent themes of blood.

All day Saturday, they kept in the house. Elenora stayed in her own bedroom which she had abandoned on Benny's arrival; Suzanne restlessly paced the downstairs, from living room kitchen and back again. She kept the venetian blinds down and the curtains drawn, dreading the knock on the door which had to come. Her brief moment of well-being had vanished in the wake of her disturbing dreams.

But nothing happened; no one came.

Late in the afternoon, the phone rang and went on ringing again and again until she could bring herself to answer it, her mouth and throat so dry she could hardly hear her own voice.

"Suzanne?" she heard Nana Chicory ask.

"Yes, it's me. What—?"

"Everything done. You don't be bother by that white man now."

"Nana—"

"I'm tired, chile—bone weary. Don' make me talk no more."

The line went dead.

And Nana Chicory's prediction was true. They heard no more from Benny—or even about him.

In the aftermath of the incident with Benny,

Elenora grew increasingly moody. Suzanne knew that she was phoning in sick a lot to her job. She would lay in bed most of the day, sleeping or staring out her bedroom window into the little weed-choked yard that was fast becoming a jungle.

Suzanne threw out all of Benny's largely filthy clothing. She cleaned their mother's room, removing every trace of him—scouring out the bathroom basin where she found his blood crusted around the faucet, near the old straight-edge razor he always had used, and even using a paste of strong cleansers to remove his traces from the mattress. Finally she took the soiled linen out and stuffed it into the garbage can. Then she threw open the windows for a day and a night to rid the stale traces of him in the air.

When her mother phoned to announce her return in three days, Suzanne took charge of Elenora. She dragged her sister out of bed, helped her dress, and made her sit in the living room and drink a cup of coffee. Elenora made no protest, offered no thanks. She just watched Suzanne with the look of a scientist watching some strange animal in a zoo.

Nana Chicory came by late in the afternoon, insisting that the younger woman share cups of herbal tea with her. Whenever Suzanne asked her about Benny, the old woman waved her questions away with an impatient gesture. Elenora seemed totally disinterested in what the other two were talking about; she excused herself abruptly. When Suzanne started to call her back, her grandmother laid a restraining hand on her own and said, "Let her go . . . you can' undo what's been done anymore than you can change what has to be."

Then Nana had insisted the two of them wash up the dirty dishes stacked in the sink. As they worked, neither of the two women said anything. Later, Nana Chicory, as she was gathering up her worn sweater and purse, leaned up to kiss her granddaughter on the cheek and said, almost sadly, "You the one chose. You got so much *power* in you, chile, I only hope you got the *strength*."

Then she was gone, leaving Suzanne to puzzle over the meaning of those last words. And to return to the pressing question of how much or how little to let slip to her mother.

But Elenora took the decision out of her hands. The moment Thelma stepped into the house and set down her suitcase, Elenora flung herself into her mother's arms, sobbing out a story—changed in many details—of how Suzanne had jealously come between her and Benny and had finally driven the man out of her sister's life, when Benny had (according to Elenora) rejected Suzanne out of hand.

A three-way argument erupted among the Raine women; their confrontation, quickly establishing battle lines between Suzanne on one side and her mother and sister on the other, opened up old wounds, buried grievances, imagined transgressions.

By the time an armed truce had settled over

things, Elenora and her mother had locked themselves in Thelma's bedroom in a welter of tears and recriminations and Suzanne was slamming around her own room, packing for the trip to New York she had so long dreamed about—but which now seemed the only avenue open to her.

She left two days later while her mother and sister stood arm-in-arm, watching stonily from the living room window, and a taxi drove her to the Greyhound station.

So she had come to New York, hoping for a career that never really took shape, unprepared for the passion and consequences her meeting with David Palmer would produce, never dreaming of the tangled web of circumstances that would lead her, so many years later, back to Oakland, to Elenora, to this once unimaginable moment.

The house was still all around her, and she was exhausted; still, Suzanne resisted, for a few more minutes, the sleep that would sweep her into a moonlit dream landscape and still another meeting with the dreamed image of her grandmother, waiting silently in a forest of silver-leaved, silver-trunked trees. The old woman's black skin would be the only relief in a field of intense brightness, save for a little pool of gathering crimson bubbling out of the ground beneath her feet.

THIRTEEN

Two days after his sister's funeral, Kirk Palmer was sitting in his room when Mrs. Custace, the housekeeper, her eyes pink as a rabbit's from private weeping, tapped lightly on the partially opened door and then came a little way inside.

"There's a phone call for you," she said, her voice little more than a whisper.

"Who is it?"

"I'm not sure. Some lady. I think she may work in your father's office. She said something about a memorial service. She said it was very important she talk to you." Mrs. Custace pulled a handkerchief out of her apron pocket and blew her nose. Kirk said, "Thanks, I'll get it." He patted her arm as he went by, feeling as inadequate to deal with her grief as with his father's grief that always turned into frightening explosions of rage.

He knew his father was coming home for the afternoon, but he hated being alone in the house with the man and knowing there was nothing he could say or do to reach out to him—or draw from him any comfort. His father's outrage and anguish left no place for Kirk in his father's thoughts. He hoped that he would come to his own terms with Amy's death in his own time, and nothing Kirk could do would hurry the healing process.

Mrs. Custace had set the receiver neatly on the table next to the upstairs phone.

"Hello, this is Kirk Palmer," he said picking up the receiver. At first he couldn't understand anything the woman on the other end of the line was saying. Something in her phrasing, in the cadence, suggested to him that she might be black. He asked her, "Please talk louder. I can hardly hear you. We must have a bad connection."

"I gots to talk fast," she said. "I 'fraid somebody gonna hear me. I know who killed yo' sister."

There was an abrupt silence on the other end of the phone; Kirk tried to sort through the thoughts and emotions suddenly tumbling pell-mell through his mind. Finally he said, making his voice sound as mature as possible, "Is this some sort of a joke?" His mouth felt so dry his tongue wanted to stick to the roof of his mouth.

"I swear to God, Mr. Palmer, what I'm sayin' is *Gospel*. The man who kill yo' sister be married to my sister. He be drunk last night and braggin' what he done. My sister too 'fraid to say nothin', 'cause that sumbitch kill her or me if he think we tell someone. But I can't go along knowin' what I know 'bout what he done."

There was another pause. Kirk's head was

spinning at the prospect of playing at least a small part in catching Amy's murderer, of helping nail the bastard. Still, he had doubts: some warning in his subconscious was alerting him to the unlikelihood of what he was hearing.

"Why don't you call the police right away?"

"I can't do that. That sumbitch find out he kill me. Kill my sister too, maybe her kids."

"Why call me? Why not my father?"

"Yo' daddy would want the police. I can't take the chance."

Something strange was happening in his head —a sudden headache, like the blade of a red-hot knife jammed between his eyes and running the length of his brain, front to back, threatening to split his skull in two. He felt recurring waves of nausea: his knees felt weak and he could feel sweat beading on his forehead, flooding his armpits. The woman's words seemed to flow into his brain, scaldingly clear, along the edge of the blade. He could feel his doubts dissolving in the heat of those words. Then they coalesced into a coal in the center of his mind and they were everything; and he was agreeing with everything. And, as he agreed to see all that was happening as plausible, the heat cooled away, the sickness left him—but he could still sense her words branded in his mind, implanted in the nerves and muscles of his body.

"How did you get this phone number?" he managed to ask, finally. Curious, not really challenging.

But she only said hastily, "I gots to go. You

wanna know what I can tell you, you *be* where I tell you. And don't be sayin' nothin' to the police or I can't give you no help."

"But how do I know what you're telling me is the truth?"

"When yo' sister died, she be wearin' a necklace. That sumbitch took the po' chile's necklace when he kill her. He was showin' it when he be braggin'—a lady's face with her hair all tangled into trees on a chain. I saw it. I ain't lyin'." He saw it too, around Amy's throat when her father had given it to her on her seventeenth birthday.

Kirk knew that she was telling the truth. The police had deliberately kept that information out of the papers to help them identify the murderer if they caught him—and screen out the cranks who always (the detective had explained) came out of the woodwork to confess to crimes they had only read about in the newspaper. There was no way the woman could know anything about Amy's necklace unless she had seen it. To see it meant she had seen the murderer also.

"Can't you tell me his name, at least?" Kirk asked.

"I gots to go!" She sounded suddenly desperate. "You meet me tomorrow night in front of the DollarSave Market at Sunrise Plaza out in Concord. Can yo' find the place?"

He hesitated, felt his final hesitation disappear in a flash of surprisingly intense, brief pain. Pain and doubt subsiding, he said, "I—*yes*—I can find it." Now his mind was racing.

Concord was a town some miles east of Berkeley and the campus. If the murderer was hiding out in the suburbs, not in the larger East Bay cities, it might explain why the police were as boggled as they appeared to be. Or, he told himself, it was logical that the woman had deliberately chosen some place far away to be sure her brother-in-law didn't find out about her meeting with Kirk. His certainty grew far faster than he could reason it all out.

"You be there 'round eleven tomorrow night. And don' tell no one—*no one*—'bout what I'm tellin' you."

"I won't."

"No police. I smell a single pig and I be gone without tellin' you shit."

"No police," Kirk promised. "Can't—"

He heard the phone slammed down into the cradle; then there was only the buzzing of the disconnected line. Feeling drained, he slumped back against the wall, feeling, for a moment, that he was drowning in the red half-light of the hallway.

Then, downstairs, he heard the front door slam, heard Mrs. Custace and his father exchanging a few words, then heard his father's footsteps approach the front of the stairs.

Now, in the midst of his thoughts, he had the sudden clear impression of his father standing stiffly at the foot of the stairs, his hand resting tensely on the lower end of the railing, knowing he must—yet dreading to—come upstairs. Kirk knew his father very well—knew the man hated to deal directly with unpleasantness, scenes, pain. It was this, more than anything else, that had kept the boy and his father always at an emotional remove. Kirk had never felt that David had been there for him—or for his mother or sister—when they had truly needed his support or simply wanted to share some emotional high with him. His father was always a "closed system," never wanting even his family to demand things—beyond a surface security and reserved politeness—of him. Nor did he want them to involve him in their separate lives.

Kirk had grown to feel *cheated*—convinced that he meant no more to David than the sprawling house on the beautifully manicured lawns, the computer banks that plugged PalmerCo headquarters into branch offices around the world, or the first-rate staff-people like Christine Lee who surrounded him, catered to him, kept the world at one remove.

It was David's secretaries (Kirk had found out) who kept track of the family's birthdays, bought the coolly appropriate gifts, kept David's schedule free on these family occasions so that one of his countless business dinners, cocktail meetings, or less-clear appointments didn't intrude. Kirk had, every early in his life, come to realize that, while he *respected* his father, he couldn't love the man. There simply wasn't someone underneath all the right things said and the carefully maintained image and the generous hand with allowance money to make contact with. David indulged his children, and liked having them around, and let them have their heads (about going to local schools or holding down Mickey Mouse jobs), but he never wanted them to complicate him in the often painful business of shaping their lives. He treated them all well; they were—*had been*, Kirk reminded himself bitterly—an ideal family unit, to show off, to make other people envious, to remind people just how successful David Palmer was as a businessman and father.

The death of Amy, Kirk decided, had complicated David's life unbearably; had involved him with police, intrusively sympathetic friends and staff; had violated the well-run, evniable *status quo* he had built for himself, with his daughter and son as central showpieces.

Kirk was astonished to find his own acknowledged hostile feelings toward his father surfacing so clearly, sharp as a knife-blade, in the wake of the phone call from the terrified, confused woman. Of course, he could not share the information with his father; he felt that his father would use the information only to get back at whoever had dared to screw up the well-run appearances of his life—that the idea of a blood repayment for Amy's life (here the image of his sister's face filled his imagination and flooded his eyes with tears) was the only thing his father could respond to. Someone had stolen his complacency, had taken away his daughter, had cut away a part of his life. And he would have his own back on his own terms. For all David indulged them, Kirk thought bitterly, he indulged them as expensive pets or hobbies—not as persons with real needs for love and comfort or simple sharing.

So now, Kirk welcomed the fact that he—*and he alone*—might crack the case and deliver his sister's murderer to the police. And his father would be forced to see that his children took care of themselves and did the best they could by one another—in life, in death—because their father, for all his posturings, could no more get to the truth of their deaths than he wanted to share in the facts of their lives.

Kirk could feel himself breathing heavily; the thoughts, rebounding through his mind like the Indian clubs of mad circus jugglers, were his own, but they were all couched in the voice of the nameless black woman who had called him. *Him.* Because she sensed that *he*—not *his father*—was the right one to make sense out of the obscenity, the *madness*, of Amy's death.

He started toward the steps to confront David, but the hall below was empty.

Mrs. Custace called from the living room, "Your father had to pick up some papers and go back to the city. He said he won't be home for dinner."

Kirk just stood and stared at the closed front door.

At nine the following evening, Kirk sat in his car in the driveway of his father's house, listening to, but not hearing, a radio interview with some rock star. His key was in the ignition, but his hand was shaking too much to turn the engine over.

"Got to—got—*got to!*" he muttered to himself aloud, loudly slapping his hands on his thighs by way of punctuation. He forced himself to take several deep breaths in an effort to calm his racing mind and pulse.

When he felt sufficiently in control, when his hands were steady enough, he started up the engine and eased the car out of the lot.

He drove as slowly as he dared to compensate for the way his hands and legs continued to shake at periodic intervals.

The road east out of the town carried him to Highway 101 and, at San Rafael, he connected with Highway 17, which ran across the Richmond-San Rafael Bridge to the east side of the bay.

The bridge was nearly deserted at this time of night; through the clear air he could see the distant lights of San Francisco to the south and the increasingly brilliant lights of the oil refineries which sprawled over the low hills at the bridge's eastern exit. Three-quarters of the way across, he felt a lightheadedness bordering on dizziness that forced him into a cold sweat, gave him a terrifying fear of losing control of the little Datsun, slamming it into one of the guard rails.

His fingers slippery with sweat, he turned the radio up as loud as possible, forced himself to sing along loudly, hoarsely, with the Ramones' oldie "I Wanna Be Sedated," and kept control of the little sedan, which was being hassled by buffeting winds that had risen out of nowhere and the shakiness of his own hands on the steering wheel.

Once he was off the bridge, his nervousness subsided somewhat.

The road curved around and eased him into the eastbound flow of freeway traffic moving along the San Pablo Dam Road toward the suburbs beyond the Berkeley-Richmond Hills.

Fifty-five minutes after leaving the bridge, Kirk spotted the "Willow Pass Road—Concord" exit and left the freeway. A few minutes later, he could make out the orange neon sunrise on the sign at the main entrance to the shopping center. The DollarSave Market was at the westernmost end of the island of stores surrounded by a nearly empty parking lot.

It was only ten-thirty. Kirk looked around and found a Little Red Hat Pizza Parlor with its neon signs still alight. Going inside, he sat at one of the long tables near the front windows, nursing a cup of coffee and watching the clock above the entrance. There were few customers and not much talk. The heavy cigarette smoke in the place stung his eyes to tears. *Or maybe,* he thought, *I'm nearly ready to cry all those tears I've been wanting to cry for Amy.*

Maybe after tonight, he thought, when he brought a part of the nightmare to an end, he could allow himself the luxury of tears.

At ten-fifty, he left the pizza parlor, walking back in the direction of his car, which he had left parked in the uneasy pale yellow light cast by the still-burning DollarSave Market sign.

He was worried about whether he and his mysterious caller would recognize each other.

He reassured himself, *Hell! If she was smart enough to find out how to call me, she won't have any problem making sure we meet tonight.* And then he remembered all the photographs of him that had been scattered through the newspapers along with pictures of Amy and his parents. *If she's read a single paper in the last week,* he realized, *she knows what I look like.*

He reached his car without meeting anyone. He stood beside the driver's door, his arms folded, trying to make himself feel as collected as his pose suggested.

He heard her before he saw her, heard the rapid *click-click* of her heels rebounding from the shuttered store fronts. He turned in the direction of the sound. In spite of the warmth of the night, she was wearing a long, dark coat, and her head was covered with a scarf in a green-and-purple abstract pattern. In the mottled light, her face seemed to alternate between black and a bleached, ghostly pale. She was walking unerringly towards him, occasionally glancing behind her as if she were afraid of being followed. Taking a cue from her, Kirk found himself searching in the direction from which she had come for any sign of danger. But the only people he saw were several young couples laughing and smoking under a distant theater marquee and clearly not the least interested in him or the woman.

He congratulated himself for figuring correctly that she would be black, as the voice over the phone had suggested. As she came closer, he saw she had a slender build, with fine hands, graceful fingers, and eyes that were so deep set, they looked like empty sockets; she seemed to Kirk somewhere in her mid-forties. The only makeup she wore was a garish red lipstick that made her mouth look like a wound so fresh it hadn't begun to bleed yet. Still, he had a vague sense of something familiar. When she asked, in a breathless, anxious whisper, "You weren't followed were you, Kirk?" he was doubly surprised to find there was no trace of a deep-South accent in her voice at all and that her voice made him recall suddenly his anger at his father the day before. Had she deliberately been disguising her voice? he wanted to ask.

Instead, he merely answered, "No. I didn't tell anyone about our meeting."

"Good boy," she nodded approval. The green-and-purple scarf fell part way to reveal a close-cropped Afro heavily sprinkled with gray.

He was impatient—eager and frightened—to get the thing over with now, so he asked, "What's your brother-in-law's name? Where is he now?"

She didn't answer directly, but took his arm, pulling him toward the empty buildings, saying, "Let's go over there in the shadows. I know it's my imagination, but I had the impression that Aaron—that's my brother-in-law—may have tried to follow me here. I'd feel better if we weren't in such an open place."

Kirk shrugged and followed her to the corner of the DollarSave Market, then around into a dark receiving area filled with stacked wooden crates. In a tiny alley formed by a loading dock and two immense metal dumpsters filled with wastepaper and garbage, she stopped and turned to the boy. Kirk thought she looked haggard and preoccupied. For the first time he noticed her prim white gloves gleaming little-old-lady-like in a patch of overhead light.

He said rapidly, trying to sound adult, but sensing that his voice was betraying him with its adolescent high pitch and waver, "Just tell me Aaron's last name and where he lives and whatever other information you can give me. Don't worry: I've got it all worked out. I'm going to tell the police I heard it from an anonymous phone caller. Once they know who they're looking for, they'll be able to piece together a case against him." He paused, searching her face for reaction, finding none. Trying another tactic, he asked her, "Does he still have my sister's necklace?"

She nodded vaguely, as if she hadn't really heard him. Then she turned suddenly, looked him full in the face, and smiled in a strange way. "You're a clever boy—just as clever as your father."

Puzzled by what she had said, Kirk just stared at her. Something in her smile and in the tone of her voice bothered him. He asked impatiently, "What's the guy's last name?"

Suddenly something clicked in his brain. He stared more closely at the thin black woman under the yellow-white lights. He recognized the woman who had come to their house shortly before Amy was killed. *What was going on here?* He felt a sudden twist in his guts, an unexpected chill.

A shadow fell across the two of them. Kirk turned to confront the silhouette of a tall, skinny man standing in the entrance to the little alley. The boy couldn't see the man's face, but something urged him to take a step back towards the woman. "Is that Aaron?" he asked her, fear making him nearly inaudible.

She laughed—a throaty, bitter, excited laugh—and said, "Not Aaron. It's only Jomo." She put an arm around Kirk in a familiar way. He tried to shrug free, but she would not let go and her embrace was surprisingly strong. He felt terrified and angry as he sensed himself caught up in a game for which no one had bothered to tell him the rules.

The man-shadow took a step nearer the other two. The woman said in an eager whisper, "Jomo, I want you to meet Kirk—David's son. Kirk, this is Jomo."

Frightened by the bizarre turn things were taking, Kirk twisted himself free of the woman's restraining embrace.

Jomo raised a hand as if he were going to shake hands with the boy. But he suddenly lunged forward, clamping his hands around the boy's windpipe, slamming him back against the cold metal surface of a dumpster. His maneuver cut off Kirk's breath and silenced the shout which never reached the boy's lips.

Stunned, Kirk was aware only of tremendous pain in the back of his head and his throat. His fear took an immediate back seat to the pain and the agonizing need to draw a full breath. He waved his arms, flailing about, trying to get a clawhold on the man's pinioning arms, to no avail. He was aware of the reality of Jomo's hands, of the ribbed fingertips of the man's gloves digging into the soft skin of his throat. Jomo pressed his face so close to the boy's that Kirk was nearly smothered by the stink exhaled from his mouth, with a gush of air that seemed not really breathing; he looked into eyes without a thought except a desire to hurt. The smell of him was fetid: like rotten meat, like something long dead.

He kicked out furiously and caught Jomo in the crotch. He expected the man to double up in pain, but the viciousness of his desperate attack seemed to cause no pain—though it *did* manage to pitch his assailant backward, off balance, loosening his grip momentarily. He scrambled around Jomo, who grabbed for him with a deliberateness which was no match for the boy's desperate speed. The woman, her face now looking as pasty-white as a skull in the light from above the loading dock, stood aside as Kirk pushed past her. She made no protest, and he realized he was going to get away.

Then he was stopped by a sudden unbelievable pain in his back, somewhere between his shoulder blades. He screamed and screamed again. But the only answer was another flash of searing pain, just below the burn of the other. His legs gave out under him as all his being drew into the twin knots of agony and wetness his back had become. His mind kept urging him frantically to *run away*, but his body buckled around him, his head collapsed onto the pavement.

It's over now, he thought abruptly, and then he stopped thinking forever.

While Suzanne wiped clean the blade of her knife with a handful of tissues, Jomo stood stupidly staring down at the boy's body. Whatever animated him him had evaporated with Kirk's final breath. Now he seemed inert as a lump of wood or clay . . . *Lifeless,* Suzanne thought. *Not even what you could call waiting. Not there. Not there until I make him be there.*

This time Suzanne felt no emotion, just a colorless realization that things were going according to plan. She would succeed—was succeeding. Everything was going to be all right. She was proving herself the perfect instrument to be all right. She was proving herself the perfect instrument of Shango's power, though much of the working out of the god's complex web she might never understand.

She looked at her temporarily moribund servant and felt revulsed by his unearthly pallor—almost a phosphorescence—his mindlessly patient stance, the offal smell of him that assailed her nostrils in the thick, warm air.

She dropped the bloodied kleenexes into her purse. For an instant she stood staring at Jomo, trying to make up her plans. She took in the way his greasy, matted black hair lay flat against his scalp; the way the worn-thin stained jacket material stretched taut over his skimpy back; the stink of death that surrounded him. She felt like an executioner standing over her next victim. A quick side-wise slash where the hair met the collar, a single thrust through the faded circle of worn red embroidery, a few muttered words taught her in a dream by Nana Chicory—and Jomo ceased to be a burden. He had almost let the boy escape. If she hadn't been prepared for such an emergency . . .

She loosened, tightened, loosened her hold on the knife. Unexpectedly, Jomo swiveled his head and looked into her eyes.

Though his pupils looked almost normal, there was a *deadness* that belied the surface correctness.

Air was expelled from the lungs in an imitation of breathing; Suzanne nearly gagged on the stench that—almost visible—enveloped her.

The voice that issued, in poor echo of a human voice, had not the slightest resemblance to Jomo's own. It said, "Patience, child. We are not yet finished with this one. He must be there at the end; his part is not yet finished."

In the whispered command, Suzanne heard a little of Nana's voice, and more of the deeply masculine resonance that spoke to her with increasing frequency in her dreams: the voice of one who touched her as lover, child, *god*. She called him *Shango*, but she sensed in him a power beyond a name, an image beyond gender.

She looked at Jomo, heard Shango, surrendered all idea of eliminating the vacant-eyed, mindless thing she called Jomo, before it was permitted.

With a sigh she slipped the knife into one of the inside pockets of her handbag and snapped it shut. She pointed to the still form of the murdered boy.

"Take the wallet out of his pocket," she ordered. "And give it to me." Jomo, moving with the stiff motions of an automaton, bent down and slid the wallet out of the boy's back pocket; with it came his car keys. Jomo handed the wallet to Suzanne. She turned it over several times in her gloved fingers, then put it in her coat pocket. Jomo held onto the key ring attached to a clear lucite rectangle with *KIRK* carved in block letters. He stared at it, apparently fascinated by the way the light caught and danced over the plastic surfaces—like an overgrown child hynotized with a shiny new toy. *Or was there more?* she wondered, suddenly. The dull ache that plagued her whenever she was Jomo's presence had suddenly intensified excruciatingly. She was suddenly aware of white-hot threads tying her mind to Jomo's—threads that were braiding together—*against her will*—into a single scalding band constricting around her forehead, temples —threatening to crush her head in a vise or slice off the top of her skull.

Confused, tears of pain stinging her eyes, Suzanne looked over at Jomo, saw a dangerous new light in his eyes as he held the lucite bauble up to his eyes and made it spin faster and faster while the light glinted and darted with sudden frenzy.

She wondered if she were dying. Keeping his eyes on the whirling plastic, Jomo sank to his knees beside the corpse. Something was wrong, deadly wrong; she was losing Jomo to the light; he was being compelled by something stronger than her. Now he was lifting the already stiffening arm, shoving the jacket back to reveal a length of arm, the flesh tanned and ironically healthy looking, lightly downed with golden fuzz.

What are you doing? She felt the words form in her mind, because the pain that was trying to split her head in two made her unable to speak aloud.

Never taking his eyes off the bit of plastic, he answered simply, *Eat. I am ... hungry. The boy had a lot of life in him, and I am hungry for life.* She could not be sure whether the words were actually spoken or had simply shaped themselves in her mind.

"NO!" she made herself scream the word, though the effort nearly made her faint.

Her word made him look away from the plastic; she felt his defiance waver functionally. In that instant, she reasserted control over him, forbidding him to look at the glitter flickering over the planes and hollows of the embossed *KIRK*. At the same time, the agony in her head subsided to the familiar dull ache.

Before any protest came from him, she summoned up a mental image of the needle diving deeply into his pink tongue. His body jerked convulsively, as if in writhing pain, but he made no further protest.

Envisioning the skull-splinter being pushed

even further into the folds of his brain, she commanded him, "Hand the key chain to me without looking at it. And forget your hunger. We've been here too long already. You are my servant until the god sets you free." When he had done this, she dropped the key chain into her purse. Then she said, "Now we have to go."

She started down the alley; Jomo paused to give the body one final, regretful look.

"Come on—*quickly!*" Suzanne warned. He followed her in silence.

It was all going so well, so well, Suzanne thought as she drove the Volkswagen carefully back to Oakland, except for Jomo's unexpected defiance. And that hadn't amounted to anything very serious so far. He was doing exactly what she had ordered him to do once again.

Still, he would need constant monitoring: his challenge to her had been dangerously strong. And his indicated desire to violate the boy's body had caught her wholly off-guard. She glanced sidewise at him, reassured herself that he was once again *servant*. Nothing in his rigid posture suggested anything else.

She relaxed a little, returning her attention to the freeway ahead.

For now . . .

For now she was at peace with herself and the sleeping world outside. She felt the god's spirit close to her, an unseen presence in the chilly, slightly fetid air of the little car.

As if in a dream, a face appeared—near enough almost for her to touch. The face seemed to serene, so deeply at peace, that she recognized it as a messenger from the spirit-world. It hovered just inches from her own face —the face of a thin-featured, but attractive black woman—almost Suzanne's twin. She longed to touch the wide brow, stretched her fingers out towards the familiar, strange visage—

Then laughed at herself when her fingertips touched the cool glass of the windshield and she discovered that face was—magically—her own.

She studied her face with renewed interest; noting how she still seemed able to detect subtle differences—as if it *were* a twin's face, seemingly identical, yet, to the practiced eye, filled with a hundred differences that stamped this the face of another. A twin: a sister who had never existed. Suzanne's only sister was—had been—Elenora.

Then Suzanne thought she was the features of Nana Chicory hovering behind the reflected features, then momentarily overlaying them, so that she looked into Nana's eyes, and then into her own surprised eyes, staring back at her from such deep settings that she might have been gazing into the empty sockets of a skull.

Then the vision dissolved in the harsh light and noise of a passing truck, and she realized she had almost missed her freeway exit.

She forced herself to pay close attention to her driving. Tonight she had just enough strength left to get them to the silent house on Manningtree Lane; she had no reserve energy to cope with getting lost. She felt drained, utterly. Tonight she would sleep deeply, and trust that her dreams would bring her the strength she needed to face the tasks yet to come.

FOURTEEN

CHRISTINE LEE tossed aside the third magazine she had tried to interest herself in in as many minutes. It hit the coffee table with a loud *thump* that made her start. She reached for her coffee cup and was surprised to find she had drained it completely. She started to get up and fix another cup of instant, then decided she was jittery enough without topping off her caffeine level. Letting herself sink back into the couch cushions, she tried to focus her mind, probe the causes of the nervous state that had followed her out of troubling dreams and had left her on edge all morning.

She was thinking of the deaths of David's children—clearly part of the same plot, but baffling to the police and her own agency. The murders had come from left field—they seemed to fit nowhere in any discernible pattern. But the police talk of a madman, with a vendetta for the Palmers born out of some insane notion, did not satisfy Christine or her co-workers. Certainly, neither David nor his man Dominic gave it any credence.

David had refused police protection, insisting that Dominic was all the protection he needed. And, recalling Dominic's face when the man talked about what he'd do if he got his hands on the childrens' killer, Christine knew he was a man you crossed only at your own risk.

She had met Amy and Kirk during one of their infrequent visits to the PalmerCo offices; she had been impressed by the two of them—and by now untouched they were by the corruption she felt underpinning a majority of David's financial activities.

And she had thought at the time that they were going to be hurt—in spite of David's efforts to keep that corner of his life clean and decent. They were either going to be caught up in the scandal of seeing their father's criminal activities made public—or they were going to be drawn in, little by little, to their father's game. To Christine, one or the other alternative would win out. Either way, Amy and Kirk would be the losers. They were strong, they were independent—but only (she saw what they did not) insofar as David let them have their head.

In time, Christine knew, from the things David Palmer said and the way she saw him use people, he would begin reeling them in, turning their strength and independence to his own ends, making them what he had determined they would be all along.

She tried to feel sorry for the man, but she was always confronted with the fact that his grief had, to her, the bitter flavor of a high-rolling gambler who has bet heavily on a sure thing, then lost everything on an "impossible" turn of the cards.

But where the true gambler might chalk it up to fate, David was chalking his losses up to someone—or several someones. Whoever was to blame for his double loss was going to pay—and pay heavily.

David had told her this, in a series of angry outbursts following Kirk's burial two days before. But it was Dominic Roselli, standing at David's elbow, who had looked across his employer's shoulder at Christine and said, "Sangu lava sangu."

David had merely nodded; but Christine had asked, "What does that mean, Dominic?"

"An old Sicilian proverb," he explained. "Blood washes blood."

He had turned, abruptly, whispered something to David, and walked quickly toward the knot of mourners, signaling his security men to clear a way from the little cemetery chapel to the waiting black limousines outside.

"David," Christine had said.

But he had simply shook his head and muttered, "I'll call you." Then he followed Dominic out into the rich Marin sunshine and into the foremost limousine. Christine had stood for a long time on the top step outside the chapel, looking out across the whorls of curving road and the rise and fall of green lawns lined with sun-bright grave markers.

Far out to the west, clouds were gathering. Though logic said it was only a heavy and early fog, to Christine it looked like massing thunderheads. She imagined an unseasonable storm, and shivered, as though a freezing, storm-driven wind had enveloped her—not the warm, still air that lay thick and lazy over the well-tended lawns and sparkling tombstones.

She thought of the two fresh graves, side by side, in the family plot. She thought of David's eyes searching for whoever had cost him so much, clouds massing on the horizon, and Dominic's words that cut to the heart of it all in an obvious and (to her) deeper way: "Blood washes blood."

Sitting in her apartment, recalling what David's security man had said, Christine was drawn back part way to her nightmares. They were the key, the thread she could trace back to—

No, it was gone. She released it, unwilling to stir up the fears that had clung to her long after the substance of her dreams had faded.

She got up from the couch and looked at the little clock on the end table. It was not yet eleven. Though it was Friday, the PalmerCo offices were closed out of respect for David's double tragedy. It seemed a good opportunity to go in under the guise of finishing some of her legitimate work and take a closer look at David's files. Outside of the security guards, the place should be just about deserted.

She headed for the bedroom to begin dressing.

* * *

The guards on the ground floor of the Palmer-Co building waved her through without even glancing at her clip-on badge with the photograph.

The third floor was deserted. On her hefty key ring, she located first the key to her own office, unlocked it, switched on the overhead and desk lights, then walked across the hall to the Director's office. It was most sensible, she decided, to go about her business openly, as if she was taking care of routine matters only. Anything else could damage her credibility with the security people—and that, she knew, would get back to David in short order.

She nudged the light switch inside David's office and watched the fluorescent panels overhead flicker into life, flooding the room with a ghastly bright light that seemed to leech the color out of everything.

Moving quickly, she unlocked the bank of files marked PERSONAL, for which she was not supposed to have her own key (it had taken her a risky couple of hours to pull off a temporary substitution and fast duplication to get the key for herself during one of David's overnight visits). At the very least, if David found she had it, he would dismiss her on the spot—that presupposed he only suspected her of spying for a competitor. There was also—given the slowly reconstructed perimeters of his connections, locally and internationally—the chance that being discovered with access to confidential documents could very easily place her life on the line as a threat, not only to David, but to other "interested parties."

Swiftly running her fingers across the obscurely coded files in the topmost drawer, Christine extracted those which seemed the most promising. In rapid succession, she repeated her rapid culling of the lower three drawers.

Quickly, her ears on the alert for the sound of an elevator or stairwell door opening, she relocked the file drawers, turned off the lights, and retreated to her own office, hesitating just long enough to make sure the Director's office was securely closed behind her.

With her own door closed, she placed the stack of heavy olive-green file folders on her desk, lifted off the first one, and began a line-by-line perusal of its content.

The first cluster of folders began to help her piece together a better composite picture of PalmerCo's interests in Bukawai.

All of PalmerCo's holdings in and around the capital city of Ajapa were the legal property of several corporate entities: the parent organization, Bukawai Central Construction, Ltd., was set up for the proposed purpose of building a new airport facility and a new highway to the coast as the key to bringing in new industrial and commercial interests—for which B.C.C. would undertake all new construction. And many of the new ventures would be PalmerCo subsidiaries to begin with. PalmerCo, through a transparent use of local personnel and government cooperation, controlled the Bukawai Development Company, established for the management and sale of commercial and industrial real estate. But the key seemed to be Bukawai Amusements, Ltd., the subsidiary organized to take charge of the gambling casinos (and, presumably, less legal "amusements" such as prostitution and drug dealing, Christine thought) brought into the tiny African nation.

She read faster, seeing more and more clearly just how thoroughly enmeshed in the Bukawai government PalmerCo was: it had the ubiquitousness of a dictatorship which had begun under the shelter of the first inedpendent government of the then-emerging nation. Then the new rulers had been too eager to make concessions to bring in foreign investors and unlimited capital. With few exceptions, the PalmerCo operations were free of income tax, profits, tax, real estate tax—even sales tax. Yet, every day, Bukawai's citizens used the airport, highways, schools, land, commercial establishments, electricity and water produced by PalmerCo's various enterprises. The supercorporation and its subsidiaries—a private, tax-exempt megalith—affected the quality of life for a tremendous number of Bukawai's residents from birth to death.

Little wonder, Christine reflected, *that the new Socialist Government, with its veiled talk of "nationalization," "ousting corruption," and "freeing Bukawai of foreign influences," was a primary threat to PalmerCo, International. How could David and his people not be involved in the right-wing attempt to overthrow the legitimately constituted leftist government that posed such a threat to PalmerCo's highly lucrative private reserve? When bribery and graft begin to fail,* she thought bitterly, *you have to set up a new situation where such time-tested techniques will work again.*

There was a soft tap on her door; she looked up, startled, closing the folders instinctively.

Billy Thompson, one of the security guards, smiled at her. "Sorry to bother you, Miss Lee. Just checking. Take it easy."

She mumbled something polite as she closed the door. Christine continued skimming the documents in front of her, seeking anomolies, inconsistencies, clues to the direct links between PalmerCo and the Bukawai civil car.

Inside a folder marked "D. Palmer—Personal Correspondence," she found, inked in David's handwriting:

> D3
> DPALM 124C41Z
> SPX B(1)

The thumbnail-sized inscription was nearly buried at the back fold of the back cover. Unclear exactly why, she copied it down on a piece of paper and pushed it to one corner of her desk.

The second-to-last file, labeled "Miscellaneous Invoices," turned up a single floppy disk of the type used for storage in the computer system on the twelfth floor data center. The label—again, in David's handwriting—read:

> David Palmer—Confidential
> No Unauthorized Use
> D3—SPX B(1)

She reached for her earlier note, instantly recognizing in David's encoded name and the string of letters and numbers an access code to the information stored on the disk. The same hunch that prompted her to copy down the codes now suggested to Christine that the disk might provide a significant piece of information.

From her desk she pulled the keys to the computer room. Locking her office behind her, she summoned the elevator and rode up to the data center.

Her duties routinely involved the use of the computers. She sat herself down at the console, slipped the disk into drive unit, and activated the video display. The single asterisk in the center of the green-tinted screen indicated it was waiting for her commands.

Her fingers moved rapidly, expertly over the keyboard.
BEGIN PROGRAM
INITIALIZE flashed on the screen.
D3. She identified the magnetic disk.
ID
DPALM 124C41

If she had read it right, this was David's personal identification code. The reappearing

asterisk indicated she was proceeding successfully, since no query of ERROR had appeared on the screen. The logical step was to access the disk's directory—if it had one—to get some sense of the information contained. Mentally crossing her fingers, she typed:
DIR-D3

Immediately the screen began tirelessly printing out:
SPX B(1)
AMCNSRT
FUTRXEN
DITRANS
BUCENCO

SPX DD(6)

EAGLEML
WESCHEM
ANCPROP

STOP

Christine interrupted the sequence. The second batch of name codes were familiar, West Coast suppliers and affiliates of PalmerCo; she screened many of their invoices daily, and doubted they had anything to do—except in the most tangential possible way—with the Bukawai question.

The first batch of names, with a (1) priority, looked worth investigating. She had also recognized the "SPX B" tag from David's note.

The machine waited, the incomplete information frozen onscreen. She coded in.

```
RECALL: AMCNSRT
AN ACCESSION NUMBER: 010875 (X)
HN     AMERICAN CONSORTIUM      /CO
       TWELVE OAKS PLAZA        CN
BC/BS  ATLANTA, GEORGIA 30301   HZ
PC/PN  1453   ELECTRONIC COMPONENTS,
TRANSPORTATION, BROADCASTING, REAL
ESTATE, INSURANCE, SAVINGS AND LOAN:
IMPORT AND EXPORT


SD     SALES MIL        $ : 28.3
EX     EMPLOYMENT       : 1,531
PS     PRINCIPLE STOCKHOLDER:
       PALMERCO (AN 011004)
```

Christine had never heard of the company before. She wondered if it was one of the "shadow" organizations, cover entities she knew existed to shield various activities of PalmerCo from government notice.

After a moment, she returned to the DIRECTORY, then typed in:

RECALL: FUTRXEN

The screen cleared, then printed out:

```
ACCESSION NUMBER 010858 (X)    AN
BN:       FUTREX ENTERPRISES   /CO
          P.O. BOX 1131        CN
          SOUTHCREST, NC 28711 BA
```

PC/PN	1156 IMPORT/EXPORT
	SALES MILL $: 5.0
EX	EMPLOYMENT : 421
PS	PRINCIPLE STOCKHOLDERS:
	PVT//
HN	AMERICAN CONSORTIUM
	TWELVE OAKS PLAZA
	ATLANTA, GEORGIA 30301
	(AN 010875 (X))

The "IMPORT/EXPORT" product code told her nothing, but the sudden reappearance of "AMERICAN CONSORTIUM" suggested a larger picture. The "PVT"—privately owned—she found also signifcant.

Christine froze, started for a moment, thinking she had heard footsteps in the corridor outside. Her fingers locked in position over the keys, she heard only the faint hum of the machines waiting patiently for her next command. Quickly she typed in.

EXPAND: FUTRXEN
ASSETS
LIABILITIES
INVENTORIES
INVESTMENTS
PROPERTY, PLANT, EQUIP
REVENUES—

She stopped it, asked it

EXPAND: REVENUES

DOMESTIC/BY STATE
FOREIGN/BY COUNTRY

EXPAND: FOREIGN/BY COUNTRY
ARGENTIAN
BELGIUM
BOLIVIA
BUKAWAI

Her fingers were moving rapidly now; some inner alarm warned her time was running out.

EXPAND: BUKAWAI
CONTINUING OPERATIONS
CASH SALES TO DATE OVERALL
CASH SALES YEAR TO DATE
CASH SALES INVOICE BREAKDOWN/YEAR/
  TOTAL ONLY/FULL READ-OUT
CASH—

EXPAND: INVOICE BREAKDOWN/1981/
  FULL READ-OUT
And there it was: invoices filling the screen with information: a record of numerous arms shipments, funneling East German heavy machine guns and submachine guns, British pistols, Soviet Kalashnikov assault rifles, ammunition—all of it going out under the auspices of "DITRANS," which (she did some fast cross-referencing) expanded to "DIVERSIFIED TRANSPORT SYSTEMS," operating out of Port Melanie, North Carolina, a wholly owned subsidiary of "AMERICAN CONSOR-

TIUM" (read: "PALMERCO"). DITRANS was shipping materials out by sea and air direct to "BUCENCO."

BUKAWAI CENTRAL CONSTRUCTION, LTD.

And BUCENCO, Christine guessed, was surely handling the details on the other end of the line, getting the illegal weapons into the hands of the right-wing Bukawai insurgents. So far, no one—not even her superiors—suspected the full extend of PalmerCo's African adventures. Everyone had accepted the reality of monetary and political meedling; no one had grasped the full extent of their involvement. They weren't merely fomenting a revolution in the tiny nation; they were supplying the hardware—enough to give the rebels twice the firepower the government could manage. Only the fanaticism of the government's supporters had kept the outcome in the balance this long. With the piped-in weapons, Christine realized, there would be little doubt of the final outcome: a bloodbath and a reign of terror that would secure the junta's dictatorship—and, just as surely, secure PalmerCo's Bukawai investments for a long, long time to come.

All Christine had to do now was get a printout of this material and—

"I figured you'd be here, since you were nowhere down on three." For a moment Christine was so startled at the voice cutting through her concentration that she couldn't place it—even though it sounded nearly as familiar as her own. The words and numerals seemed to glare accusingly off the screen at her. Between one breath and the next, she flipped the "off" switch darkening the display screen.

As she swiveled around in the operator's chair, she deftly slid the tell-tale disk out of the drive unit slot, setting it with forced casualness on the ledge to the right of the keyboard. Then she was face-to-face with the newcomer.

Dominal Roselli was watching her from just inside the door to the data processing room. His head was tilted slightly to the left, and shaded by his right hand against the glare of the fluorescent panels overhead. The heavy-set man's eyes were hidden in the shadow of his beefy hand: Christine could not make out any expression—if, indeed, Roselli could be said to have an expressive face under any circumstances. He was wearing a dark suit and tie; twin ketchup smears on his tie and right lapel seemed right in keeping with the slept-in look of his shirt front.

"Dominic," she began, "I—"

"You're a workaholic. I know. We're a lot alike in lots of ways." She tried to read his face, his words, but found her eyes and ears unable to pull anything out of his expressionless face, his nearly toneless voice. "Security thought you might be up here. David—Mr. Palmer—had a hunch you'd be in today."

"David is here?"

"In his office. He sent me up to find you. He wants to see you."

Something in the man's voice put her on her guard. For the first time, she was truly frightened of him. She felt she had glimpsed something chilling—brutal, cold, calculating, which was the substance of the man, far more than flesh, bones, blood.

"What were you working on?" he asked, a genuine note of curiosity in his voice.

"The Blaylock Report—just trying to get a little ahead." She strained to keep her voice even, casual. She picked up the disk and, with a show of routine efficiency walked to the "B" storage drawer and filed it. "I've done enough for today—let's not keep David waiting."

As they headed toward the elevator, Christine let Dominic close up and secure the data center behind them. She walked thoughtfully, refusing to let the threatening presence of Roselli spook her.

As they rode down to five, Christine was aware of the man's sweat, the faint reek of onion, the gagging smell of his drugstore-close-out aftershave.

He watched her, his eyes betraying neither hostility nor friendliness—not even an old familiar horniness. She felt like some insect under the eye of a collector who would, soon enough, chloroform it or leave it to wriggle its life out on the end of a pin—

The doors slid aside; she walked ahead of Dominic toward the open doorway of David's office. She dismissed the panicky thoughts she knew could—if given in to—destroy her effectiveness as an operative. A little healthy edginess was fine; too much, and you might as well disqualify yourself.

David was standing by the window, his back

to her. When he heard her step into his office, he turned and smiled. "Christine. No—" this last to Dominic who had started into the office behind her, "I want to talk to Christine alone."

Out of the corner of her eye, she saw Dominic shrug and draw back, closing the door behind him.

When they were alone, David said, "Jesus, I missed you—" His voice had the soft sluggishness that betrayed his bone-deep weariness.

She began, "If you'd only called—"

He shook his head. "I move by fits and starts these days. I'm so busy trying to—" sudden anger flooding him, sweeping aside his weariness, "find out what the *hell* is going wrong—what I can do to get back in control. *And I am going to re-take control.*" He slammed his fist into the window frame; the impact made her start. She couldn't get an accurate read-out of his anger. Was it the terrible loss of his daughter and then his son? Or was it the fact that events—"persons unknown"—had dared turn his life inside out? Either explanation seemed to apply. With surprise, Christine realized how little she knew this man. She could only guess at his real feelings: she felt like a swimmer who suddenly looks down to find she has left the shallows unwittingly and is making her way over unimaginable depths in which frightening shapes glide and wait. Out of seemingly nowhere came the unwelcome thought that David had been hiding most of what he was from her. Now, for whatever reason, he was letting her see more clearly into just what deeps she had ventured.

He suddenly grabbed her, pulled her to him. His lips covered hers; his tongue probed past her lips, half-parted in a stifled protest. Locking his hands behind her head, he pulled her face toward his throat, while he whispered huskily in her ear, "Come with me now. Home. I need to make love to you. Jesus, I need you!"

He was crushing her face against his skin now, she could feel his whiskers abrading her skin, nearly smothering her. Her nostrils were clogged with his *Van Cleef & Arpel* cologne. She pushed free of him, taking a deep breath, laughing a little uneasily as she warned, "Easy now—*easy.*"

He let her pull back a fraction, but the circle of his fingers and thumb slid down her arm to lock around her wrist. She looked questioningly into his eyes, and saw in his face that she had no choice in the matter. "I've given the housekeeper a week off to visit her sister. Except for the security people Dom has arranged for, we'll have the place to ourselves. I'm not going to be alone tonight." This last was a statement of absolute fact.

She said, her protest sounding weak, "My work—the reports—"

"They'll wait. I won't. Come now." The grip on her wrist tightened just perceptibly. In another of her unwelcome flashes of insight she sensed for the first time how much strength the man was—barely—keeping in check. She glanced down at his hand imprisoning her wrist, saw the way the tanned fingers were dusted with light golden hairs—and saw that those fingers could snap her wristbone with minimal effort. "My car is in the lot," he said.

"I'll get my jacket—it's in my office."

He released her, then followed a pace behind her while she crossed to the door and opened it.

Roselli was leaning against the wall opposite. He had turned off the fluorescent lights immediately overhead. In the muted light of the hallway, he was scratching at the stain on his tie, scraping away the dried ketchup.

He looked up inquiringly as they exited David's office. David, pausing to lock the door behind him, said, "Christine and I are going back to my place."

Dominic, smoothing his tie down over his rumpled shirtfront, asked, "Want me to come?"

Christine, crossing to her own office and retrieving her coat, heard David say, "No. You finish up here. Come by this evening. I'll want a full report later."

Roselle nodded as Christine came out, slipping into her windbreaker and locking her own door.

The three of them rode down to the lobby in silence. On the main floor, Roselli turned aside to talk to his security people and David, his hand cupped under Christine's elbow, urged her toward the main entrance.

As she walked along nearly double-time-march to match David's impatient pace, Christine found she was dreading her visit to the house which had been so filled with death.

And she was even more mistrustful of the

man beside her who was no longer the familiar —if dangerous—commodity. In her acutely sensitized imagination, she now saw him as unknown territory to which nothing—not her "company" briefing of her own experience— provided any map. The familiar landmarks were gone. As the two of them stepped out into the cooling, fog-flavored afternoon air, she sensed unmistakable danger where she had needed only exert reasonable caution before. Somewhere inside her brain, she heard a child's cry—the child she had once been?—fading, fading, as though tumbling into a darkness deeper than forever.

Get ahold of yourself, Christine warned herself. *You're too close to the big payoff to go to pieces now. Twenty-four hours and the game is yours.*

"My car is over there," David said.

Inhaling a deep, calming breath, Christine followed him toward David's parked Mercedes.

FIFTEEN

CHRISTINE OPENED her eyes on a room filled with diffuse gray light. She turned her head to the side and saw fog pressing damply against the bedroom window. Exhaling deeply, she rolled onto her back and let her dream dissolve—already, for the most part, forgotten—in the chilly air of the unfamiliar room. She ran her hands back and forth over the sheets beneath the blankets, luxuriating in the unreality of it all.

His side of the bed was empty. A quick glance at the clotheshorse in the corner of the room showed that his shirt and pants were gone too. She must have been incredibly tired not to have felt him leave the bed or heard him begin dressing. David was never able to do such things quietly. *I must have been dead to the world,* she thought.

She remembered what she found the day before: the computer disk with the information about PalmerCo's Bukawai connections. *The disk.* It was still buried in the storage bin. And the confidential files were still stacked in her desk drawer. *If only David—*

She was fully awake now, kicking free of the covers and sliding from bed.

Where is David?

Careless of the chill on her naked skin, she slid from the bed and began to gather up her clothes from a tangle on the floor near the foot of the bed.

The bedside clock showed 10:17. *Jesus! How could I have slept so long?*

She threw on her clothes, then hurried into the bathroom to pull a quick comb through her hair. She had to get back to the office, recover the disk, and hide her tracks. Then call Harry, and put the whole operation into final phase.

Christine splashed cold water onto her face and toweled it off quickly. She was buttoning her blouse as she stepped into the hall and ran down the staircase, to make a quick survey of the house—then make her call to Harry if David had left her on her own for whatever reason.

David was sitting on the couch as she stepped through the wide archway into the living room. "Good morning, Christine," he said. But his voice was toneless, edged with steel. His eyes locked on hers with the same contained ferocity she had felt in his grip the day before.

Dominic Roselli, rising from a wingchair just outside her line of vision, said only, "I think you left this in the wrong file, Miss Lee." He was holding the computer disk in his hands, as he added, "I think this more properly belongs in Dr. Palmer's office."

She turned to run out, Roselli was too fast for her; he threw himself at her, and caught her by the arm—nearly wrenching it loose—spinning her halfway around, then slamming her into the wall. The impact turned the side of her face into a dizzying swirl of pain.

Stunned, Christine felt Dominic half-drag, half-carry her back to the living room and shove her brutally into the chair he had vacated only seconds before. When she immediately tried to push herself to her feet, he slapped her once, viciously, and she collapsed back into the cushions, her head ringing. A dull inner voice throbbed in time with the pain, telling her relentlessly, *It's over. You're finished. It's over. You're finished.* Tears of pain and frustration blurred her field of vision. She could hardly see the two men. But she could hear them clearly enough.

"Dominic did some filing yesterday," David said. "You were very careless, Christine. This file belongs in my office—not in storage in data processing. I'm afraid such carelessness merits immediate reprisal. This is going to cost you your job—"

Christine said nothing; she moved her fingers to her face and discovered her nose was bleeding. She wiped the blood away as best she could.

"This," David added, "is going to cost you a lot more. When you play for high stakes, you forfeit a lot when you lose."

"You're going to have hell to pay yourself," she said, her voice sounding liquid through the blood and mucus filling the back of her throat. "Industrial spying for a competitor doesn't give you the right to assault and—"

"Save it!" David said. She could see his palm upraised to her in a cut-off gesture. "We know who you're working for. It's just a question now of finding out how much you know. How much *they* know. And what we have to do to keep things from blowing wide open."

She had blinked away most of the tears now. She could see him turning the incriminating disk over and over in his hands, never once taking his eyes off her. "I didn't want it to turn out this way," he said, more to himself than to either of the others in the room. "But everything goes to shit, sooner or later." Now he was looking directly at her. "Sooner or later, it all comes down to saving your own skin. And for you to win, means somebody elses loses. That" the disk, cradeled inhis fingers, was still now, "is a fact of life."

She considered making a break for it; but she *felt* as much as saw Roselli looming like a watchdog over her. She decided to bide her time and hear David out. She might learn something useful she told herself—refusing to accept the likelihood that nothing she knew or learned would make the least difference in a very little time.

"I had a son once. A daughter," David said, playing with the disk again, seeming to speak to it. "They're gone. Maybe you had something to do with that—"

"*Never!*" she shouted, sickened by the idea, the horror of what he was suggesting momentarily obscuring the danger of her present position, "I could never—"

"Shut up!" David said, tossing the disk carelessly into a corner of the couch. "You don't talk. You listen. And—later—you *talk*. You tell us everything we need to know."

"But—"

"Dom—" David said, gesturing to his security man.

Roselli loomed closer, his fist upraised.

Christine shut up.

"For the moment," David said, in the same impersonal tone of voice he used when dictating letters, "we are going to move you to the guest cottage in the grove at the back of the lot. That's for," he paused, then smiled mirthlessly at her, " *'preliminary questioning.'* As our guest. If we, um, don't get everything we want, we're moving you to my cabin in Sonoma for a longer stay and what we will *politely* call 'more extensive questioning.' "

Crazy, she thought. *Jesus-God, the man is crazy.* But she said nothing; she kept her eyes locked on his, while her mind formulated and discarded plan after plan for escape.

"Dominic," David said, with a little sigh, "can be a *most persuasive* questioner. He would have done the Inquisition proud. Dominic is a man born too late for his time; he rarely gets the opportunity you'll be providing him."

She shook her head frantically back-and-forth, but did not dare open her mouth.

"On the contrary, *yes,*" David corrected. "For my kids, it's all over. But for you, Christine, it's only just beginning."

He gestured again and, before she could say anything, or even move her head, Dominic punched her on the side of the head and she lost consciousness.

On the Oakland side of the Bay, the fog was beginning to burn away. Suzanne, dressed in one of Elenora's shapeless, warm housedresses, padded down the upstairs hall in a pair of Elenora's scuffed slippers. Her arms were folded across her breasts; she had pushed the sleeves partway up; and now she chaffed her skin, trying to warm herself enough to get the stiffness out of her wrists and fingers.

Her mind was a jumble of thoughts, with one certainty only: *she would have to move quickly.* In her mind, she could sense Jomo asleep. But he would awake long before evening—hungry for lifeblood again, harder for her to control—soon, she knew, he would slip beyond her control and be worse than useless. He would be a threat to her. She could feel the flooding, building hatred in him. The longer he hovered between life and death, the longer the ultimately irreversible—only delayed—process of corruption had to work its way on his flesh, the more aware of his own state of death-in-life he grew, the greater his hatred of her became.

In a short time, his rage at his own disintegration would overcome all her commands, all the waning magics she could command. Nana Chicory had warned her of this in recent dreams, many times over. Soon he would reach a point where he would fall on her and tear her piece from piece if she lowered her guard for a moment. She would have to act fast, act soon.

She went downstairs to the kitchen to fix herself a cup of Nana's special tea. She felt tension throughout her body: a near-panicky feeling that time was running out too fast for her to take care of everything yet to do. She was bound to a sequence of events that she dared not violate, but the time element was all screwed up. Jomo had taken away a margin of hours—perhaps days.

Sitting in the kitchen watching curls of steam twisting up off the tea in front of her on the littered table, Suzanne sorted through a maze of thoughts, trying to formulate a plan.

David must die now, she realized.

She thought again of Jomo—growing more unruly as he grew stronger—and wondered how long she had before he broke free of her control altogether. He would have to be eliminated—his physical body destroyed completely—before he would die a second, unalterable death.

Time is running out, she warned herself. Then she realized there were still things she could do, powers she could make use of.

She crossed to the wall phone near the door to the back porch. Dialing from memory, she called David's home in Marin.

After several rings, David Palmer answered. "Hello. *Hello,*" he said impatiently.

The sound of his voice momentarily immobilized Suzanne; the receiver in her hand suddenly threatened to burn her. She gripped it as though it might come alive and writhe free of her hold.

"Damn it! Who *is* this?" David demanded.

Suzanne got control of herself. She tightened her grasp on the instrument and created in her mind the picture of a needle that was really the deadly sharp extension of the phone cord she held fisted in her free hand. In the time between David's one audible breath and the next, she pushed herself to the limit of her power, reaching through the phone line to touch her mind to his. It was an intimacy, a violation, a melding of the two of them beyond anything she had experienced while they were living together. She felt it as a sexual rush and a gross obscenity. Simultaneously, she wanted to open herself to him, and she wanted to vomit the sudden intrusive sensation of him out of her physical body.

She imagined the white-hot tip of the thick, rigid wire probing the soft gray folds of the man's brain, stimulating compliancy here, a false sense of well-being there. The envisioned wire-needle had a white-hot extension into her own brain.

Suzanne heard David gasp—in pain or surprise or both—and dearly hoped she was able to hurt him, even in this limited way.

"Who—?" he began again; but now the anger

and impatience were gone from his voice. Only a mixture of fear, confusion, and pliancy remained.

She started to speak, but found the steadily intensifying pain in her head and the links (physical and mental) with David had robbed her of her voice. She licked her lips and swallowed several times, before she could make herself audible. "Where will you be today?" she finally managed to ask him.

When he failed to respond, she ordered, *Tell me!"*

"Here," he answered woozily, like someone rousing himself ineffectually from a deep sleep. "I'll be—here. I have—things to do."

"At the house—your house?" she questioned.

"Yes—no. Not always." He paused; Suzanne had the impression he was struggling against her control, floundering toward volitional integrity like a drowning swimmer struggling towards the surface and air.

The pain in her own head threatened to burst it apart. The phone in her hand, against her ear, felt molten. She could almost feel the skin of her fingers, the side of her head, charring where flesh met plastic. "Be exact," she commanded. "Where will you be?"

"Here, for a short time. Then, in the—the guest cottage in—in the—grove of trees, behind the house."

"How long will you be there?"

"As long as it takes—to—to learn—to learn what I *have*—to know."

"Who else will be there?"

"Roselli. Chris—Christine."

She could not go on. The pressure in her ringing ears, behind her throbbing eyes, at her throat—the unmanageable pressure that was threatening to blow her apart could no longer be contained. Unless she released David, let the mental wire-needle dissolve, she risked aneurism, hemorrhage, death.

Fighting against the flaring pain-centers and pressure as intense as that on a submarine plummeting out of control into unimaginable deeps, Suzanne forced herself to tell David, "When you hang up, you won't remember any of this. It was all a—wrong number."

"Wrong number," he repeated.

"Hang up on this wrong number now, David," she told him.

He did.

Her head aching, Suzanne hung up the phone. Ignoring the pain as best she could, she reviewed everything that David had told her.

Once again, she found herself wondering if—in time—she would be able to kill at a distance by intensifying the powers of control and suggestion she had.

But time was a commodity she had too little of.

And, she sensed, the real problem, as always, was her own emotions. When she had too much of an emotional stake, as when she imagined hurting David, she lost the control she needed to focus her gift in and project it like a pencil-thin laser. When she imagined David's face, voice, body, she lost the power, felt it diffuse in a hundred different directions. She had barely been able to use it on David's son over the phone; the confrontation with his daughter had so filled her with unexpectedly confused emotions that she had been unable to use it at all.

David, she thought bitterly, was protected simply because of her bone-deep hatred of him. Paradoxically, her desire to strike back at him served to shield him from Suzanne's unruly power.

Her tea had grown cold; but she continued to sip it anyway, while she waited for the worst of her pain to subside.

David's voice, the feel and taste of him, stirred up memories in her like unexpected currents might churn up the sediment at the bottom of a stilled, almost forgotten pool . . .

Though it was early morning as she sat in the kitchen of her sister's house, drinking cold herb tea, Suzanne's mind was no longer in Oakland: she remembered herself sitting in the semi-darkness of her old apartment in New York. Elenora's stiff-backed kitchen chair had been replaced by a wooden rocking chair Suzanne had bought in a secondhand shop on Bleecker Street. She was feeling dizzy; the slight forward motion of the rocker kept threatening to pitch her onto the carpet, in which was wine-colored with a pattern of sprinkled black roses. Her head was throbbing; she felt almost ill.

The silence disturbed her. She wanted to play the radio, but she remembered the child was asleep in the tiny bedroom down the hall.

She moved her right foot carelessly over the rug in a arc, back and forth. On the third sweep, her foot connected with some glass. She leaned back and discovered she had knocked over a nearly empty wine glass. A few drops had spilled onto the rug; but, since the wine and carpet were nearly the same burgandy color, it didn't seem to matter much. Only the baby mattered, anymore.

David was becoming a stranger to her. Only the child, Nathan, mattered; and he was sleeping safely in his crib.

She nudged the glass with her toe, sent it rolling a short distance. How much wine had she had? She couldn't remember. *Too much*, if she couldn't remember.

She looked at her hands, clutching like an old woman's hands at the carved rocker arms. Like Nana Chicory's, the last time she had seen her grandmother.

He had made her this way; he had given her the child, but he had taken away everything else —himself. She was adjusting; but there were still moments when she felt old, tired, lost.

She was alone tonight because he was out at a political meeting. Or so he said. When she challenged him, he no longer bothered to deny her challenge that other women were the real reason.

When they had first become lovers, she had managed to convince herself that something real was happening between them. Loving him as much as she did, she had allowed herself to become disoriented, capricious, helpless in the wake of emotions no one had ever stirred up in her before and too which she swore—*swore*—she would never fall victim again.

She stared regretfully at the wine glass she had knocked over, aware that he still had more of a hold over her than she liked to admit.

The apartment smelled of grease and dust and the overripe stench of the thick, hot, moist summer air that pushed in through open windows and closed doors with equal persistence.

It had rained just before dark: warm, oily, flat drops which turned the streets and alleys into a steambath.

And where was David? He knew how afraid she became when she was alone at night. But he had stormed out of the apartment that morning shouting—as he had shouted so many times before—that he would not be coming back to her sullenness, her accusations, her coldness. To the child he feared because it was her only tangible claim on him.

What time was it? she wondered. She made an effort, and this time succeeded in reaching the window. She pulled back the drapes and looked at the clock on the building just across the street. 2:10, according to the clockface framed in a double circle of blue neon. Overhead, the New York City sky-glow hid the stars behind a veil of light.

She remembered that she had promised

herself a nap at some point earlier in the evening—but she had never intended to sleep so long. She turned, facing the half-closed glass doors into the hallway; she listened, but there was no sound from the child asleep in the next room. She remembered how upset Nathan had suddenly become earlier in the evening: he had worked himself into a frenzied crying until she had managed to soothe him. He must still be exhausted now, sleeping peacefully.

She flattened the palm of her hand against the cool glass of the window, then pressed it to her face, transferring some of the coolness to her burning skin. Was it the wine? Or did she have a fever?

Suzanne froze suddenly. She had heard the faintest sound—the least whisper—from somewhere back in the apartment.

Had Nathan cried out?

She listened, her back to the window, staring into the darkness. Her right hand held to the window frame: she still felt unsteady on her feet.

Simultaneously she heard the sound of something smashing in her bedroom and the startled cry of her child. Thinking only that her baby was in danger, she lurched across the room towards the tiny hallway. There were more sounds, careless sounds, from her bedroom. The door, open when she had last checked on the child, was closed now. From beyond came the crazy sounds of random breakage and soft, ghostlike mutterings. Through the door filtered also the frantic yells of her son. Her only thought was for his safety.

She threw the door open; saw no one at first; grabbed the baby from the corner of the crib where he stood, leaning into the angle formed by the juncture of railing and head of the battered old second-hand crib. His foot was caught in a tangle of sheet which she frantically unwound.

She had just freed Nathan, when a fist slammed into the small of her back, smashing her against the crib slats and knocking the wind out of her. She guessed instantly that her assailant had hidden behind the door when she pushed into the bedroom.

Somehow, she managed to hold onto the hysterical infant. Gasping for breath and forcing herself not to be sick, she pulled him tightly to her. She didn't dare turn around.

Then a hand slapped her a ringing blow across the side of the head and a voice said, "You pay *attention* when I talk to you, woman!"

She was spun around to confront her attacker, a slender young white man. His thin, olive-colored features were dewed with sweat that glowed in the orange light from the single lamp she had left burning in the room.

The man pushed her roughly back against the crib. Her eyes on the intruder's face, she set the screaming child back in the crib.

"Please," she said. "My baby . . ."

"Shut the little bastard up. *Now.*"

His eyes had an odd, dilated look to them. He

blinked continuously, as if even the muted light in the room hurt them. He moved in abrupt spasms—foot out, leaned on, drawn back; arm suddenly thrust out, pulled back, dropped to his side.

Suzanne placed her fingers on the child's lips, saying, "Oh, Honey, don't! Hush now, quiet for Mama. Baby, it's going to be all right." Her hand was trembling; she begged Nathan, "Be still, for the love of God, be still." Now her hand was shaking violently; she was soaked in sweat; her stomach hurt where she had been slammed into the side of the crib. She fought back the taste of vomit.

"You see, you see—it's the money I need." The man was talking compulsively, though most of what he was saying was incomprehensible to Suzanne. For the main part, he seemed lost in a tirade against someone who had been "riding" him for a long time, a man, apparently.

There was an explosive sound as the nightlight was swept from the dresser and hurled across the room to smash in the far corner. The room was plunged into darkness, except for streetlight filtering through the thin curtains. *My God*, Suzanne thought, *where are the neighbors? Sure to God someone downstairs must wonder.* Should she scream? Did she dare? She couldn't: her mouth was too dry, her throat was paralyzed with fear.

Nathan struggled free of her fingers to begin screaming again as loud as he could.

She could hear the man muttering to himself

as he walked back and forth behind her; he was breathing heavily, almost painfully. The room smelled of sweat and fear. Suzanne felt dizzy, but hung onto consciousness for the sake of her child. She must protect the baby at all costs.

Nathan yelled with all the desperate energy his tiny body could produce.

"I told you, shut him *up! I told you!*" He lunged for the crib. Suzanne screamed, "No!" and grabbed at the man as he fumbled for her child. He shrugged her off, but she clawed at his shoulders, feeling the shiny fabric of his shirt give, digging her nails into the sweat-soaked, unexpectedly soft skin underneath. She shouted, "You *won't. I. Will. Not. Let. You. Hurt. Him."* She threw herself backwards; her fingers having found firm purchase, she pulled him off balance. Her nails tore deep furrows in the sweat-gleaming flesh.

The man bellowed and jabbed his elbows back into her midriff, winding her. She let go, doubling over with pain; then she dropped to her knees.

Her head lolled back on her shoulders; she discovered he was looming over her, like a violent shadow. Then his suddenly immense fists rose and slammed down on her again and again, until she was too battered to do more than try to shake her head and plead for him to stop. But she had no voice, no will, and finally, not even a protest to make to this merciless shadow that was filling her mouth with the taste of blood, her ears with ringing, and her mind with a kinder darkness which swallowed up her pain and fear until there was nothing but the darkness and Nathan's terrified screams which penetrated the darkness when nothing else could.

Then even that was gone—

She awoke to stillness and only gradually became aware of the distant sound of a neighbor woman calling her name. She was lying on her back. Her lips were bruised and swollen; she could taste blood in her mouth, though her questioning tongue could discover no missing teeth. There was blood at the back of her nose and throat.

Her head was throbbing; the ringing in her ears rose and fell in intensity. The front of her blouse was ripped away; she was aware of a burning, stinging pain between her legs. Everything was dark, so she pushed her hand down, discovered her skirt in a tangle around her hips; her panties had been pulled down around her knees. She touched her genitals and, frightened, brought her fingertips to her nose. They smelled of blood and sperm.

She began tossing her head from side to side, sobbing, "No. . . no. . . no . . ."

There was a hammering on the front door of the apartment; a male voice was shouting, "Police! Open up!"

Something she had forgotten—

More pounding and shouting.

Something that was more frightening than her pain, than the . . . violation of her very being. Something she had forgotten—

She forced herself into an upright position, sitting on the floor. She didn't trust her legs to support her. She inched he way back until she was leaning against the wall.

Heavy hammering at the front door; the sound of splintering wood; the protest of the safety chain being ripped from the doorjamb.

Her back still against the wall, she used her legs to push herself up far enough to reach the light switch. Her hands shook with fear of what the light would reveal, but she made them fumble the lights on.

The room exploded from darkness to mind-wrenching clarity.

She gagged, pressing her hands to her bleeding mouth, when she saw the bloody wreckage amid the red-spattered crib sheets—

Then she found her voice and the screaming began—

And continued to this moment in every corner of her soul.

Suzanne was on her feet now, moving aimlessly around the kitchen. She had pushed away so violently from the table, she had overturned her tea cup, spilling the dregs. She was not healed yet; she would never be. Though she had let herself remember what had happened, she was—as always—unprepared for the violent emotions remembering still aroused in her.

She hugged herself tightly as if she could console herself for a misery that filled every corner of her being.

But when her remembered grief had become

almost unendurable, when only pressing both hands across her mouth could hold in the screams which, unvoiced, strained her throat muscles to near bursting—then her grief was (as it always was) transmuted into a different emotion: hatred. And she found once again the reasons it was necessary that she never forget: her memory of that night was the ultimate assurance that she could and would do everything that was demanded of her.

She thought again of David Palmer. And she saw in her mind his two green-eyed children as they appeared in the gold-framed photographs.

Hatred flashed in her fingertips and face, feet and stomach; it ignited every nerve of her body.

She blamed David for the death of the child. She knew—*knew*—the truth of her accusation, though her friends, her doctors, the social workers, the police had all conspired to convince her that she was imagining things, trying to transfer her guilt to her common-law husband, who had somehow managed to absent himself from the aftermath of the child's death, who had made it clear on the one occasion when she got through his many phone screens to David himself, that he no longer wanted her in his life. He had hung up on her. And she had begun screaming and smashing the receiver of the phone against the wall of the phone booth, imagining she was pounding his face, while the fragments of plastic flew like black chips of bone and several astonished male passersby tried to force open the accordion door of the booth she was stubbornly holding shut with her other hand . . .

But it had not all come together until she had bought a ticket to see David's candidate speak at a fund-raising benefit. She had gone hoping to have a chance to talk to David, wanting to give him the chance to lay to rest her terrifying suspicions.

She had sat in the stuffy hall, fidgeting uncomfortably on an unsturdy wooden chair, hearing nothing of the candidate's empty promises, but watching David, who sat on the dais with two dozen other apparently rapt listeners, their pale foreheads gleaming damply under the overly bright lights.

Then, amid the waves of applause and the rush of enthusiastic supporters and patrons to crowd around the speaker, Suzanne made her way across the speaker's platform and behind the curtains, determined to confront David with a catalogue of her grievances and her hopes.

She stopped, her hand grasping the material of the drapery alongside her.

She saw David, talking angrily to the thin-faced white man the police had never been able to trace. She saw the two men yelling at one another, then saw David shove some cash at him —saw the man stare at the money in his hand, then angrily grab at David's arm, only to have David turn around, slam his hands, palms outward, into the man's chest, tumbling him backward into a cart of electrical equipment, upsetting it.

Blue-uniformed security guards hurried to intervene. The man began to yell something, but he was silenced—one meaty hand was clamped over his mouth, a fist slammed into his stomach. The man slumped in the guards' arms. The three guards glanced at David, who shrugged, made a single quick gesture of dismissal. In her gut, Suzanne knew the thin murderer was finished—just as surely as she understood that David had sent the man to eliminate her and the child. Only, in his drugged state, he had somehow botched it.

She knew she had seen his death warrant signed.

She wanted to scream out everything David had done and was doing—to her, to others. But what she had seen terrified her, froze the words in her throat.

Then David's eyes locked on hers; she felt her lips forming words that meant nothing to her.

There was only raw hatred in his eyes; he signaled the guards.

She ran for her life, terrified to seeing him sentence her to non-existence with a quick movement of his finger across his throat. She shoved her away through the crowd of annoyed, astonished onlookers, while, behind her, David's security forces shouted for her to stop.

Then she ran on the street, running, running —afraid to go home. She rode the bus until 3:00 a.m., when she deposited herself, gasping for breath and sobbing, at the apartment-house of a social worker in Brooklyn who had expressed sympathy for Suzanne's case when when she had visited the latter in the hospital.

Days later, when she had pulled herself together enough to decide that bringing David to some sort of justice was the most important thing in her life, Suzanne had begun the endless rounds of talking to sympathetic non-believers in a variety of professions.

They had all concluded the horrors she had undergone had deranged her temporarily. They patiently explained to her that no agency had turned up a shred of evidence to link David to the murder of her child. Repeated investigations confirmed that no one vaguely resembling the man she described in such detail had ever been seen around David. David's friends and associates had closed ranks defensively around him.

When no one would listen, she talked to herself during the days and to Nana Chicory and other shadowy figures in her dreams.

Then David's candidate was discredited, the government began investigations into his alleged underworld connections with his campaign, and David himself disappeared from her view—from everyone's.

But now she knew. David had simply walked out of her life and into another life: replaced her with a real wife and produced a son and daughter to substitute for his real, only son who had been murdered. He had built himself a new life and left her forever among the ruins of her own. For a long time, her feelings of guilt (she *had* been drinking; she *had* forgotten to lock the window near the fire escape; she *had* lost her head and panicked when she *should* have *forced* herself to remain calm for the sake of her son) had nearly overwhelmed her. It was only the dream-talks with her grandmother that made her realize that none of that mattered at all. David had engineered the murder, which had only failed because it had not eliminated her too. She and the baby were an inconvenience to his plans; the death of Nathan and the attempt on her life had been, for him, an easy out.

Small wonder that she hated him. Her hatred had brought her back several times from the brink of suicide, with the vow that she would not rest until David had been repaid for the suffering he had cost her. He had no right to another family, another start, another life. He no longer had a right to life at all.

So much he had to account for, even before one considered the murders and anguish he was purchasing half a world away in Africa.

His children. Then him. As her dream-visitors had commanded. Her way was clear to David; now she had taken all the necessary preliminary steps to bring her to the moment upon which all the complexity of event-threads were converging.

Satisfied that she was pursuing the only possible course of action, Suzanne left the kitchen. She did not bother mopping up the spilled tea. Such things simply no longer mattered to her.

She would dress; she would rouse Jomo one

final time. In the early evening, together, they would go out to David's and exact the blood payment Shango's infinite wisdom and her own aggrieved soul demanded.

SIXTEEN

LATE AFTERNOON sliding into early evening. Under the scattered trees on the rolling hills surrounding Tiburon, the pooled purple shadows lengthened eastward across the green-brown landscape.

Suzanne, who had insisted on driving, had parked Jomo's sorry red Volkswagen under twin oak trees beside the road leading out of Chetwynd a few hundred yards short of the entrance to Balboa Court. She could see the little white-painted gate set tidily in the carefully cropped, waist-high hedge. The house, partially shaded by oak and fir trees lay cool, distant, intensely white—as though it had somehow absorbed the afterglow of the rapidly westering sun. Smudges of cloud marred the deepening blue sky; heat lay thickly over the landscape; swarms of midges floated in the comparative cool of the shade under the interlocking branches of the oaks. No breeze came in through the rolled-down car windows—only a press of heat that lay, like warm cloth, against

Suzanne's face. The gagging odor of corruption filled the car to near-choking.

Suzanne concentrated on the house, trying to gauge what lay hidden beyond the blank, two-story facade. Her searching eyes picked out details with almost more-than-human ability; the flecks of red blossoms on the massed rosebushes along the driveway; the slightly off-center tilt of the white-painted post that supported the old-fashioned mailbox; the thick, rich green paint on the window-trim, shutters, front door.

The door opened. A heavy-set man in a dark suit stepped part way out onto the porch. Both hands were bracketed over his eyes, as though the mellowing light of eventide was too glaring for him to bear.

She watched—not even, at the distance, and screened by the roadside oaks, as she was, daring to breathe or move, for fear he would discover her and (in some *sensed*, though not clearly *understood* way) threaten her plans.

Never removing his hands, the man swiveled left to right and back again several times, surveying the grounds and the deserted court beyond. Then, evidently satisfied, he stepped back inside and closed the door behind him.

Suzanne dared breathe again.

The sensation that had come to her when she first spotted the man lingered like a metallic aftertaste of blood and danger in her mouth, a warning pressure against her jaw and at the back of her head.

She licked her dried, cracking lips, and said, "We'll wait a little, till it gets dark. It should be easier to get inside then." She swallowed, tasting the blood-taste, feeling the tightness in her throat, adding, "But we can't go directly, that's too risky. We'll have to try another way. A back way." She closed her eyes tight and listened for the whispered voice that manifested itself so deep inside her ear that it might have originated in the very substance of her brain.

After a moment, she smiled grimly, and said, "We'll go along the far side of the property—there, on the other side of the garage." She could see, beyond the lawn and corner of the garage with its three wide doors drawn down shut, part of a tall fieldstone fence. It divided the Palmer property from the undeveloped, weed-burdened adjoining lot. "We'll find our way in over there."

Jomo, his eyes hidden behind sunglasses, said nothing. He stared silently along the road with the same impassiveness which he had demonstrated on their drive from Oakland into Marin county. In the still, cloying air, the smell of Jomo quickly became almost more than she could handle.

She knew that Jomo, for all his illusion of life, was secretly corrupting. She had seen the greenish tinge on the skin over his distended belly, the bloated skin prying apart the filthy-silky black shirt, straining the buttons to near-snapping.

The stink was as much a part of him now as

the pallor of his skin. She guessed it was the result of putrefaction as the tissues of the intestines broke down. The gases of decay were pushing the too-elastic skin outward, straining to the point where the body would burst like overripe, dropped fruit, unable to contain its own rottenness. How soon, she wondered, would it be until the decaying flesh begin to split, disgorging its unspeakable secrets, while he continued to stare down an empty, heat-soaked road, indifferent, waiting for her next order, waiting to serve her and those she served? Or would he, in those final moments, turn on her, recognizing the lie that he had become, the obscenity she had made him?

She roused herself out of such disturbing, unanswerable questions. She made herself think of fire, of the fire she would set in dead Elenora's house to cleanse the physical evidence of the place where the supernatural had thrust hands into the stuff of the natural world, bending it, shaping it, using it to set right old (and new) wrongs with an implacable demand for blood.

Jomo sat; the gnats, attracted by the smell, came closer. Suzanne stared out across masses of shrubs with oily-green leaves—like a dusty, dark-green sea—and refused to think of the figure beside her. She concentrated on the man hidden somewhere in the vastness of the white house and grounds beyond the neat white fences, the tree-shaded lawns, the carefully tended flower gardens.

Time moved imperceptibly, measured by the

minute changes in shadows rather than the stilled hands on the dashboard clock.

The two figures in the car sat, frozen in place. Waiting.

Christine regained consciousness slowly. Every fiber of her being resisted wakefulness. She hurt too much to hurry back from obliviousness. For a long time, she continued slipping from half-awareness to blessed unconsciousness. But, over her body's resistance, her impatient mind tugged her forward finally out of the safe blankness into the wretchedness of full consciousness.

The right side of her face was a single sheet of agony; her right eye was swollen shut. When she moved her jaw, white-hot pains shot through it, splaying into her brain like burning wires and running in scalding waves down the side of her neck to fan out through her chest with such excruciating fire that it threatened to stop her breathing, it was so jolting to her system.

Her right eye was swollen shut; she forced the tip of her tongue past her numbed lips and swallowed weakly, tasting blood. Her hands were tied behind her—they felt like dead weights. Clearly the ropes had cut off circulation in them.

She was lying slightly on her right side facing a hard, raised half-circle of brick hearth in front of large, cold fireplace. This must be the guest house buried deep in the trees at the back of David's property. She had the crazy thought that she was trussed like a sacrificial victim on an altar, waiting only for the swift slash of the priest's hand, the terrifying pain of feeling her living heart tipped out—

The fluorescent lights nestled in between the redwood beams of the ceiling were all on; but, as far as she could tell, she was alone in the room. Muted daylight was still visible through two of the small, high-set windows, but it had the thickening quality of late-afternoon light. She guessed she had been unconscious for several hours. *Jesus, that motherfucker Dominic really walloped me,* she thought.

Experimentally she tried the knots on her hands: they seemed too secure to undo. Because her hands below her bound wrists were without sensation, she pressed her right wrist down as hard as she could, moving it around, feeling for some jagged brick edge to saw at what felt like strands of hempen rope from the way it prickled. She found no likely rough spot. She then considered rolling off the edge (she guessed the drop was a foot or so) and, since her feet were untied, trying to escape with her hands tied. David had shown her the guest house on one of her infrequent visits to his home; now she racked her memory for recall details of the place. She berated herself for not having committed more useful information to memory.

Christine began the slow, painful business of turning onto her back, steeling herself against the searing pains that ran from her shoulder, up the side of her face, and across her scalp. She would have to hook her legs over the edge and force herself to a sitting position, being careful not to throw herself onto the floor and maybe worsening her position.

With a last groan, she flipped onto her back—

And found herself staring through her good eye at Dominic, who had apparently been standing all this time just out of her line of sight, enjoying her efforts.

"Are you just getting more comfortable? Or are you up to something?"

She sighed and relaxed the tension in her body slightly, letting her weight come to rest on her bound hands. Finding the position too uncomfortable, she tried to return to her original position on her side.

But the man reached down and put enough pressure on her ankles to prevent such a change of position. He shook his head and smiled, saying, "Uh-uh! Since you got yourself into this position, you can just stay there."

"Bb-Bastard," she managed to whisper.

He shrugged, but the smile disappeared. He watched her the way someone might watch a TV report of a convicted killer's execution.

She stretched her neck, seeking a fractionally more comfortable position, closing her one eye to take what comfort she could in the darkness behind her lids, while her mind raced through thought after thought, seeking a solution. She made herself get out the word, "David?"

"Oh, he'll be back shortly. But, I'm afraid he's as angry with you as I am. Anyway—we've decided to move you, late tonight, to Mr.

Palmer's cabin in Sonoma. No matter how much we learn from you now. Even if you tell us everything we want to know before we leave, we're still going to make a private party of it." Dominic gave her a big grin, showing his coffee-stained teeth with a large peppercorn lodged between his lower front incisors. "David has given me what you might call *carte blanche* to deal with you. I'm going to help even the score for him."

She could feel her head swimming; she was soaked in sweat and her mouth and throat were dry and gravelly. She fought back a need to vomit, afraid she would drown in it, like a junkie too helpless to turn his head. She closed her eyes, forcing herself to take deep breaths, making the threatening nausea subside.

"Open your eyes, when I talk to you," Roselli snarled. Before she could respond, he clamped her jaw in one of his huge hands, squeezing cruelly for emphasis.

The pain was so shockingly intense that Christine fainted.

"We're going now," Suzanne said, after a glance at her wristwatch showed 6:30 p.m.

Jomo turned his head slightly at the sound of her voice. She sensed him watching her from behind his impenetrable sunglasses, but he said nothing.

She opened the car door on the driver's side and climbed out. After a moment, he opened his door, and did the same. It was a relief for her to get out into the cooling fresh evening air and out of the car interior so saturated with the smell of her companion.

With Jomo following a few paces behind, she set out between the oak trees and carefully picked out a path that wound through the shrubs and trees that bordered the house on the left—or western—side. Suzanne was alert to any signs of police or private security people, but she could detect nothing. *How very much like David,* she thought, *to mistrust any official protection and trust absolutely in his own ability to take care of himself.* She also recognized his obsession with keeping his private life free of intrusion by anyone— and especially free of the very authority that could call him to account for unlawful acts that ran the gamut from corporation cheating and deceptions to borderline treason and outright murder.

The tangle of shrubs and trees dissolved onto a jumble of waist-high weeds. The thick mass of brambles and thistle was roughly circular in configuration—but flattened at the eastern end, where a head-high fieldstone-and-cement fence marked the periphery of David's estate. Beyond the choking grasses and weeds, she could make out the cross-bars of a rusty metal gate topped —as was the stone wall—with tangles of barbed wire, effectively barring entrance to the elegant grounds just beyond. Eight upright metal poles were embedded in horizontal crosspieces at top and bottom, and there was a single waist-high crossbar in which the lock was set. The whole was uniformly coated with rust, the color of dried blood.

Suzanne stepped up to the gate and took hold of one of the upright bars. When she satisfied herself that the gardens were empty, she rattled the gate experimentally. She tried again harder, feeling the rust powdering under her hands, but the gate remained sealed fast. Releasing it, she stepped back a pace, trying unsuccessfully to brush the gritty red powder from her hands.

"Jomo," she said finally, "you try."

From where he had been standing behind her, presumably watching her ineffectual efforts, Jomo moved through the tall weeds to seize the gate in both hands. He shook it with a quiet ferocity: the only sounds were Suzanne's breathing and the rattle of the gate in its sockets. Jomo continued shaking it until she ordered him to stop; then he just stood in place, his arms dangling at his sides. His hands and jacket cuffs were smudged with rust.

Suzanne considered. It was impossible for her to get through. Yet all her inner guides, which had led her this far, assured her that she could not take a single step backward from the course on which she had embarked. She was at an impasse. She had done all that was humanly possible. She realized that those others who reached through to her in dreams, in flashes of intuition, in the deep-rooted assurances that gave her the courage to proceed from one step to the next with certainty that she had never taken a false step during the whole of this venture—those others would have to help her as they had never been able (or willing) to help her before.

"Nana," she said aloud, but in a normal speaking voice, feeling the old woman's presence very near her left hand, "Nana, help me. Maitre Shango, help me. *Os pretos velhos*, help me. Help me as you've never done before."

An unexpected cloud-fragment swept across the sun; the cloying warmth of the day was replaced with a sudden chill.

Suzanne repeated her appeal, but her voice had dropped to little more than a whisper now.

Impossible thunder roiled out of the sky; the world was caught in the throes of a capricious summer storm. The sky abruptly shaded down from pale blue through indigo to gray-black to black. No rain fell, but flashes of violet sheet lightning seared the darkening air.

"Nana. Os pretos velhos. Maitre Shango," Suzanne said, or thought, no longer certain whether she had spoken the words aloud or only formed them in her mind.

Diffuse sheet lightning funneled itself into forked lightning, poured in a triple stream out of the sky, focused its concentrated energy onto the metal gate, which was suddenly sheathed in violet light that danced in waves of raw energy over the metal. With a hiss, the violet incandescence turned white-hot, forcing Suzanne to turn her face aside to save her eyes from being boiled in their sockets.

When she dared look back, the metal bars—uprights and crossbars—had turned molten, had melted into slag between the stone walls. A few drops of rain fell, turning instantly to steam where they touched the superheated metal sludge.

Ignoring the still-raging heat, Suzanne stepped over the seething metal, through the gap that had been a gate, and ordered Jomo to follow her.

Overhead, the storm clouds churned furiously, bellowing thunder with increasing frequency.

Suzanne ran across the storm-riled gardens, across the lawns flecked with still-hesitant raindrops. The house loomed silent and dark in front of her in the twilight to which the storm had given a nightlike cast. She looked over her shoulder once, and saw Jomo loping along behind her.

She made her way unhesitatingly past he rain-dappled pool to the patio and the french doors beyond. This time, the doors were unlocked; she yanked them open in a single exhuberant gesture. The deserted, shadowy living room lay beyond: thickly carpeted, filled with heavy furniture, empty. She crossed to the center of the room; heard Jomo follow her as a pair of sliding soles crossing the thick pile generating crackles of static electricity, felt the wind follow them in through the open double doors and saw it scatter papers off the coffee table and agitate the curtains at the windows that girded the room.

Suzanne extended her hands out in front of her, waist high, stretching her fingers out as far as they would go. She studied them as if they had become something no longer quite part of her. Instinctively she reached out, pressing her palms flat against the rich, gold-flecked wallpaper of the room.

She felt the house around her, felt the walls, floors, ceilings and the emptiness each contained. She had a *certainty* that it held only herself and Jomo, and no one else.

Still keeping her hands in contact with the wall, she let her new-found awareness flow out in expanding circles, like the ripples of a still pool. One ripple encountered, then flowed thickly through a tangle of human impressions. They seemed to be moving unhurriedly through the house—away from the house—to another place at a short distance from where she stood.

Then her foremost awareness ripple slammed into a cluster of consciousness. One was a woman, in pain, only partly awake, struggling to free herself from some very great danger. The second was a male, with a cold, snake-like quality—a desire to inflict pain—a dangerous man, for sure.

The third, another man, was a garble of conflicting emotions—his ego like the calm eye of a hurricane at the center of a rage of desires, fears, regrets, ambitions, and a hunger to lash out at anyone or anything that stood between him and his goals or was responsible for taking away from him anything that he considered his. A lesser being would have flown apart psychically, Suzanne realized, shredded by such devastating crosscurrents. But this man had such a strong ego that his center held—kept all the tempest in his soul battened down by sheer will power. He was—

David! She jerked her hands back from the wall, as if it had turned white-hot. The rush of hatred, tinged by something uncomfortably like *fear*, through her—together with the action of breaking contact with the wall—dissipated the sensations. She felt her awareness implode, folding back in on her until, in a moment, there was only herself, and Jomo.

Her hands were shaking spasmodically. She was awash with hatred. And fear. She tried to reestablish her mental parameters, but her body was emotion-torn, as surely as the sky outside was storm-tossed. She could no longer touch those other minds.

But David was close, very close. Suzanne felt an ingathering certainty. *Now. It was all whirling down to this. Here. Now. Now—*

"*Now*, Jomo, *now!*" She roused herself from the emotional confusion to make herself a strong center—just as she had experienced David as the diamond-hard core of his whirling, spinning, energy—his kaleidoscoping inner world. Out of her stormy inner self, she fashioned a resolve as compact and strong as the green-and-purple-veined thunderstones that the Shango of legend was said to fashion out of the torrential energies of African storms.

"Come with me," she directed Jomo, leading him towards the sea-green tiled entranceway she could see beyond the entrance to the living room.

Urged on by impressions that floated into her consciousness, Suzanne led them through the hall and out onto the shadowed porch. The sky was a raging cloud-mass from horizon to horizon; a rising wind swept out of the east. She felt it sting her face, as she sought to make sense of the strong, intermingled impression of a woman and two men that she was certain was the point toward which she must make her way at any cost.

To the north, through the storm-obscured air, she could just make out a thick grove of trees.

With the interior certainty of a compass needle locating true north, Suzanne traced out the graveled path that led from the foot of the front steps on an erratic course toward the wind-shaken cluster of trees. She was not choosing her path; she was simply following more and more rapidly the path that was set out for her. The tempo of events had increased to a near-dizzying pace. *Very soon*, she guessed, *everything will be ended. One way or another.*

Motioning Jomo to follow her, she made her way through the gusting wind and rain, along the path that had become the whole of the world to her. With every step she took, the world behind her dissolved into insubstantial mist; the grove ahead was the only reality in a universe as wispy as a dream. Jomo, matching her pace for pace, was the only bit of substance she brought with her out of the melting world at her heels.

The rain fell with renewed vigor; it sizzled on

the leaves of the matted branches above her as she entered the grove.

And then, through the screening trees, she saw a nearly circular structure built of fieldstone and redwood beams. The path approached it from the rear, apparently circling around to an entrance with a westerly exposure. She felt the thinning fringe of trees along the path would screen them from anyone who might possibly be watching from one of the small, oval, head-high windows set at regular intervals in the massive fieldstone walls. Suzanne's whole being was focused on the curving stone wall in front of her.

She could feel David was just inside, and every fiber of her being was shouting: *Now*.

Christine regained consciousness even more slowly this time. The fire on the side of her face and in her jaw had subsided to a dull ache that flared into agony whenever she moved her jaw experimentally. She suspected a part of it had been shattered by Dominic.

With her good eye, she made out Dom and David talking together near the door of the cottage. While they talked, she managed to angle her hands out from under her to the edge of the hearth, then began sawing at the ropes on the sharp edge of the coping.

"Let's finish it, right now," Dominic said. "Every minute we keep her here, we're taking a bigger risk."

David made a sound that might have been a

laugh. "Risks are the name of this game, Dom. You don't win big playing penny-ante. There's a hell of a lot of money riding on this game—not to mention a couple of whopping jail sentences if they can nail us for any of the African deal. I want to know how much the Feds know—you can be sure she's involved with them up to her twat."

David turned and glanced across at Christine. She looked into his face with her eyes, trying to make some—any—kind of contact with her. *If he would just talk with her, maybe—* She worked her lips, but no sound resulted.

David's face grew hard. He turned back to the older man, rejecting her mute attempt to an appeal. Her hands, hidden beneath her, resumed sawing at the ropes that bound her as soon as he turned away.

Dominic's voice reached her. He was saying, "In that case, whatever you want to know— that's what I'm going to find out. *Any*—ANY— way I can. Now. I'm gonna *fine-tune* her till she sings every song we want to hear."

Christine saw David's hands clench and unclench several times, but he made no move to interfere with Dominic. Instead, he remained locked in place, watching.

Dom came and stood over Christine. With his right hand he draw a switchblade out of his rear pocket, never once taking his eyes from Christine's face.

With a *swittt!* the knife-blade locked into position. Light from the fixtures set tidily between the overhead beams seemed to gather silver-white along the finely-honed, razor-sharp edge.

Christine instinctively inched backward toward the maw of the cold fireplace behind her.

"Easy. *Easy*," said Roselli. His left hand grabbed a handful of her hair, pulling her head up off the hearth bricks. She strained at the partially cut ropes, but her bonds held. "I got eyes in the back of my head, you know. They tell me you haven't missed a word we've been saying. That's good, that saves time. You know what we want, so you tell us. Maybe we'll strike a bargain." Dominic grinned down at her; her whole being was suddenly concentrated on his uneven teeth, on a drop of perspiration trembling on his stubbled chin the color of a bruise.

"No-nothing. I can't—" she somehow managed to get out.

"Oh, but you *can*," Dominic said, "and you *will*. You will." He nodded more to himself than to her. She was afraid he was going to slam her head back onto the bricks; she braced herself for the shock.

But, his fingers still painfully twined in her hair, he merely lowered her head back onto the hearth. Then he sat beside her, for all the world like a parent on a child's bed at nighttime.

He held the blade out over her face, studying it in the light. Then he brought it down in a sudden slashing motion, slitting the material of her white blouse between her breasts. With his free hand he pulled back the halves of material, exposing her bra.

In horror, she felt him slide the blade up her abdomen, from her navel, aware that the faintest pressure would draw blood. She breathed as shallowly as she could, feeling the sweat pouring off her body, soaking into the rough surface of the bricks below her.

Then she stopped breathing as the knife blade slipped below the elastic band joining the cotton breast cups, continued up and up until the very tip of the blade touched the hollow of her throat and the hilt of the knife caught momentarily on the narrow elastic.

For a moment Dominic stared down at her chest, as though trying to decide whether to continue thrusting up into her windpipe.

Then he ripped the blade upward, with a quick sawing motion that severed the brassiere, leaving her right breast exposed, her left still covered. With a smile, Roselli used the blade point to flip the protecting cup off her left breast.

She felt her nipples stiffening as he, with delicacy a hair's breadth from cutting her, retraced a line with a knife point from her throat, down between her breasts, coming to rest just above her naval.

"Tell me what you know," he asked, his voice as threatening as the blade he held.

"I—noth—nothing—" She drew her feet up part way, preparing to make one desperate lurch back, away from the knife, then kick at the man.

He said, "First, I'm going to remove the nipples—"

She tensed—

There was a thunderous, explosive sound followed by a sudden rain of window fragments as the sliding door to the deck outside erupted inward. Christine jerked around to see what had happened, thinking freak lightning might have struck the entranceway. She was wildly unprepared for what she *did* see.

SEVENTEEN

A WOMAN'S VOICE screamed.

Christine saw Roselli, startled, turn just in time to be thrown backwards by the lumbering attack of a thin, silent young black man, whose hands clamped on the older man's shoulder and throat, even as his loping, foward rush sent the two of them tumbling backwards, slamming Dominic into the floor and knocking the wind out of him. But Roselli managed to somehow keep his hold on his knife, even though his grunt of pain told Christine just how heavily he had fallen.

At the same instant, a wild-eyed black woman, wielding a knife herself, launched at David herself through the now-empty door frame with a scream. "Murdering bastard!" she shrieked, lunging at him with her weapon outthrust toward his belly.

David moved quickly, instinctively. He sidestepped the deadly thrust. His hands shot out, grabbing the woman's arms, preventing her from maneuvering, then getting both her wrists in locks. At such close quarters, his greater weight and strength turned events in his favor, now that she no longer had the element of surprise.

Christine only gave herself a second to take in what was happening, then she twisted to reposition herself and began frantically sawing at her bonds, ignoring the pain she was causing herself as the sharp edge of the coping sometimes gouged into the tender flesh of her wrists.

Dominic, struggling on the floor, still underneath his assailant, doubled up his right knee and brought it up into the softness of Jomo's belly; a sudden gush of fetid breath caught him in the face. Jomo, his eyes on Roselli's throat, his mouth a grin that was almost a rictus, managed to hold the older man's hands pinioned to the floor. Dom strove to free his hand just enough to use it. He refused to let himself be distracted that, though much of the young black's clothing was in tatters, and the skin lacerated ferociosly by his explosive passage through the heavy glass door, *there was no blood on him*. The wounds looked wet and gangrenous, *but they did not bleed*. The two men rolled from side to side, Dom trying to throw Jomo off balance enough to get some control; Jomo, however, was managing to counter the older man's efforts effectively, maintaining the upper position. Roselli's heavy breathing was the only evident sound; to his frantic awareness the other man was was not even breathing heavily—*seemed not to be breathing at all*.

David, grappling with the woman, who was

considerably stronger than her slight frame and graying hair would indicate, found that the mad forocity in her eyes unnerved him more than the weapon she held. He did not see a woman, he saw a frenzied killer. The woman's eyes glittered with fanatic fire; her mouth was twisted into a line of mingled pain and hatred and irrational rage. David had recognized her the instant she had hurled herself on him, brandishing the knife.

He recognized, in the skeletal figure, in the faded hair, in the terrifying eyes, Suzanne— whom he had chosen a long time ago to forget.

He had thought her dead or forever out of his life. Now, wild-eyed, her distorted face framing chaotic eyes, she was his long-buried past ripping its violent way into the present.

Here was one of the dead, burst from some grave in his mind, vomited into his present, filling the instant with incoherent, deadly madness.

He could make no sense of what she was saying. He had a spasmodic memory of a child he had seen hit by a car; he remembered the girl's head thrashing from side to side, spittle and blood from her nose mingling, her eyes with the same horrible glassiness and disconnectedness from sanity that Suzanne's now held.

The girl had been dying; and this woman, he sensed in his gut, was dead to the rational world. Whatever was driving her, he could expect no reason for mercy. Her eyes were filled with an unfathomable, dark obsession that left no room for anything but its own purposes. She was a black angel, a mad angel, an angel of death who was a dead thing herself. Mad, mindless, hopeless, dead.

These thoughts tumbled through his mind in a fraction of a second. His head reeled. In less than a second, everything had collapsed into insanity. He was locked in a life-and-death struggle with a nightmare memory. It was like having his dead come back to haunt him—to drag him down with them into the grave and whatever hell lay beyond.

"You know me, don't you, David? I'm Suzanne. Suzanne!" she screamed, pushing her face up close tho his, while she struggled with the mythic strength of the insane to break free of his grip. He brought his knee up suddenly connecting with her wrist. The impact forced her fingers to open convulsively; the knife clattered to the hardwood floor. With a kick, David sent it spinning across the floor, through the glass fragments, toward the shattered door. Wind and rain gusted through the opening unheeded. She writhed in his hold like a creature of superhuman energy, growing stronger. He sensed he could not restrain her very much longer.

"You let our child—*my* child—die. I've taken your family away from you, and now—" Her taunts died away into grunts as she struggled to break free.

David hung on, refusing to let his mind be distracted by her nearly incoherent ramblings. The only thing that mattered to him was his survival. But he recognized the very real possibility that she was in some way responsible for Amy and Kirk's deaths. The realization gave him the added force of his own anger and hatred. He yanked down on her arms, nearly wrenching them out of their sockets. The pain made her screech, startled her enough to weaken her efforts for a moment.

She tried to curse him, but words failed her utterly; a dam inside burst in raw sound. Screams and moans of frustration at her inability to twist free of him, the tenacity with which he clung to life in defiance of the dead and the living—

Blood cried in the brain and heart, exploding like a geyser, like a gusher of poisonous brown water, as if her heart had burst like an overheated, worn-out radiator filled with filthy, brown, scalding hatred. Like blood festering in a wound suddenly lanced—

She felt the poison pouring out of her; she vomited out the years of held-back pain and hate—

Enough of this to drown the world; enough in her heart to drown the world a thousand times over—

Screaming and screaming and screaming until the sound of it filled the room and her raw throat was incapable of making any sound at all.

She broke free, she charged at him, her hands groping for his throat because there was no time to retrieve her knife.

He jumped aside, so her momentum carried

her forward into the space he had just vacated. At the same instant he pivoted, locking his fingers together and extending his arms full length, continuing to pivot as she went past. The second she halted her forward rush and turned to come at him again, she met the arcing sweep of his joined arms full in the face, feeling her nose pulped as it impacted with his arm somewhere between his wrist and elbow.

Suzanne spun backward. The impact of David's blow threw her back and over, so that she crashed into the fireplace coping with a shout, "Jom—," suddenly snapped off by the impact.

She came to rest, her head thrown back and grotesquely lolling on the fireplace, inches from Christine's ankle. Only the steady trickle of blood from her ruined nose and burst lip signaled the life still in her.

Her cry connected with Jomo. For a moment his head spun around in the direction of Suzanne's shout; distracted, he let his grip on Roselli loosen just enough to allow Dominic to wrench his knife hand free. With a bellow of victory, he buried it in Jomo's stomach, just above his belt buckle, and slashed upward, feeling the knife rip through skin and muscle that had the consistency of soft cheese.

With a hideous *popping* sound, stinking gases and fetid matter more like pus than a man's insides were expelled over Roselli's shirt and pants, covering his hand which was still gripping the hilt of the knife, so deeply embedded in Jomo's ribcage. Dominic couldn't withdraw it.

Feeling his own guts churning within him from the smell and feel of the foulness, Dominic tried to shove the obviously dead man off him, wanting only to get as far from the reeking corpse as he could.

Then the impossible happened.

Jomo's head swiveled around to lock again on Dominic's eyes; his hands moved erratically, as though under only imperfect control, but still able to seek out the older man's throat.

All logic screamed at Roselli that there was no way anyone who'd been gutted from navel to sternum could be alive, purposeful, still a threat.

But the filthy hands with the cracked and broken fingernails were relentlessly closing on his throat.

"Jesus—Sweet Jesus—he won't die! *He won't die!*" Dominic screamed. "Jesus—make him die. He's got to be dead."

He began kicking wildly, but Jomo straddled him, took a firm hold on his throat. With every moment, more of Jomo's pustulous insides spilled cold and slimy onto the shuddering, now frantically screaming man beneath him; the room was filled with a vileness, a miasma— the odor of the charnel house.

David, his heart pounding, his breath coming in ragged, heaving sobs, saw his man struggling beneath what looked and acted like an animated corpse. He heard Roselli's shout, "*He won't die!*" He stared at the . . . *thing* . . . Dominic's knife still buried to the hilt in its chest, methodically strangling the older man.

Then David looked around frantically for the knife he had seen fly out of Suzanne's hands, but he couldn't locate it. Christine, her eyes wide open and terrified, lay helplessly, her hands bound behind her, on the hearth. Suzanne, her breath coming in liquid, bloody gouts from her injured mouth and nose, still was collapsed unconscious against the fireplace.

No time for the knife, his mind screamed. His eyes scanned the walls, the bar surface, looking for a weapon. He grabbed first for a wine bottle from an ornamental rack, then spotted a hatchet, nearly buried in a pile of kindling in an alcove behind the fireplace.

He snatched it up as Dom began to scream horribly, yelling, "He's biting me—into me—" His voice became an incomprehensible bellow of pain.

Turning, ax in hand, David saw the dark, nightmarish creature riding Roselli's thrashing body. Only—now the finely shaped head was buried in the right side of Roselli's neck. For a moment, David froze, transfixed by the sight, staring helplessly at the back of the man's head —the tight, oily-looking curls of hair completely hiding most of Roselli's own head—the curve of the back stretching the shiny, partly shredded, greasy fabric of his shirt taut. That shirt, to David, looked even filthier than the blue-black jeans over thin shanks rocking up and down in almost orgasmic motion, while Dom's legs, jutting out beneath, beat a weakening, agonized tattoo on the floor.

Dominic gave a truly horrific scream, his whole body arching in incredible agony.

David stepped forward, brought the ax down with a wet *chunk* square in the middle of the man's back, burying the blade three-quarters of the way into the flesh that gave too easily, seemed *too soft*. With a quick wrench, he pulled the ax-blade free, as a mixture of coagulated, stinking, dark blood and white corruption oozed out of the wound, like the split in an overripe fruit.

Dom's legs went suddenly still; but, incredibly, the body straddling him didn't topple forward. It began a slow revolution to face its assailant. David, his ax hand at ready, but mesmerized by the impossible thing that was happening, watched the rotating neck helplessly.

His immobility lasted until he saw the face, grinning past a bloody gobbet of Dom's neck the size of a man's fist. The chunk of bloody flesh was clamped greedily between the stained, yellow teeth. He looked down at Roselli's limp body, and saw the dead eyes staring up at the beamed ceiling in a grimace of terrified, unbearable pain.

The blood which had gushed out of Dom's torn jugular had pooled around his head, though blood barely seeped from the wound now.

With an incoherent cry, David broke free of

his stasis and swung the ax down aslant the *thing's* face, shearing away the lower half of the face from below the nose to just behind the jaw. The gory mass of muscle, bone, nerves, flesh welled blood with unreal slowness; from the throat opening gushed black bile. Still the hands reached up for him.

"Die, damn you, die, die, DIE!" he shrieked, and buried the ax blade squarely between the eyes—

—which continued to fix on him, refocusing from either side of the blade which he had smashed almost to its haft in brain matter and—

—still the hands moved up to grab at him, pull him down to death.

Then he went crazy—overwhelmed by the horror of it. He stumbled backward, tearing the hatchet free, then yelling, "*Die!* Die! Die! You son-of-a-bitch!" Chopping down-down-down, with his blade each time, he severed right hand from arm, forearm from elbow, upper arm from shoulder—then swiftly repeated his work on the left hand and arm. And when he looked again and saw the eyes, still blazing with hatred, looking out at him from the ruin of a head, he gave one final curse and swung the ax, the blade whistling, in a deadly, right-on-target arc that decapitated the monstrosity, sending the obscene tangle of pulp and matted hair bouncing across the polished wood floor to *thump* to rest against the far wall of the room.

His chest heaving, he watched the still-upright torso, straddling Roselli's corpse, whispering a challenge for it to keep up the struggle. But, with a wet sound, the remains of Jomo tilted to one side and slumped to the floor.

David backed away, not ready to believe the horror was really dead. A muscular spasm in one of the dismembered hands sent him skittering backwards, ax raised. Then the flesh was still; an expectant quiet settled over the room.

David sank to his knees, almost dead himself from the exertion and the horror. While his left hand wiped away sweat and gore from his face, he used his right hand to drop the darkly clotted ax on the edge of the fireplace not far from Christine's head.

His hands on his thighs, his head hanging below his shoulders, he waited for the room to stop spinning around him, rocking underfoot, wondering if he would ever pull his head together enough to make sense of any of this. At the moment, he seriously doubted he could find the strength to even move.

During the struggle between David and Jomo, Christine, letting herself concentrate only on the ropes holding her, continued to saw at them. She ignored the stinging pain. She did not look at what was happening, but she could follow the hideous struggle through Dominic's shouts, his screams, and obscene sounds of the ax blade gouging flesh with dull, wet sounds that were— in some insane way—*all wrong*. Just before David delivered the final blows, to Roselli's tormentor and (apparently) murderer, she felt the last strands of her bonds beginning to part. She was almost through, when David decapitated the human ruin, and fell back against the brick coping while the remains of his victim collapsed over the blood-soaked body of Roselli. She heard the ax *chunk* onto the hearth bricks only inches from her head.

She immediately hid her hands under her again, trying to gauge her best course of action. She angled her head to consider David, and realized that he was, for the moment, so exhausted by his efforts and distracted by the complex questions his dead and his momentarily incapacitated assailants represented, that he had forgotten her entirely. Seizing the moment, Christine gave up all pretense at secrecy, and sawed frantically at the last few fibers that held her prisoner.

Suzanne had also begun to come around, pulling her head foward, away from the stone coping, with a tremendously painful effort.

The room in front of her seemed washed by waves of darkness and light—alternating patterns of blindness and clarity that were connected somehow with the rhythms of the blood she felt pounding at her temples and throat.

When her perceptions lightened to soft, gray shadows behind her closed eyes, she could hear the yells, grunts, curses, *chopping* sounds of the struggles she could not quite turn her head or open her eyes to see. When the shadows thickened to easeful, caressing darkness, she sensed the room crowded, *choked* with a multitude of people. Black people. Several times she wondered if she was going blind, or if so many ebony-skinned bodies were pressed in around her that there was no space for even a sliver of light to slip in between. And when this latter state of blackness was on her, she heard a ringing-roaring in her ears that resolved itself into a few words in English. And many words and phrases in a language that she could not understand—though there was a tantalizing familiarity about it.

Light. Darkness. (Sounds of fighting.) Light. Darkness again.

One female voice floated above the others. *Nana Chicory's.*

Nana, help me . . . help me know what to do now. With a great effort Suzanne formed these words in her mind, because her mouth was filled to bursting with the blood-taste, and her throat was swollen shut with unimaginably constricting pressure. She could barely draw a breath down her occluded windpipe.

She strained into the darkness outside and inside her mind, listening for Charlotte's whisper. When it came to her, the familiar raspy voice said simply, *Listen to Shango, he closes the trap.*

Then Nana's words broke into motes of sounds scattered amid the babble of voices and incomprehensible, alien words.

Light again. (Human voices, raised in anger, pain, confusion.)

Darkness.

But now some powerful force, contained within the darkness in which she drifted, was gathering up the jumbled words, voices, sounds, consciousnesses, and weaving them into one sound, one voice, one roar, one cosmic presence.

The buzz inside her head and ears was crescendoing into thunder; the churning darkness inside her eyes and brain was split with violent slashes of violet-tinged lightning. She could no longer distinguish the roaring inside her head from the sound of the rain-and-thunder-lashed wind rushing through the shattered door.

From the fire-lashed turmoil that had become her soul, Suzanne felt as much as heard a single word coalesce and erupt from her throat in an inhuman bellow.

"BLOOD!"

Shouted aloud, the sound split apart, shattered into a cacophony of sounds—

Nana Chicory's rasping laugh—

A woman sobbing—

The hissing of a whip against flesh—

Moans and weeping and the rattle of chains—

Machine-gun bullets echoing in a jungle clearing—

Pleas and cries of the dying—

Terrified wail of a baby—

A woman screaming down a nightmare corridor as long as eternity—

Inside and out. Screaming.

The darkness, voices, the confusion drained away in her screams. She saw the lighted room clearly around her ...

Heard the dull sound of what was left of

Jomo's head rolling across the floor . . .

Managed to turn her injured head just enough to see David slump back against the fireplace exhausted. He did not look at her. All her screaming had been only in her mind: she had been screaming and shouting into a place that was neither the room she and Jomo had invaded nor some corner of her mind. She had touched —if not the place where the god dwelled, at least the place he had to cross from his world to hers.

Shango was present, was the word that filled her whole mind, her whole being. *Blood*. It was the god's reality. *Blood*. It was the magic that summoned him, sustained him in this world. *Blood*. Linked her to a violent past, a violent present, a violent destiny. *Blood*. The price demanded and the price to be exacted. *Blood*. The god's ultimate commandment.

With a cry that was little more than a groan, Suzanne summoned up every bit of strength that was left to her and hurled herself at David, catching the man off-guard.

There was an exhausted, slow-motion quality to her attack and his weary defense. Suzanne felt like she was moving underwater, or in a film that was suddenly winding down.

David tumbled clumsily onto his side as Suzanne let her weight carry the brunt of her onslaught. The man, attempting to defend himself, felt as though he was thrusting his arms through glue. He found he was nearly incapable of coordinating his muscles properly; his vision blurred. His hands groped ineffectually toward Suzanne's face, which seemed to bob above him like a helium balloon. Everything about his body and hers seemed out of joint in time and space; he had the sensation of being a swimmer caught in some freakish undertow, so disoriented and lightheaded that he no longer knew up from down. The only thing that reached through his fuzziness was the sudden realization that death had come unexpectedly close in the person of this woman he had thought dead to him.

One flailing hand struck her bobbing face. His nail caught in the corner of her left eye; he dug deeply into the flesh with teeth-grinding satisfaction, scratching across the soft fold of her lower lid, deeply enough to partially blind her. She screeched and jerked back her head too late to spare herself the pain. Angry and frustrated, blood coursing down her cheek and filling her eye, she slammed her fisted hands at his head with a futile gesture that gave him a momentary advantage. He grabbed her wildly swinging hands, wrenched them together in front of her over his stomach. Then he twisted suddenly to the side, spilling Suzanne onto the floor as he rolled on top of her, pinioning both sets of hands between their tightly pressed bodies in a grotesque parody of one of their long-ago sexual embraces.

While she tried to break free of his body press, he worked one set of fingers around part of both her wrists and pulled his right hand free. Balling his hand into a fist, he smashed her one-two-three times on the mouth and chin. "For Amy! For Kirk! For *me!*" he hissed through clenched teeth. He felt her lips mash wetly, softly against her teeth—felt some of the teeth themselves break. Saw, with satisfaction, how his upraised fists came away blood-stained each time before he hit her again.

Stunned, nearly unconscious from the beating, she ceased her struggles, her head lolling to one side.

His hands, no longer need to restrain her, were at her throat in an instant, crushing her windpipe.

If only she had died with the bastard, he thought, *if only the fool he had hired had finished the job he had begun in the sweltering New York apartment so many years before.*

For years David had ceased caring if the bitch was alive or dead; his new life had been everything to him and she had become less than a memory. Now he had only one wish, one need, one focus: to finish what he had so badly bungled years before, to destroy her utterly, to make her pay for not being dead, for not leaving him in peace, for disrupting the pattern of his new life, for taking away his dreams of a dynasty, for reducing him to this gore-spattered *monster* in his own house.

He was certain now she had been the cause of his children's death and—if for no other reason —she deserved to die for having stolen from him what he perhaps loved, certainly took a just pride in, and what was irreplaceable and therefore, beyond price—even a blood-price. Though that was the most he could exact and that was the price he demanded, the price he intended to take as his bare hands shut off the last thin trickle of air from her lungs, as his fingers dug crushingly into the cartilage of her throat—

Suzanne felt herself dying, felt her body feebly resisting, knew that it would soon erupt into convulsions which would signal the end of control, fight—the end—

Frantically, she tried to free her hands from David's grip, tried to twist her head just enough to let a little air into her bursting lungs and buy herself a few precious seconds of life and hope. But he was too strong; he seemed to feed off her faltering struggles, sucking her dissipating energy into himself, fattening on her life while he sent her down to death.

Physically her struggles were at an end. She had only one hope: whatever power was left in her mind. Some fragment of the gifts Nana had brought her from the god ... Fighting to remain alive even a few seconds longer, she focused her last resources on thrusting a part of her consciousness into David's mind.

Fighting the waves of darkness of which floated a flotsam of voices and shadowy consciousnesses, resisting the terrifying, deadening silence welling up from the deepest places inside her, Suzanne imagined herself peeling aside the flesh and bone of David's skull to burrow inside—

Imagined her hands inside.

There.
Deep inside.
There.

Over the involuntary panic and demands of her dying body and the pain in her head that felt as though the inside of her own skull had gone red-hot, then white-hot, she felt her envisioned mental hands bury themselves deep in the soft wet tissue of David's brain. Concentrating on the sensation (now surprisingly easy because, with the suffocating lack of oxygen, all other sensation was leaving her body), she made those invisible hands take on enough substance to not simply *be* in his brain, but to actually touch it—

—take hold of it—

—begin *tearing* it—

David's fingers at her throat suddenly froze, spasmed open, tightened again—but not so firmly. Suzanne sucked air greedily into her lungs during this momentary respite.

She dug her visionary fingers even deeper into the wet soft center of him.

His mouth opened and closed soundlessly, like a fish yanked out of water. One hand flipped up, away from her throat to clutch convulsively at empty air. His back arched; he hung onto her throat with his remaining hand only by some supreme effort of his will. She dug in ferociously again, feeling tissue begin to loosen, give—

She felt the sudden bulge of an erection swelling at his zipper, pressing against her stomach through the thin material of her blouse. His whole body spasmed in a death-throe orgasm—

In a moment, she knew, she would have won.

Then her nostrils were filled with a cloying, drowning sensation of blood. It flooded her brain, filled her remaining good eye with red, and swept away her desperate concentration. She was filled with a hopeless terror, the possibility of failing, even greater than her near-death at David's hands.

His head all raging pain, desperate David recovered his hold on her throat. With both hands he tightened, *tightened*—

Suzanne knew she had lost . . .

She could not find her way back to the mind-power in time. The redness flooding into her mouth, nose, lungs, brain was thick with the metallic smell of blood and the stench that had increasingly clung to Jomo, whose body, while not entirely dead, had nevertheless suffered the corruption of the truly dead.

The redness behind her eyes was filling with blackness veined with purple, green, blood. David's hands were inexorably crushing the life out of her. But a peacefulness engulfed her; she saw her grandmother Nana sitting backward, naked, on a night-black horse galloping away from her down a grassy-green slope dewed with blood toward a distant horizon limned in violet. She was a little girl again, and her sister was with her.

Hand in hand they ran after the young stallion and the aged rider who called to them in a language Suzanne did not understand and understood fully. Together the three of them raced into the violet forever—

David got slowly to his feet, watching the body below him for any signs of life.

Suzanne lay unmoving, exactly where she had fallen.

Only Christine remained; better to get it all over with now, he decided.

Once and for all. Finished. Then—

But his mind was too confused to think through more than a step at a time.

Christine was still sprawled on the brick ledge, her hands under her. He started to reach for the ax, but he saw the blade of Suzanne's knife gleaming amid the glass shreds, not far from him.

Much cleaner with a knife, he decided. *There's been enough messy killing tonight.*

He half-stumbled across the room, holding his side, which nearly bent him double with the pain, with one hand, while he retrieved the knife with the other. Still breathing heavily, he said, turning to look at the bound woman, "Sorry, baby—you're still a liabil—"

Christine, who had cut herself free during the last moments of Suzanne's and David's struggle, stood up and brought the ax down in a single, clean blow, angled so that it splintered his clavicle and cut far into his chest, the edge of it just touching the muscle of his heart.

While David fell backward, a silent look of astonished horror on his face, Christine sank to her knees, unmindful of the glass that cut cruelly into her flesh.

In a minute, she would find a phone, call help, bring everything to an end. But, for now, sobbing for breath, she could only bury her face in her hands and pray that the nightmare had finally ended as surely for her as it had for the other still figures scattered around the mercifully darkening room.

EPILOGUE

CHRISTINE LEE and Harry Metzger stood in the sunny living room of the house on Manningtree Lane. "It's warm in here," Christine said, slipping off her pale-green sweater and setting it on a sideboard, moving aside several tall, purple-tinted glasses to make room.

Harry idly picked the ebony Shango-cult figure off the mantel. He turned it around and around in his hands, studying it intently for a moment. Then he shrugged and carefully replaced it, before turning to say quietly to the slender young black woman, who was staring past him at the woodcarving, "I'm still not sure why you wanted to come here. You're on extended leave. You should be miles away from here, forgetting—all this." He gestured vaguely around the room. "Hawaii—the Company has some nice condos in Honolulu. Or New Orleans. You've always talked about having an urge to see New Orleans, even though you've never been there."

Christine shrugged, tearing her eyes from the statue, then touching the right side of her face, which was still tender and bruised. "I can't give you a reason, Harry. I just had to—that's all."

"Well, after breaking this case wide open, you're entitled." Then he added wearily, "This whole case is a mess like nothing I've seen before. I doubt we'll ever sort out all the pieces. Our people have moved in and shut down the supply lines to the rebels in Bukawai. The situation there should begin to 'normalize' in pretty short order. Everyone's breathing a little easier, now that we aren't going to see full-scale civil war erupt and spill over the borders into a few shaky neighbors. We could have had a major crisis on our hands."

She nodded, only too familiar with what Harry was saying. She asked him, "What about Suzanne Raine? And that—the other one?"

"Her nephew? The kid seemed to have been almost dead of gangrene or some sort of weird disease."

"He was dead before he killed Roselli," she said, hearing her voice edge into a higher register. "He—wasn't human."

"Let it go, Christine," Harry said wearily. "You've been around and around this already."

"Yeah, and I got an extended leave, more for 'stress' than for having the shit beat out of me," she snapped. Then she quickly apologized. "I know you went to bat for me, Harry." She reached out to touch him briefly on the arm. "Thanks again, for that."

He smiled at her, then said, "For my sake as well as yours, stick to what's possible, forget the ghost stories." Not waiting for her to respond, he continued, "As for Ms. Raine—we've traced her back to New York, where she just about scratched out a living as a singer in some higher-class Harlem clubs. There's a chance that we'll track down some connection between her and Palmer back there. But we're talking about something years ago—and neither Palmer nor Raine have left us many clues to work on. It's all pretty moot at this point."

Christine moved to a window, looking out onto the side of the house, where a head-high mass of bougainvillea was dying from lack of watering. It affected her with a sadness, but stirred her with a deeper restiveness. This was not merely a house of the dead. Some inner compulsion was promising her that something vital waited for her to discover it.

"Walk with me through the house," she asked her companion.

"Sure," he said, "but you won't find anything new. Everyone's been over this with the proverbial fine-tooth comb. Several times."

But Christine would not be put off.

They went upstairs, then, to continue their room-by-room search. The house seemed preternaturally quiet; the air was unmoving, stale. Christine was aware of a faint odor of corruption, and a much more pronounced metallic tang—like fresh blood. But, when she commented on this to Harry, he sniffed the air and shrugged. She knew he was attributing it to her overactive imagination.

They entered the first small bedroom. It was airless and hot; the windows, firmly shut, appeared not to have been opened in a long time. The narrow bed was neatly made; the chocolate-colored spread was smoothed out without a wrinkle.

Harry, sounding to Christine like a tour guide in a waxworks to great crimes, said, "When they opened the drawer of the desk, they found Kirk Palmer's key chain, a broken necklace with a medallion identical to the one Amy Palmer had been wearing the night she was murdered, and a few fragments of photographs which, pieced together, are shots of Amy and Kirk. It looks like she'd been planning the murders for some time. Probably they were just a preliminary—"

He broke off as Christine suddenly walked across the room and jerked open the closet door.

While Harry watched, uncertain how to respond, Christine rattled hastily through the few items of clothing on hangers, and opened and shut the single green-and-brown plaid suitcase. Then she quickly checked out the flimsy pine dresser, opening and slamming shut the drawers, assuring herself they had held nothing of importance.

Guardedly, Harry said, "This was all examined as carefully as anything else. There's nothing here."

But Christine, to his consternation, had her head cocked frantically to one side, away from him, as though she were listening to a voice he could not hear.

Afraid for her now, he said, gently, "Christine, I think—"

She warned him to silence. Then motioned him to help her push the little drawer from one side of the closet to the other. He complied with the air of a doctor humoring a patient until an orderly arrived with help and sedatives.

When the bureau was out of her way, Christine dropped to her knees and ran her fingertips searchingly over the baseboard behind, still in an attitude of listening. With a sudden nod of satisfaction, she gripped a portion of the baseboard and yanked it away from the wall, revealing a dead space beyond. Harry immediately guessed it was the result of some of the haphazard remodelling with which the Manningtree Lane house abounded—and of which Harry's trained eyes had spotted, then dismissed, ample evidence.

Christine reached far back into the recess. After a minute, she extracted two shoeboxes, which she handed out to Harry, who accepted them without comment.

Harry set these side by side on the narrow bed, then sat on the edge himself. The first contained only several carefully tissue-wrapped stones. They were of different sizes; but all of them were nearly spherical and smooth. Each was veined purple and green. Christine recognized "thunderstones" immediately but said nothing.

Christine stood aside, her arms folded, while Harry unpacked the second tissue-packed shoebox.

"Jesus Christ!" Harry exclaimed. "Crazier and crazier!"

Sandwiched between the wads of yellowing tissue were the bones of an infant. He couldn't bring himself to touch them—just stood staring down into the box while his partner looked over his shoulder. The bones had a look to them like fine old ivory; they were pressed so firmly into the packing material that the hasty removal and opening of the shoebox hadn't disturbed them.

"A kid. Sweet Jesus, that poor, crazy woman was toting around a dead kid all the time. I've seen a lot, but this—"

Christine said softly, "You'll have another homicide investigation now. See there: that indent in the skull, and, see, the wrist looks like it was broken clean in two. This child was beaten to death." Her voice held certainty, not the tentative quality of a guess hazarded.

Harry accepted this without challenge. Then he asked, "You think she murdered this kid too?"

"No," Christine positively. "She never murdered the child. He was killed by—someone else."

This time her companion was less willing to accept her statement. "I'd say the odds are better than ever she killed this one." Christine shook her head vehemently, but he ignored her, adding, "This may even, in some crazy way, connect up with the other murders."

"It does," Christine said.

But Harry didn't seem to hear her this time.

"Poor kid. Poor a lot of people," he said, staring at the pitiful remains.

After a moment, he repacked the tissue and gently closed the box. Then he set both shoeboxes carefully in the green-and-plaid suitcase Christine had retrieved from the closet. He stood up, hefting the case by its green plastic handle. "We'll have to take this along as further evidence." He shook his head. "As if there isn't enough craziness in this case already."

Neither one of them seemed to have any interest in exploring the house further.

As they descended to the first floor, Harry asked, "What tipped you to the hiding place?"

"A hunch," Christine said offhandedly.

"Hell of a hunch," Harry muttered. He looked closely at Christine, "You all right? You seem— awfully preoccupied."

She paused, her hand resting lightly on the bottom of the stair bannister. "I'm fine."

"Let's go then. This place gives me the willies. Especially finding this." He tightened his grip on the suitcase. He had almost reached the door, when Christine said, "My sweater. In the living room. I almost forgot."

She ran back into the other room, hearing Harry open the heavy front door at the end of the abbreviated hall.

She grabbed her sweater off the sideboard. Then she turned to the fireplace, letting her fingers slide slowly along the lip of the mantel, until they came to rest in front of the Shango-cult carving. For a minute, she gazed at the ax-shaped headdress, the generous breasts, the faint fracture line that showed where the wood had been mended with glue.

Then she grabbed it off the mantel, prompted by an impulse so strong in her it might have been a command spoken aloud. Burying the ebony statue in the folds of her sweater, she hurried to join an impatient Harry on the porch.

Also by Robert D. San Souci:

EMERGENCE

LEGEND OF SCARFACE

SONG OF SEDNA

THE SACRIFICE

Nana Chicory paused some distance away. "Those who would take the most powerful magic into themselves must first show the *orishas* their willingness to make great sacrifice to claim such power."

Dream-Suzanne nodded as if she already knew what her ancestor was going to tell her.

"In the homeland you would be required to present the *orishas* the skull of the person you most deeply love among the living. This alone will entitle you to safety and success in wielding the power Shango would place in you—and which you so deeply desire to possess. Whoever means the most in your life must be slain by you. Only then will you be able to claim in full the powers the *orishas* wish to give you in order to carry out their wishes and the commands of your own heart. These are one, as the power that will let you fulfill both is one."

"But who . . . ?" she asked.

The old woman's lips curled into a brutal smile. She said, "There is another value in killing one you greatly love. Once you have done this, no other death you may cause will ever bring to you the horror you feel when you kill the one you love."

"Who is it?" Suzanne in her dream demanded.

But the old woman was already hastening back to the gray boundaries of the dream. "You know. As soon as I spoke the great one's wishes, you knew."

THE GOD GAME

Ralph Hayes

HE WAS ALL-POWERFUL AND HALF-MAD— AND SHE KNEW IT!

Curtis Gabriel's disciples had followed him deep into the New Guinea jungle, blindly worshipping in his self-created Church of Eternal God. Among them was Jody Summers, who soon discovered that Gabriel was a power-mad fanatic who wielded the power of life and death over his devoted flock. Her only hope of escape lay in the man named Gage, yet she feared to trust her life to this enigmatic stranger...

LEISURE BOOKS

PRICE: $3.25 US/$3.75 CAN
0-8439-2026-2

LOVE'S UNEARTHLY POWER

Blair Foster

THEIR PASSIONS FED ON FLAMES OF HELL!

Sultry daughter of a Louisiana sharecropper, Gisela Dupin knew little of love until her first breathtaking encounter with Johan Simeon. Once she had tasted his lips, she knew she would stop at nothing, not even witchcraft, to make him hers forever. But Johan was the heir to a vast estate, and betrothed to pretty, docile, and wealthy Marianne Manuel. Obsessed by demonic lust, Gisela and Johan's desire for one another transcended all other obligations, compelling them to barter their very souls!

LEISURE BOOKS

PRICE: $3.50
0-8439-2039-4